What others are saying about *The Girls of October*:

"A wild ride! Just when you thought you knew where it was going, it takes you to another level."
— Solon Tsangaras, Author, *Detour to Armageddon*

"*The Girls of October* is just plain genius. And it's so unorthodox that initially, we don't know what we're getting into. But 50 pages in you'll realize that this is more than just a unique piece, it's also a supremely wrapped gift to the horror fans of the world."
—*Horror Novel Reviews*

"Josh Hancock's novel reads like a true-crime book inspired by the John Carpenter film *Halloween*. I was completely sucked into this incredibly realistic horror story."
—Zakary McGaha, Author, *Sea of Medium-to-High Pitched Noises*

"*The Girls of October* is an engrossing read from beginning to end that's sure to entertain even the most desensitized horror fans."
—*Rue Morgue Magazine*

"As the pages turn, the movie reel inside the mind cranks with suspenseful intensity, contemplating what horrors will come to pass in the next scene of pure terror. Hancock delivers what true horror fans have been ravenous for and provides a new nightmare vision on every page with a uniquely genius storytelling template... "
— David J. Fairhead, Author, *The Fall Of Tomorrow, Dwelling In The Dark* and the voice and talent behind *Kettle Whistle Radio* Podcast

Other books by Josh Hancock:

The Girls of October

The Devil
and My Daughter

JOSH HANCOCK

Burning Bulb
PUBLISHING

The Devil and My Daughter
By **Josh Hancock**

Burning Bulb Publishing
P.O. Box 4721
Bridgeport, WV 26330-4721
United States of America
www.BurningBulbPublishing.com

Cover designed by Gary Lee Vincent with the following elements used under license from Fotolia.com:
- Black Magic Ritual © Heartland Arts and
- Camera Photo Lens © Booka

First Edition.

Paperback Edition ISBN: 978-0692676080

Printed in the United States of America

Acknowledgments

Thank you to those who helped bring the creative scope of *The Devil and My Daughter* into gruesome focus: Brittney Aresta, Sharylen Hesterly, Travis Leland, Peter Razavi, Savannah Rugg, Hanna Scheuerman, and Kate Stephani. Thank you, as well, to Gary Vincent and everyone at Burning Bulb Publishing for their unwavering support of this book. And a heartfelt thank you will always be reserved for my wife—my constant adviser, best friend, brightest star, and forever love. I dedicate this book to her.

Foreword

When I was thirteen, my favorite television show was *Mannix*, a weekly series that depicted the lawful adventures of hardboiled Los Angeles cop Joe Mannix. This Armenian-born detective could solve any crime, held a black belt in karate, and drove a racing-green 1968 Dodge Dart convertible with chrome wheels and flamethrower driving lights. I was hooked on the series after the very first episode, and my younger brother Mark and I tuned in every Saturday night to watch Mannix's daring exploits. Our father, at the time a 16-year veteran of the Oakland Police Department, noticed my interest in the show and sat me down one evening after dinner to set the record straight.

"Not everyone can be a police officer," he said. "It takes a man who is responsible and courageous. Loyal and compassionate. A man willing to sacrifice a part of himself in order to provide for others."

My father then explained what he saw as the biggest difference between fictional cop shows on TV and real-life police work. "Mannix works alone, putting away the bad guys without much help from anyone else," he said. "My job as a homicide detective isn't like that at all. To solve a murder, I rely on the input and expertise of my fellow officers, my superiors, and the citizens of our community."

In addition to being a dedicated cop and parent, my father was a devout Catholic who attended church every Sunday. One night, after an episode of *Mannix* that found the gun-toting detective infiltrating a religious cult, Dad told me a story I would never forget.

While searching a house in the "Lower Bottoms" neighborhood of west Oakland, my father and his partner, a gentle giant of a man named Stephen Janowski, were forced to defend themselves after two gangbangers opened fire on the detectives with a pair of shotguns.

"I should've been killed that day, reunited with your mother in heaven," my father said, not realizing that his chilling words would fuel my nightmares for weeks to come. "Stephen and I were like ducks in a shooting gallery, just waiting to be picked off. Even as I returned fire I found myself praying—praying that I would live to see you and your brother again."

"What happened?" I asked. I had forgotten all about Joe Mannix by then. Dad was a commanding storyteller, his timber voice booming throughout our bungalow-style house. Mark, equally transfixed, squeezed in next to me on the living room couch to listen.

Our father explained that, as he scrambled behind a poker table to avoid being struck by bullets, rays of white light flooded the room. "Bullets ripped up furniture and tore into walls," he described. "A window above me exploded on impact, spraying glass everywhere."

"I had no idea where this strange light was coming from," my father added, "but it was warm and oddly comforting. Our lives were on the line, but I wasn't nearly as scared as I should've been."

"I couldn't see Jano anywhere, and I could only hope that he was okay," Dad continued, his powerful voice increasing in volume. "I heard a loud *thump*—and somehow I knew it was one of the shooters throwing his shotgun down on the floor because it was out of ammo. I would have only a few seconds before he reached for another weapon and started blasting. With white light buzzing around me like an enormous halo, I stood up from behind the table and emptied my magazine in the direction of the two men."

My brother and I sat entirely still, hanging on our father's every syllable. Our mother had died two years before, and Dad had become our entire world. As he shared this dramatic and intimate story of his life and career with us, I felt waves of unconditional love pass through my body.

That's my old man, I thought. *And I am a hero's son.*

"When the smoke and dust settled," my father said, "both of the shooters were dead. I found Jano slumped behind a couch; he had only been able to get a few rounds off before a shard of glass had fallen into his eye." Dad paused and looked intently at me and Mark. "Do you understand what I'm saying, boys? A higher power saved my life that day—call it God, the Holy Spirit, or my very own guardian angel—but divine intervention stepped in and protected me when I was at my weakest and most vulnerable."

My father then looked me sternly in the eye. "Johnny, those cop shows will depict as much crime and violence as the TV censors will allow," he said, "but they'll never have the guts to truly show the role that spirituality and faith play in a lawman's life—in all of our lives."

Eventually, my obsession with Joe Mannix faded, and though it was my brother who ended up in law enforcement, I never forgot my father's story. To this day, his words underscore an important tenet in my life: if you believe in God, then you must believe in the Devil. Dad was rescued by an angel of mercy that afternoon, but he could just as easily have been destroyed by a demon. As the Bible says in Peter 5:8, "Be sober; be vigilant; because your adversary the devil, as a roaring lion, walk about, seeking whom he may devour."

Let me tell you another story.

In August of 1987, my brother, a police officer for the Oakland Police Department, responded to an emergency call from Mercy Care, a medical center near Lake Merritt in the heart of downtown. This book will detail the events of that tragic afternoon, so I will keep my summation brief: that day, Mark became involved in the fatal shooting of a young woman. After the shooting, he was placed on paid leave while the OPD investigated the incident.

In the next few weeks, I visited Mark often at his apartment in Emeryville, an industrial city between Oakland and Berkeley. He didn't feel like talking much, so we often found ourselves eating Chinese takeout, watching sports, or playing Texas Hold'em. Mark sometimes spoke of his ex-girlfriend, a pretty paralegal named Ashley, but his reflections on their relationship were often spiteful and cold.

Then the "visitor" came.

It first arrived inside the walls of the apartment, tapping on the plumbing, scrambling inside the heating duct like a frightened mouse, and short-circuiting the electrical cables.

Over the next several days, we heard the tapping throughout the entire apartment—inside the cupboards, inside the refrigerator, under the coffee table, under Mark's bed. There were other strange incidents as well: lights in the apartment would flicker repeatedly, the TV would turn off by itself, and the bathroom sink was always clogged with thick, gummy strands of brown hair. At night, when the tapping ceased long enough for Mark to be able to fall asleep, he had terrifying nightmares about the shooting. In his unpublished memoir, *Demon by the Lake*, my brother described what it was like to experience these nightmares: "I dream in blood, and when I wake my entire skull feels wrapped in butcher's twine, cutting into my skin like a knife..."

As the intensity of the late-night rappings increased, Mark grew despondent. He relied heavily on prescription medication and alcohol to function. The nightmares continued, each one more gruesome than the last. Mark became disoriented and moody, and he often complained of aches and pains throughout his body. To lend him support, I began spending nights at his apartment; however, the anomalies continued. Family photos were found ripped to shreds; the tap water turned brown and reeked of fetid earth; the temperature in the apartment became icy cold; and the barn-stink of horses and other livestock filled the air. Convinced that some sinister force had taken hold of both the apartment and Mark, I called our father for help.

Now retired from the police force, Dad listened patiently to my story. Then, as calm as could be, he said, "I need to make a few calls and gather some things from the house. I'll call you in the morning with a plan. In the meantime, keep an eye on your brother and monitor all paranormal activity in the apartment. If you suspect your lives are in danger, don't call the cops. Don't pack your stuff, don't think you can fight it and win—just get the hell out of there."

In the year following these events, I learned what my father did next. He collected several religious items in a travel bag, including his Bible, a crucifix, a rosary, and a Saint Benedict medal; he also packed a fully-loaded Glock 21 pistol. He walked to the Catholic church down the street from his house and gave his confession. He then placed an urgent phone call to his long-time friend and spiritual advisor, Father Joseph Coyle, and made several private inquiries.

Whatever was tormenting my brother must have caught wind of our father's preparations. That night, I awoke with an excruciating migraine; my head felt like it was being crushed in a vise, my temples lanced with sewing needles. Suddenly I needed to be sick. I hurried to the bathroom, hit the light, and stumbled upon an awful scene.

Dressed in a wife-beater and cargo shorts, Mark was slumped in the tub. He had slashed his arms with a knife, then smeared his blood all over the white-tiled wall. Through swooning waves of horror, I saw that he had been trying to write a name.

Moloch.

I found out later that Moloch was an ancient Ammonite god, the most ferocious fallen angel in Milton's *Paradise Lost*, and a symbol of genocide and human sacrifice.

My recollection of the rest of that night comes in pieces of some horrific jigsaw: the bloody knife on the floor; the flashing red and blue sirens; Mark's clown-mask grin; and the accusatory eyes of the responding officers, who for some reason regarded me with derision.

Considered a danger to himself and others, Mark was admitted to a nearby psychiatric hospital. His hold was supposed to last for 72 hours, but there he remained for almost 13 months, a prisoner of his own mind. During that time, he was cleared of any wrongdoing in the fatal shooting in Oakland. According to the 68-page report issued by the Alameda County DA's office: "Officer Mark Tanner reasonably perceived threats of deadly force against himself and others and acted accordingly. As a result, no criminal charges will be brought against the officer for his participation in the shooting and resulting death."

But despite this good news, and despite the fact that Mark was receiving expert medical treatment, his mental and physical condition declined. He was crude to the staff and other patients. He had violent outbursts and emotional breakdowns, with lengthy jags of crying and cursing. When I visited, we no longer talked about movies or sports; we no longer teased each other, or told off-color jokes, or reminisced about all those carefree Saturday nights we spent watching our favorite gumshoe on TV.

Instead, Mark screamed at me. Screamed at me to get out of the room. Screamed at me to fuck off. To let him die. And when Mark screamed his voice was ferocious and guttural and hate-filled, like the howls of an animal driven to slaughter.

I agreed to participate in this book because I am convinced that Mark's life is in grave danger. I want his story—his truth—to be told. As fervently as I believe in God and all the angels of heaven, I believe in the Devil and all the demons of hell. And I believe one of these demons, the bull-headed "fire god" known as Moloch, has come to possess my brother's soul.

For some, this is an egregious claim, one that could only come from the mind of a lunatic; they will most likely not make it through the rest of this introduction. Others have picked up this book because of their interest in the paranormal and the occult. Some readers are fans of Debra Morrow's horror film, *The Devil and My Daughter*, which plays a critical role in this story, as does Alexander "Judas" Grimm and the rock band Carnal Season. Still others are seeking "campfire" tales for their next Halloween party.

And then there are those who already *know*. The countless men, women, and children who have fought and bled at the hands of the "old serpent" himself—or perhaps one of his infernal legion. I suspect that my father, who passed away earlier this year, had encountered the beast in his lifetime as well.

No matter your experience or belief system, and no matter your reasons for reading this book, you hold in your hands a complex and incredible story of demonic possession.

This is not a campfire tale, a ghost story, or a cheap knock-off of *The Exorcist*. It is not a hoax or an urban legend. There is no need for fiction when the truth is frightening enough.

John F. Tanner
Berkeley, 1991

Preface

A floating red balloon. The spinning wheels of a rusted tricycle. A fanged clown in a rainbow frightwig, blood trickling from her mouth.

These images comprised the entire plot of the first movie I ever made, shot on a Canon "Autozoom" in 1977. The movie had no sound, the shots were unsteady and out of focus, and the blood was actually a mixture of Heinz ketchup and cocoa powder. My best friend, Charlene Worsley, played the role of the killer-clown with reckless abandon—she danced, skipped, and prowled the crowded city streets, oblivious to the stares of those around her, all while I held the camera with chubby fingers and mimicked being a "director." It was summer in the San Francisco Bay Area, and Charlene and I were two 10-year-old movie geeks having the time of our lives.

Years later, while we were both studying at community college, Charlene would star in my first feature film, a shot-on-video attempt at exploitation horror called *The Devil and My Daughter*. No doubt you are familiar with the movie, not due to its cinematic merits but to the violent tragedy that occurred after its release. Immediately, the media latched on to the gruesomeness and sinister implications of the events that took place, an understandable reaction that ultimately led to the compilation of this book. Arranged in loose chronological order, the content inside—interviews, newspaper clippings, essays, scripts, legal documents, and more—has been collected to give you what the news agencies, even the tabloids with their screaming headlines, have failed to report—that is, the *real* story, arranged much like a David Hockney collage, the small pieces joining together to tell a much larger truth.

And it is a horrible story—outrageous and blood-soaked. But unlike the media would have you believe, I admit to my own culpability in it. I will never make another movie, and I will never have another friend like Charlene. She was gentle and tender-hearted and kind to animals. She was the one who taught me how to make apple dolls and shoebox dollhouses when we were seven. She was the one who introduced me to John Stanley's *Creature Features* and Black Sabbath's "Iron Man." When we were thirteen, she tutored me in math, took me to the stone labryinths in the Oakland Hills, and snuck us in to see *Halloween II*. And when we were sixteen, she held my hand at my mother's funeral. But just three years later, *American Investigation* would describe Charlene as "an instrument of genocidal evil." The tabloid magazines would call her "a satanic monster." Talk-show host Geraldo Rivera would label her "the most diabolical killer since Charlie Manson."

Please understand—I'm not asking you to forgive Charlene. I only want you to see her as a real person who suffered a tremendous deal, no matter how you might judge her by the final page. This book was not published to elicit your pity, nor is it a book of excuses. Rather, it represents an effort to lay all the grisly facts bare—and allow you to make up your own mind as to what they might mean.

Before we get started, I would like to thank the courageous John Tanner, who wrote the foreword to this book and whose commitment to the truth has filled many dark moments with light. Special thanks are also due to Paul Leonard at *Monsters & Mayhem*; Matt Porter for his essay on *The Devil and My Daughter*; Noelle Ramsey of *Intrepid* magazine for her oral history of the Mercy Care Murders; Cindy Bray of Crime Victims and Their Families (CVTF); and Harmony Allen and the publishing team at *Dark Roads* magazine for helping to make this book possible.

I would be remiss if I did not give one final recommendation—a warning of sorts—before you begin reading.

I mentioned that there were sinister implications to this story. I hope that you will consider these implications seriously, regardless of your faith, regardless of what books you keep on your bedside table at night. Consider them—for your safety and the safety of those you love.

Surround yourself with bright lights and loving family and good friends—and "put on the full armor of God."

Debra Morrow
Los Angeles, 1991

"Pre-Teen's Song Lyrics Cause Controversy" by Theresa Cacciatorre (originally published in the *San Mateo Daily Journal*, September, 1978, p. 2):

SAN MATEO - A student's musical performance at a junior high school in Pacifica has caused quite a stir among school administrators and parents.

The song was written by Alexander Grimm, 13, a student at Jefferson Middle School. Alexander is the singer and guitarist for a heavy metal band called The Creepazoids, a group he formed with two other Jefferson students.

Titled "Rise, Demon, Rise," the disturbing song was performed during the school's Creative People Festival, a talent show designed to recognize the artistic abilities of the students. Pupils wrote stories, played live music, and took photographs as part of the festival.

The lyrics to the song tell the morbid story of a boy who uses a "satanic" prayer to conjure a murderous spirit: "I spend every night / hopin' to get it right / Those razor-sharp horns, that majesty's tail / with you by my side I'll never fail."

When the boy's father punishes his son for getting in trouble in school, the boy asks the spirit to get revenge: "Got in a fight at school / My father laid down some rules / Grounded me from all my thrills / Demon, please kill, please kill."

The evil spirit agrees to the task, but first requires that the boy surrender his soul in return.

"Our children are supposed to be taught reading and math, not exposed to satanic music and violence," the mother of a student who heard the tune said. "I thought this was a good school!"

In the third verse of the song, the boy burns an effigy and casts his father into the basement where the horned creature awaits: "Set this paper bull aflame / drop it in the spirit bowl and call your name / I'll be your slave, I'll inhale the smoke / Throw Dad in the basement and watch him choke."

According to a parent who attended the show, the performance of the song included an actual satanic rite that Alexander Grimm had discovered in a book about ancient religions in the public library.

"New York City was terrorized by the 'Son of Sam.' Women in Los Angeles are being raped and killed by the Hillside Strangler Clearly, Satan's legion knows no bounds!" the parent argued. "And now our own children are singing songs about murder and demonic rituals? It's no wonder the fabric of our society is coming apart at the seams."

Another parent, who admitted she did not hear the song, agreed that the lyrics represent a frightening decline in traditional American values.

"I understand that the boy worked hard on his music, but that doesn't mean our children should be subjected to it," she said.

However, several Jefferson students and the three teachers in charge of the festival disagree with the complaints.

"The song was performed only to the upper classmen who chose to see the show, not to the grammar schoolers," one eighth-grader explained. "Plus, heavy metal music is everywhere now. Bands like Black Sabbath and AC/DC are much cooler and more popular than mainstream rock!"

Marjorie Harker, one of the instructors who helped organize the festival, had previewed the controversial song prior to the screening.

"The lyrics were definitely spooky, but the song wasn't any more offensive than what's on the news or these tabloid TV shows. I have known Alexander for many years, and this is the kind of subject matter he enjoys. He's an avid reader, especially the works of Poe and H.P. Lovecraft, and he just finished a book by Stephen King called *The Shining*," Harker said.

"Alex is very talented musician, and I stand by our decision to allow his group to play. The notion that the lyrics to the song or the live performance were harmful to the students is just absurd," the teacher added.

Though the Creative People Festival has now ended, the uproar surrounding the student's performance has yet to go away. In a recent letter to Jefferson Middle School, a parent wrote:

"Here is a student who made the deliberate choice to frighten his peers and teachers; a student who has expressed a genuine interest in ghoulish subject matter like Satanism and witchcraft. Have you listened to the words? Are you aware that the boy attempted to conjure an actual demon during the live performance? If the young man in question is not expelled immediately, then I will be forced to withdraw my daughter from the school and encourage other parents to do the same with their children."

"Loose Bull Causes Fatal Crash in Barstow" by Wade Kurtz (originally published in *The Desert Dispatch*, October, 1978, p. 3):

BARSTOW – A bull caused a fatal car accident on Friday after it ran into the road on CA-247 near Barstow.

A semi-trailer truck that was hauling bulls to a nearby farm was heading south on the state highway when the incident occurred.

According to a statement issued by the San Bernadino County police, the driver of the truck swerved to avoid an armchair that was laying in the road. As a result, the trailer doors swung open, and the bull leaped onto the highway.

Several cars had to swerve into the next lane to avoid hitting the animal, and some drivers were forced to veer off onto the shoulder of the road. The driver of the truck managed to pull over and lock up the trailer before other bulls escaped.

The rogue bull darted in and out of traffic, causing some drivers to bring their vehicles to a complete stop. Jackson Pelletier, a veteran trucker of over thirty years, was one of those drivers. According to Mr. Pelletier, the bull was on a "suicide mission."

"He was charging at the oncoming cars, his eyes filled with rage, like he knew he was going to die," he said. "But he was going to try to take someone down with him."

Samantha Franklin, who had pulled her vehicle to the shoulder, watched in horror as the bull rammed the side door of her car before turning around and bolting north down the highway.

"It was a huge animal, huffing and snorting. It was running against traffic, defecating in piles all over the road, scared out of its mind. It was going to cause an accident at any second," she said.

As the bull charged down the road, Henry Grimm, 43, slammed on the brakes of his truck to avoid crashing into the animal. The vehicle careened to the left, splitting the guardrail in two.

Grimm exited his truck, seemingly in a daze from the crash, his hands on his knees. The bull then whirled around and gored the man from behind, killing him instantly.

The accident happened shortly before ten in the morning on the southbound lanes near Barstow Station.

"The bull knew what it was doing," Pelletier said. "The person that died was driving a red pickup, and we all know that red is the color that makes bulls angry."

California Highway Patrol officer Tim Moya, who responded to the scene and helped to navigate the bull off the highway, clarifies the issue.

"Bulls are actually color blind to red and green," he explained. "The animal was scared, disoriented, and it was probably responding to the rapid movement of the vehicles more than anything else."

With the assistance of motorists and the truck driver who was hauling the bulls, Moya was able to corral the enormous bovine into a grassy area off the highway.

"It was a terrible accident and easily preventable had the truck driver properly locked his livestock trailer," Moya said. "Today a wife lost her husband, and a son lost his father."

The southbound lanes of the 247 highway were closed down for hours as police cleared the scene. It is unknown whether charges will be filed against the truck driver who enabled the bull to escape.

"Boy Suspended for Casting Spells and Acting Spooky" by Adrianna Landen (originally published in *San Mateo Daily Journal*, November, 1981, p. 3):

PACIFICA - A high school in Pacifica has reportedly suspended a 16-year-old boy for acting out scenes from his favorite scary movies and for "causing fear and disruption among teachers and classmates."

According to a spokesperson for the San Mateo County School District, the trouble started when the student was overheard reciting lines from a recent made-for-TV horror movie called *The Possessed*, which tells the story of a reincarnated priest who attempts to save an all-girls school from the clutches of a bloodthirsty demon.

During lunch over the course of several afternoons, the student acted out spooky scenes from the supernatural movie, playing the role of the satanic demon and encouraging his classmates to join him.

According to a statement released by Cedarburgh High School, the boy was seen writhing on the ground, "purposely rolling his eyes into the back of his head" and play-acting a "rough stabbing motion" against other students.

When the teen's make-believe antics continued throughout the week, students alerted the school principal, Tanya Palacios. When Palacios rushed to the cafeteria to investigate, she observed the boy making "distorted faces," trying to "possess the soul" of a classmate, and "casting a witchcraft-like spell." Palacios deemed the incidents in violation of the school's safety and security policy and demanded an immediate suspension of the misbehaving student.

"My son has a vivid imagination and a creative spirit, but he would never hurt another person. He enjoys school and his friends," the student's mother told the *Journal*.

The mother said that she was unaware her son had watched the horror movie on TV, but also indicated that she probably would have given him permission to see it.

"I encourage my boy's interest in the arts. He's a gifted guitar player and songwriter, and his talents have helped him cope with the death of his father. He knows the difference between fantasy and reality, and I'm disappointed that this school district isn't also aware of the difference," the mother said.

When asked at the district office about the suspension, Palacios refused to comment in depth, only indicating that it would be "a short one, lasting only two days."

Though this incident marks the first time the student has been suspended, it is not the first time his unusual behavior has concerned his teachers.

At age 13, while attending junior high in another neighborhood, the boy performed a heavy metal song before his school, singing lyrics about a vindictive child who enters into a murderous pact with the devil. The performance angered many parents and teachers who felt that the material was inappropriate and even dangerous.

More recently, the student has garnered several on-campus infractions, which have involved injuring another student with a sharpened pencil, bringing books about serial killers to class, and singing rock songs about stabbings, murder, and occult practices.

"The other kids make fun of my son. They call him names because he has bad acne and because he has morbid interests. Music has become his only comfort, his only escape," the mother argued. "It's the administrators who are stifling his creativity and having a knee-jerk reaction to all this."

Meanwhile, the San Mateo County School District has stood firm in its decision, citing school and student safety as its primary concern. A spokesperson for the district has commented, "Suspension is a strict penalty and one we take seriously, but schools can't be afraid to implement it when their students are at risk."

"High School Student Wows USF Film Archive" by Kenneth Lowery (originally published in the *San Francisco Chronicle*, October, 1983, p. 8-9):

SAN FRANCISCO – On Saturday night, a Bradley High School junior premiered her documentary at the University of San Francisco Film Archive's "Artful Docs" competition and won second place. She received a laminated certificate and a $150 cash prize for her winning entry.

A "straight A" student and a devoted cinephile at only 16-years-old, Debra Morrow began working on her documentary as part of a school assignment. She focused her film lens on Oakland native Ruth Worsley, whose photographs of the historic city have been featured in galleries and museums throughout the country.

"Ruth is my best friend's mother, and I have always appreciated her work. The way she frames her photographs, the feel and texture of them, the colors—it's just so beautiful!" Debra said after receiving her award. Two other Bradley High School students were also recognized in the 8th annual competition, which considers non-fiction movies in categories such as politics, science, art, and entertainment.

"Ruth's photography is powerful because, even through a single image, she can tell an amazing story," said Debra, whose 7-minute film showcased Worsley's photographic renderings of famous Oakland landmarks, including the Arlington Hotel and the one-story Victorian cottages that pepper the city's most popular neighborhoods.

"I want to tell stories through films the way Ruth does through pictures," Debra continued. "Her work has a transformative feel to it. You can watch the city grow and evolve in each of her photographs. She's definitely the kind of artist I would like to be one day."

Displaying dedication to her craft, Debra spent several weeks with Worsley while making the non-fiction film. Titled *Portraits of My City*, the documentary captures candid moments in the Worsley home (including a heartbreaking exchange in which Worsley and her teenage daughter, Charlene, talk about the pain of divorce), but its main focus is on the photographer's ethereal body of work.

"There's always something new and fun to discover in Ruth's work. You could look at her pictures a thousand times and not see the same thing twice," Debra said.

Debra, who will be the first person in her family to attend college, said she will always be open to making another documentary film, but that she is far more interested in the fictional horror genre.

"Ruth captures these incredible structures and shows how unique they are," Debra said. "I want to accomplish a similar goal with female characters in horror. I want to make them different, intelligent, and strange. I want to discover the beauty in them that transcends the physical. Hopefully, college will give me the chance to do all that!"

The popularity of student filmmaking has increased in the past several years, according to Steven Hogue, the Visual Arts teacher who gave Debra the assignment that sparked her documentary. "And now, with the release of the Betamax camcorder, making your own movie just got a whole lot easier," Hogue said. "I think we're going to see a lot of talented kids give the Hollywood big-wigs a run for their money."

Hogue may be on to something. For the 1983 competition, USF Film Archive received over 100 submissions from students across the country. The documentaries covered a wide range of topics, including the death of comedian John Belushi, Atari video games, and the Holocaust.

"I think Debra, and all of the kids who entered movies in this year's competition, have a real shot in the filmmaking business," said Hogue. "If they stay committed, if they don't allow negative outside influences to corrupt their vision, then these young students are set to change the world."

"Failed Novelist Confesses to Killing Family Dog" by Ewen Morrisson (originally published in the *Oakland Tribune*, October, 1983, p. 1-2):

A former adjunct English professor at Hayward State University claimed that it was a combination of "drugs and depression over his divorce" that led him to poison and kill his family dog, a Lhasa Apso named Bandit, in 1982.

Frank Worsley, 48, pleaded guilty to one count of first-degree malicious cruelty to an animal and was charged with a misdemeanor on Monday.

Worsley, who was fired by Hayward State University in 1979 after allegations of fraud and plagiarism, has also been charged with breaking and entering, third-degree domestic violence for criminal intimidation, and threatening to kill his ex-wife and 16-year-old daughter, according to court records.

During his plea hearing Worsley broke into tears as he confessed to using powdered rat poison to kill Bandit at a time of day when he knew that his former spouse and daughter would be out of the house.

"I didn't want them to see this terrible thing I was doing. I knew it was wrong, it was sick, but I couldn't stop myself," Worsley, who no longer lives at the residence where the crime took place, told the judge.

"I wanted to hurt my wife," Worsley added. "I wanted her to feel the same pain that I was feeling. I broke into the house like a common thief. I wasn't thinking straight!"

Prosecuting attorney Richard Cabriddas demanded that Worsley describe to the court the painful details of the killing of the dog. After a brief explanation of his drug use, including marijuana and cocaine, Worsley responded: "I mixed the poison into Bandit's food and then locked him in the bedroom to die."

A struggling writer, Worsley also confessed to feelings of jealousy over the success of his ex-wife, a freelance photographer, and his young daughter, a burgeoning actress who has appeared in a number of local theater productions for children and teens.

"Though the defendant has been separated from his family for three years, which includes a brief stay in a rehab facility, he has still managed to inflict as much mental and emotional damage on them as possible," Cabriddas said. "This arrest and prosecution were essential to the safety of the Worsley family, especially the young daughter."

Alameda County Chief Deputy Nathan Spears, who oversaw the unusual case, agreed that prosecuting Worsley was critical to the well-being of the teen. "The hardest part was watching her testify in court with tears in her eyes, describing all the bad things her father did, but also saying how much she loved and missed him," Spears said. "It was one of the most emotional courtroom appearances I've ever seen."

Worsley ended his statement to the judge by apologizing for his actions and even offering up a short prayer for the adorable pet that had been a loyal family companion for so many years.

"I had a dog growing up myself, a black Lab named Shadow that I loved very much. He was my best friend. I don't know why I did this to my poor daughter. Perhaps I am mentally ill," Worsley said.

Worsley stated that he became addicted to drugs after a colleague alleged that Worsley had plagiarized his first novel. As a result the book was pulled from publication. Worsley then lost his teaching job and his wife filed for divorce in early 1980. He moved out of the family home in Oakland and began living in motels and hostels throughout the Bay Area.

"I know I look like the worst husband and father in the world right now, but my wife isn't entirely innocent. We ran a very loose household. We threw parties, we held poetry readings and film screenings, with strange people coming and going at all hours of the night. There were infidelities on both sides," Worsley insisted.

After the divorce, Worsley said, he grew apart from his daughter. He became concerned by abrupt changes in the teen's personality, but felt powerless to help. According to his statement in court, Worsley had used cocaine on the day that he poisoned Bandit.

"I locked the little guy in the bedroom because I couldn't stand to see what I had done. I could hear him throwing up. It sounded like he was having a seizure, like he was crying out for help," Worsley said. "Then I went back into the kitchen and wrote this sickening letter to my ex-wife and child."

According to court documents, the letter described in gruesome detail the ways in which Worsley planned to kill his former spouse and daughter, including shooting them or stabbing them with a knife. After leaving the letter inside the house, Worsley checked into a sober-living facility, where he said he had intended to commit suicide.

"Hanging myself was going to be my grand exit, like something out of Shakespeare," Worsley revealed to the judge. "But I'm standing here now, asking for your mercy instead."

Though none of his immediate family members were present at the hearing, Worsley ended his plea to the court by staring off into the far corner of the room, referring to his daughter by name, and saying that he hoped she would forgive him for his past behavior. "Not only for what I did to Bandit, but for being a deadbeat dad," he said.

Worsley was arrested in August by police at an Alameda halfway house after being charged with cruelty to an animal. Detectives used photographic evidence, eyewitness testimony, and a veterinarian's necropsy report to piece together their investigation.

According to police documents, Worsley had been arguing with his ex-wife, over the phone and through letters, for several weeks leading up to the incident. Authorities determined that the bulk of their fights had to do with their daughter and Worsley's belief that his ex-wife conducted several extra-marital affairs during the course of their marriage.

Depending on the outcome of the case, Worsley hopes to return to both teaching and writing. He also told the judge it is his intention to be a part of his daughter's life despite the "errors of his past."

Letter from Grant Lessom, Vice-Principal of Bradley High School, to Ruth Worsley:

December 15th, 1983

Bradley High School
1222 Federation Street
Oakland, CA 94601

Ms. Ruth Worsley
[address omitted]

Dear Ms. Worsley:

The staff of Bradley High School works diligently throughout the academic year to provide a safe and healthy learning environment for our students. We would not be able to achieve this goal without the input and cooperation of the entire Bradley community, which includes teachers, administrators, counselors, and the parents of our impressive student body.

I am writing today with deep and genuine concern for your daughter, Charlene Worsley. Though Charlene is one of the most academically-gifted pupils in the junior class, her teachers have recently noted a troubling pattern of disruptive behavior that is cause for alarm.

These behaviors include a) unexcused tardies and absences; b) talking out of turn in class; c) using inappropriate language; d) writing about extremely morbid subject matter, including the "sacrifice" of animals; and e) smoking cigarettes.

In addition, Mrs. Hargrave, Charlene's English teacher, has come upon a rather disturbing movie script that Charlene inadvertently left inside her desk. The screenplay, titled *Monsters in Your Pants*, appears to have been written by Charlene and includes scenes of bullying, explicit sexual language, and horrific depictions of body mutilation and killing.

Our concern is two-fold: we do not want Charlene's disruptive behaviors and somewhat gruesome interests to interfere with other students in their pursuit of academic excellence, nor do we want Charlene's grades or emotional health to falter during this very important school year.

As of this writing, Charlene has received countless verbal warnings and three demerits (also called "bummer slips") for her unexcused tardies and absences. My sincere hope is that these disciplinary reprimands do not extend any further, as they may jeopardize her post-secondary educational goals as well as her desire to one day become a successful actress.

Finally, it has come to my attention that there has been some recent commotion in your household, including a divorce and a tragic court case involving a deceased family pet. I understand that these events may be having a temporary impact on Charlene's attitude and behaviors, and I offer my sincere condolences.

Should you have any question regarding the incidents outlined in this letter, please do not hesitate to contact me during school hours. I am entirely confident that, working as a united front, we can all help Charlene work through this difficult time.

Yours Sincerely,

Grant Lessom
Vice-Principal

Monsters in Your Pants by Charlene Worsley (final shooting script, December, 1983):

1 INT. CLASSROOM - MORNING

HILLARY MATTHEWS, 12, sits at the back of a classroom. Though we hear the sounds of other girls in the room, our CAMERA stays on Hillary as she grips her pencil and jiggles her legs.

The teacher, MISS PERKINS, lectures at the front of the room.

> PERKINS (V.O.)
> Now, ladies, this morning we are
> going to talk about a rather sensitive
> issue that pertains to all young
> women. I will need each of you to pay
> close attention as we open our Family
> Life textbooks to page 32...

Our CAMERA close on Hillary. Her expression pained. Worried. She can't stop jiggling. A brunette girl, PAMELA, looks over at her and giggles.

> PERKINS (V.O.) (CONT'D)
> ...the most important change a young
> woman will experience during puberty
> is when she begins to menstruate--also
> known as "getting your period." Your
> period is a sign that your body's
> reproductive system has started to
> work.

Uncomfortable laugher in the room. A whispered chorus of "Aunt Flo," "on the rag," and "riding the cotton pony," among other slang terms. Our CAMERA stays close on Hillary's hand, white-knuckled around the pencil.

> PERKINS (V.O.) (CONT'D)
> Ladies, please--I must have your
> complete attention if we are to get through
> this lesson! Now--I'm sure you have a lot
> of questions, but before we can understand
> why menstruation happens, we need to study
> a few key terms. If you'll turn to the

diagram and glossary in your books please.
Samantha, can you read aloud the first word
you see there?

> SAMANTHA (V.O.)
> "Vagina."

Hillary clutching the pencil, a bundle of nerves.

> PERKINS (V.O.)
> Thank you, Samantha. "Va-gi-na." The
> vagina is the small opening between
> a woman's legs. It is surrounded by
> outer folds of skin called the labia.
> "La-bi-a." It is also the opening that
> babies come out of and...
>> (with some difficulty)
> ...the one that penises go into.

Another short burst of laughter from the class. The
teacher has just about reached her limit.

> PERKINS (V.O.)
> Silence! All of you! Have a little
> respect. For your bodies! For yourselves!
>> (after clearing her throat)
> Now--moving on. Dawn, read aloud the
> next word, please.

> DAWN (V.O.)
> Um..."urethra."

> PERKINS (V.O.)
> Very good. "U-reth-ra." The urethra
> is a narrow passage just above the
> vagina. It is the opening where our
> urine comes out.

Hillary's eyes widen. Our CAMERA drops beneath her feet
to find a few drops of pee on the floor.

> PERKINS (V.O.)
> Hillary, can you read the next word,
> please?

SNAP! The pencil breaks in Hillary's hand. The sound of laughter. Hillary mortified. She clamps her legs together.

> PERKINS (V.O.)
> Hillary Matthews, were you not
> listening again? How many times must
> I ask you to pay attention? Wait--
> what is it you're doing there?
> Stop that jiggling and sit still!

CUT TO:

The brunette girl, Pamela, smirking.

> PAMELA
> She has to go to the bathroom, Miss
> Perkins. She's holding it in.

> PERKINS (V.O.)
> Thank you, Pamela. That will be enough.
> (to Hillary) Hillary, is this true? If
> so, speak up, child!

With great embarrassment...

> HILLARY
> (barely a whisper)
> I...can't.

> PERKINS (V.O.)
> Hillary, you are disrupting our entire
> class. If you need to be excused to the
> ladies', then please say so!

> PAMELA
> She's dribbling, Miss Perkins.

> HILLARY
> I can't go. I can't!

> PERKINS (V.O.)
> This is a waste of valuable class
> time. Hillary, excuse yourself to the
> washroom. And Pamela--make sure she gets
> there and returns immediately.

Both girls hesitate, unsure of what to do.

                    PERKINS (V.O.) (CONT'D)
    Go! This instant!

2 EXT. SCHOOL CORRIDOR - SAME MORNING

Hillary and Pamela head down the corridor toward the restroom. Hillary walks with her thighs close together, desperately trying to hold "it" in.

                    HILLARY
    Pamela, I'm begging you. Go back to
    class and leave me alone.

                    PAMELA
    And risk getting detention from Pudgy
    Perkins? No thanks. Let's just get
    this over with.

They reach the ladies' restroom. Hillary hesitates outside the door, squirming like crazy.

                  PAMELA (CONT'D)
    Are you kidding me?
        (shoves Hillary inside)
    Go in, already!

3 INT. LADIES' RESTROOM - SAME MORNING

The restroom is spotless, the tile gleaming. Three stalls. Two sinks. Sanitary napkin dispenser on the wall.

                    HILLARY
    Wait outside for me. Please?

                    PAMELA
    Fat chance. You'll just hold it in
    as usual, and then I'll get busted.
    I'm not going anywhere.

                    HILLARY
    Please! You don't want to be here!

                    PAMELA
          Damn right I don't.

Pamela pushes open one of the stall doors. It BANGS
against the wall.

                    PAMELA (CONT'D)
          But I'm gonna watch you pee, anyway.

Hillary looks inside the stall. The TOILET lid is open,
the water a bright disinfectant blue.

                    HILLARY
                    (shyly)
          We used to be friends.

                    PAMELA
          Yeah, well...that was a long time
          ago.

                    HILLARY
          So...so what happened?

A beat. Pamela hesitates. Shows a glimmer of the friend
she used to be. Then her Medusa-face returns.

                    PAMELA (CONT'D)
          I'm a child of divorce. I have Daddy
          issues. I'm a bitch. Who gives a
          fuck? Get in there and pop a squat!

Hillary wobbles into the stall on shaky legs. She backs
up to the toilet, lifts her skirt, and slowly pulls
down her underwear.

                    PAMELA (CONT'D)
          And I want to hear it, girl. Like
          Niagra Falls.

Hillary sits down on the toilet seat. She looks up at
Pamela with woeful eyes.

                    HILLARY
          I warned you.

A tense pause. Hillary strains.

THE DEVIL AND MY DAUGHTER

                                                    CUT TO:

Pamela, arms crossed, impatiently tapping her foot.

                    PAMELA
          Sometime today would be nice.

Hillary "pushes" again. Suddenly--we hear the sound of
liquid SPLASHING into the bowl. Then a HISSING noise,
like gas escaping from a tube.

                    PAMELA (CONT'D)
          What the hell was that?

Hillary's face scrunches in pain...

                    PAMELA (CONT'D)
          Eww! Gross, Matthews! You stink!

More sounds. Flesh PULLING apart. Liquid GUSHING into
the bowl. Blood and ooze begin to spill over the toilet
bowl and onto the floor.

                    HILLARY
          It's coming!

                    PAMELA
          What the fu...

Pamela backs away but slips on the wet floor. She falls
smack down onto her butt. Our CAMERA rushes to her face,
capturing the panic in her eyes.

                                                    CUT TO:

Hillary sits up from the toilet, her blood-soaked
underwear bunched around her thighs. Convulsions pass
through her body.

                    HILLARY
          Oh, God...it hurts...

                                                    CUT TO:

Pamela, her mouth open wide with terror.

CUT TO:

Hillary, her entire body shaking. We hear a wet SLITHERING sound. Then a SPLASH in the muck at her feet.

> PAMELA
> What...what is <u>that</u>?

Pamela's POV:

On the floor, something long and bloated, like a fat sausage casing. It's inching toward Pamela, slug-like. We can barely see it, but it might be SNIFFING the air.

> PAMELA (CONT'D)
> Get it away from me! Get it away!

Hillary looks on, exhausted and relieved, her breath coming in gasps.

> HILLARY
> There's nothing I can do now.

The sausage-thing inches toward Pamela. She looks on in sheer horror before...

> PAMELA
> Oh no...

...her skirt darkens with liquid. Pamela's just wet herself.

> HILLARY
> It wants you now. (beat) It wants to
> be friends.

The sausage-thing SCREECHES, splashing on the wet tile, excited by a new scent in the air.

Pamela tries to scoot away, but the parasite sloshes forward and slithers beneath the folds of her pleated skirt.

There's the RIPPING of fabric. Then a sound like a SUCTION CUP. Pamela's stomach suddenly BULGES, as if with a huge vibrating tumor.

She SCREAMS.

FADE OUT.

FADE IN TITLE: "MONSTERS IN YOUR PANTS."

FADE OUT.

"Mutilated Body Found at Linda Mar Beach" by Geraldine Mercurio (originally published in *Pacifica Tribune*, October, 1985, p. 1-2):

PACIFICA – The Pacifica Police Department is urgently seeking the public's help in identifying a mutilated female corpse that was discovered along the banks of Linda Mar Beach on Wednesday of this week.

In a press conference this morning, homicide detective Stanley Basso asked the public to come forward with any information about suspicious persons they might have seen on or near the popular beach throughout the past weekend or early in the week.

"Any homicide scene is inexcusable, but at Linda Mar we have an extremely savage murder. Cold-blooded, animalistic in nature. It was calculated, planned, and we need your assistance to solve it and bring the person or persons responsible to a swift justice," Basso said.

In what some are labeling a ritualistic murder, the victim's head and arms were severed from the rest of the body. Found against a sandy bank and hidden by trees, the corpse was wrapped in sheets of black plastic and tied up with rope.

"At this time, we're not going to comment further on the crime scene, but it's obvious there are sinister elements involved," Basso said at the press conference.

The remains have been identified as those of a black female, 63 to 65 inches in height, and weighing 105 pounds. The body suffered several injuries, including deep puncture wounds in the breast area, lower abdomen, and backside.

Shortly after the press conference, investigators released photos to the press of several items found at the crime scene, including a torn spool of cassette-recording tape. Police are in the process of piecing the tape together so that they can hear what, if anything, is recorded on it.

Pacifica has the second lowest crime rate among its neighboring cities, with only three murders in the past decade. "It's a safe place to live and visit, a beach community, which is what makes this crime so shocking," Basso said.

In addition to the identity of the victim, investigators are trying to determine the location of exactly where the murder took place. Based on evidence collected at the scene, they believe the victim was killed elsewhere and then dumped at the secluded beach location.

"Dismembered Body Identified as Prostitute" by Geraldine Mercurio (originally published in *Pacifica Tribune*, November, 1985, p. 2-3):

The Pacifica Police Department has identified the young woman whose mutilated body was discovered two weeks ago on Linda Mar Beach.

The victim has been named as 23-year-old Jeannette Conway, a prostitute who worked in both the Pacifica and Colma areas. Conway was last seen at the Seahorse Saloon on San Pablo Avenue in Pacifica, sometime between midnight and 1 a.m. on the morning of May 3rd.

According to an official police statement released at the time the body was discovered, the killer severed Conway's head and arms, wrapped the body in plastic, and tied the corpse with rope. The body was then dumped in a secluded area on Linda Mar Beach, where it was discovered by a local surfer.

Despite an extensive search of the beach by investigators and an active tip hotline at the police station, the woman's killer has not been arrested, nor have her missing body parts been found.

Detectives are considering the possibility that the murderer has held onto the body parts as a grisly "trophy" of the killing, or that they were used in some kind of ritual or occult-like ceremony.

Supporting the latter view are the many "satanic" images found spray-painted near the crime scene, including an upside-down cross, a pentagram, and the number "666" drawn on a nearby rock wall.

Jeannette Conway was identified through the tattoos located on her chest and shoulders. The dismemberment of the body makes identifying exactly how Conway died an impossibility, but the autopsy revealed that the murderer made several post-mortem blows with a large weapon to hack through the neck.

Conway was born in South San Francisco, and had only recently moved to Pacifica, where she lived with a roommate in a duplex near downtown.

Investigators believe that Conway met her killer at the Seahorse Saloon, or that she was picked up by the assailant somewhere along San Pablo Avenue. Police are hoping that her roommate can provide information about whom Conway might have "dated" on the night she disappeared.

A spool of music-recording tape found at the scene was spliced together by a sound technician working for the police department.

According to the official report, the tape contains fragments of music, but police have not revealed from what type of instrument. The search of the beach for further clues will continue into next week.

Investigators are considering bringing in a dive team to plumb the ocean for the missing body parts.

"The signs of ritual murder can be subtle, but there are incisions on the victim's body that are unusual. We're keeping an open mind as to what, if anything, they might mean," stated Detective Stanley Basso of the Pacifica Police Department.

"To dismember a body, to wrap and tie it up in plastic, to keep the dump site free of blood—these things require time, effort, and privacy. This homicide took place somewhere else, most likely in a private wooded area or inside a secluded house.

"If we can find the victim's missing body parts, that will help to generate more clues, more evidence, and then we can find Jeannette's killer," Basso said.

Conway's roommate, Darcy Bridgewood, spoke to KTSF-Channel 26 about her murdered friend.

"Jeannette was sweet. She believed in people, believed that they were good inside, but she just trusted the wrong dude," Bridgewood said through clenched teeth.

"She was fun. She was silly sometimes. She was a really good drawer, and she would play music, like heavy metal music, as loud as she could get away with in the apartment."

As part of their investigation, police are studying similar crimes in order to determine if there is a connection between cases. The body of Viola Arrendondo, age 21, was found in May in a drainage highway in Colma. A prostitute, Arrendondo was mutilated and then drowned in shallow water.

"We are actively pursuing every lead, and possible links to other homicides with ritualistic undertones," Basso said.

From "Prostitute Killer on the Loose?" (originally aired on KICU-TV's *American Investigation*, November, 1985, 17:00 ET):

THIS TRANSCRIPT MAY NOT BE IN ITS FINAL FORM AND HAS BEEN EDITED FOR COMMERCIAL BREAKS.

RONALD GRANTHAM, HOST: Tonight, an unflinching look into the dark and dangerous world of prostitution and the murderous toll that these poor women are subjected to every night they work the streets.

We have two young female bodies, hacked, mutilated, perhaps even sacrificed, found in close proximity to each other. Now, a third woman, a runaway, has gone missing. Time is slipping further away and police in two quiet Northern California towns don't seem any closer to catching the sinister—and some say, satanic—culprit.

For 23-year-old Jeannette Conway, life had never been easy. A prostitute since the age of 17, Jeannette spent most of her time on the streets, earning money whenever and however she could. Selling her body, pushing dope, stripping at parties. Her corpse, naked and sliced open with a knife, was found on a beach in Pacifica by a surfer out to catch some early-morning waves.

And then, nearby, in Colma, a town known for its abundance of cemeteries, another body turns up. Another prostitute, just like poor Jeannette. 21-year-old Viola Arrendondo, an attractive Hispanic girl with long, honey-colored hair. Stabbed, drowned, found dead in a drainage ditch. And guess what, folks? News out of Pacifica yesterday morning—an 18-year-old runaway named Patty Howard, confirmed missing. It's safe to say we have a serious problem on our hands.

This is *American Investigation*—the only TV news-magazine of its kind. I'm Ronald Grantham, and I want to thank you for watching this very important coverage. Tonight, we'll go live to California and share with you two stories of heartbreak and one of hope. Currently, the search for 18-year-old Patty Howard is in full force, and Bay Area police are hoping the young runaway can avoid the tragic fate of the two prostitutes before her who were found killed, their bodies stabbed and dismembered—perhaps "marked" by a satanic cult. Patty Howard is the missing woman—young, pretty, a light-skinned Afro-American. Her purse, along with her ID and a small bundle of cash, was found by the side of the road in a chilly beach town called Pacifica.

Is there a connection between the two prostitute slayings and the disappearance of Patty Howard? Is a satanic cult, or a lone serial killer, running loose in Northern California, looking for young female victims to murder and sacrifice? And is there a correlation between heavy metal music—what some people call death metal or satanic rock—and the brutal end to these women's lives?

(BEGIN VIDEO CLIP)

STANLEY BASSO, PACIFICA POLICE DEPARTMENT, HOMICIDE DIVISION, *standing outside the Seahorse Saloon*: This was the last place Jeannette Conway was seen before she was abducted and killed. Jeannette came to this bar and grill in Pacifica almost every weekend, to dance, listen to music, and to find a "date" or two for the night. She did drugs here. She met a lot of different men here. Bikers, musicians, surfers—all types.

(END VIDEO CLIP)

GRANTHAM: That was Detective Stanley Basso of the Pacifica Police Department, and we'll be hearing from him throughout the evening. But now, let's go straight to the source, the place where Jeannette's body was found in a sandy grave on the beach. We've got investigative reporter Reed Bentley on the ground in Pacifica right now. Reed, can you tell us what you've learned so far?

REED BENTLEY, INVESTIGATIVE REPORTER: Well, this is where Jeannette Conway's body was found, Ronald, right here, tucked into this little beach enclave, about fifty yards from the shore of Linda Mar Beach. Her body stabbed repeatedly, tied up, wrapped in plastic, the head and arms severed from the corpse. And detectives still have not found the missing body parts. I must tell you, Ronald, standing here, underneath these trees, with the sun going down behind me…it gives me a real bad feeling.

GRANTHAM: I don't blame you, Reed, but that's nothing compared to what Jeannette Conway must have felt, the absolute fear and terror she must have felt when she realized what was going to happen to her. And the killing, the dismembering, had to have happened somewhere else, because detectives found very little blood where you're standing. This is such an awful killing, and to think how carelessly her body was dumped there, in the cover of darkness, it really packs an emotional wallop. Take a listen to this, folks.

(BEGIN VIDEO CLIP)

BASSO, *walking along the Seahorse Saloon porch*: On the night she disappeared, Jeannette visited the Seahorse Saloon, possibly because it was "Metalhead Night," where they play heavy metal songs on the jukebox. Hardcore acts like AC/DC, Iron Maiden, and Megadeth, performing what the kids today call "death metal." This event draws all sorts of unsavory characters. They get drunk, and they migrate out here to the road looking for trouble. We think Jeannette got picked up here on San Pablo Road, most likely by someone she met at the bar or someone who was on their way to the bar.

DARLENE CONWAY, JEANNETTE CONWAY'S MOTHER, *sitting at home, holding a photograph of Jeannette*: I failed my daughter, I see that now. The way she turned out, the choices she made. I could have given her more guidance in life. She wanted to be an artist, but we never had the money for fancy paintbrushes and paper. Just a little watercolor set, that's all she had. Now I keep all her drawings next to my bed and I look at them every night before I go to sleep.

(END VIDEO CLIP)

GRANTHAM: That is tough to watch. So, Reed, Jeannette was killed, dismembered, and dumped on the beach. And satanic symbols, like the pentagram and the inverted cross, were found graffitied nearby. What can you tell us about the murder of Viola Arrendondo, the 21-year-old prostitute whose body turned up in Colma, no more than six miles from Pacifica? Are there similarities between these two homicides?

BENTLEY: There are some connections between the victims and their murders, Ronald. Jeannette and Viola were minorities, which makes investigators believe that there is a racial element behind the gruesome slayings. And as we already know, both of these girls were prostitutes, which has led police to think that the killer has a psychopathic anger against women, specifically against women who sell themselves out on the street. Now, Viola Arrendondo was stabbed and drowned. Three of the fingers on her left hand were chopped off and have not been found by police. And just like at Jeannette's crime scene, a pentagram was discovered—drawn on the dirty concrete near the body.

Now, some details—Viola was last seen outside a pool hall in the gloomy city of Colma. I say gloomy because the city has more bodies buried in its cemetery than it does actual people who live in town. The pool hall is called The Corner Pocket, and it's located on an industrial road frequented by prostitutes and drug dealers. On the night that Viola went missing, a local band called Skeleton Skin played a show at the pool hall, and Viola was seen inside the joint. Police believe that, like Jeannette, Viola was most likely picked up by her killer. So he has wheels—most likely a van or a truck, perhaps with tinted windows. Viola thought it was just another customer, but he turned out to be something much worse.

GRANTHAM: Reed, I've just been told that Jeannette Conway had some unusual wounds on her body. There were punctures and lacerations on her stomach and on her perineum.

BENTLEY: Yes, that's right. I've spoken with Detective Basso earlier today, and he confirmed those details with me. Since then, I have learned that Viola Arrendondo had nearly identical wounds— abrasions on the stomach and a deep puncturing in the perineal region. I'll word this as delicately as I can, Ronald—the perineal muscles are located in that delicate patch of skin between a woman's reproductive area and her rear end.

GRANTHAM: I see. Have you gotten any details about what type of wound was found in that region?

BENTLEY: I've spoken only to the medical examiner who completed Jeannette Conway's autopsy. But according to him, Jeannette's injuries included a tearing of the subcutaneous tissues and deep perforations of the abdominal wall. This was a brutal stabbing, inflicted with extreme force, that occurred most likely when the victim was on her back and with her knees raised—maybe trying to scramble away from her attacker—or perhaps from behind, trying to get away on all fours.

GRANTHAM: This makes no sense to me. I've reported on prostitute murders before, Reed. They are usually killed by strangling or by your basic stabbing, but this is mutilation. It sounds like these two women were gored to death in some sort of sick ritual.

BENTLEY: You're not far off the mark there, Ronald. When you begin to put the ugly pieces together—the shocking brutality of the crimes, the missing body parts, the heavy metal music with messages of death and murder, hanging over these cases like a poisonous fog— you have to wonder what connection might exist between it all.

GRANTHAM: (OVER PHOTOS) I want to go to some photographs if we can because, you know, you hear this word "prostitute" and a bad image forms in your mind. But take a look at our split-screen here—that's Jeannette Conway on the left, probably around 13 or 14-years-old there, and that's Viola Arrendondo on the right, in the Jimi Hendrix shirt. She looks 16 or 17 in that picture. These are precious young girls, not at all like someone you would expect to make a living sleeping with strange men.

Okay, previously in the video segment, we heard from Jeannette Conway's mother, Darlene. Darlene is joining us now—on the phone. Thank you, Darlene, for being with us, and I am so sorry for your loss. Can you speak to us on what detectives have told you about the killing of your daughter, your beautiful Jeannette?

CONWAY: They're working very hard. I see them working hard on my daughter's case, trying to find the man who did this terrible thing. I want them to know that I appreciate that. They don't look down upon Jeannette because of what she done.

GRANTHAM: He's not a man, he's a monster, Darlene, a maniac, and I hope you don't mind me saying so. A maniac who will be caught and brought to justice if Detective Stanley Basso has anything to do about it. Have you met Detective Basso, Darlene?

CONWAY: Yes, he's been very helpful, very gentle with me. He helped me pick out the best pictures of Jeannette to put on the TV.

GRANTHAM: That's good. You know, folks, I hate to say this, but this police department, not only there in Pacifica but in all of San Mateo County, has had its share of serious problems over the years. Illegal drug seizures, bribery, paying out huge cash rewards for confidential informants. But from what I know, Detective Basso is one of the good guys, a top cop. Darlene, has he given you any information about who committed this atrocious crime?

CONWAY: No—just that they're looking for him, that he probably met Jeannette at the bar. That maybe he was into this heavy metal music. They found some tape at the scene, a piece of a cassette tape—

GRANTHAM: Yes, I have that information in front of me. You haven't heard what's on the tape, have you, Darlene?

CONWAY: No, but I've been told that it's that loud rock music that all the kids are listening to these days. No words, no singing—just screaming guitars. Detective Basso called it "death metal."

GRANTHAM: Once again, we return to the music angle in these two cases—heavy metal music, groups with terrifying names like Skeleton Skin, groups with songs about the occult and devil worship. And it makes me think that the police, or maybe Tipper Gore and all those "Washington Wives," know something we don't. We saw heavy metal's sickening impact in 1981, when Kim Goytia, just 13-years-old, a heavy-metal fan and Satanist, fatally shot her younger sister in cold blood. We saw it again in 1984, with that vicious murder committed by Ricky Kasso. From the "devil horns" hand gesture that has become a disturbing symbol of its growing fanbase, to certain music groups entering into Faustian pacts with the devil, occult elements in heavy metal are impossible to ignore. So the question remains: could these same elements have played a role in the deaths of Jeannette Conway and Viola Arrendondo?

Let's return to Pacifica, about 20 miles south of San Francisco, where Detective Stanley Basso of the Pacifica Police Department has met up with a dive team at Linda Mar Beach. Detective Basso—thank you for taking time out of your busy day to join us. We've got you live on our state-of-the-art video feed as we speak. What can you tell us about the investigation into these savage murders?

BASSO: Well, first, I want to give my condolences to Darlene, and to the family of Viola Arrendondo. I can't speak definitively about the Arrendondo case, as her murder occurred in a different jurisdiction. But I empathize with the families of these young women. Now, as you can see, we've got a dive team out here today because we have reason to believe we might find evidence in the water of Jeannette Conway's murder.

GRANTHAM: Now, you're talking about the missing body parts, am I right? You're talking about the head and arms of Jeannette Conway.

BASSO: Any evidence, including body parts, yes.

GRANTHAM: Detective Basso—point blank. Is there a serial killer on the loose in Northern California, and, if so, do you think he has Patty Howard in his clutches as we speak?

BASSO: We can't answer that yet—it's one of many possibilities that investigators from both departments are considering. We don't want to cause any undue alarm, as we have only two victims at this point.

GRANTHAM: "Only" two victims, Detective?

BASSO: I'm just clarifying for your audience how we are directing our investigation and the labeling of these crimes.

GRANTHAM: Well, let's see—you have two killings right next door to each other, both with satanic undertones. The bodies mutilated, with body parts missing. You have a missing girl, a runaway. All three of these women are minorities, and at least two of them are prostitutes.

BASSO: We're just being careful in our approach. Collecting evidence, canvassing the neighborhood, and asking people in the community to come forward with information if they have it.

GRANTHAM: Follow-up question. Do you think the murders are the work of some kind of satanic network?

BASSO: A network? Well, that remains to be seen, though both cases do contain subversive elements. Suspicious graffiti was found at both sites, and investigators are looking into exactly when those markings were made. Now, the unusual wounds on Jeannette Conway do have a ritualistic element to them, which we take very seriously.

GRANTHAM: And let's not forget that three of the fingers on Viola Arrendondo's left hand were removed and taken by the killer. Now, folks, hear me out—for centuries, Satan has been associated with the left hand, in the Bible and in folklore stories from around the world.

BASSO: That's an interesting point, but it would only be speculation as to whether the assailant made those same associations. Believe me, if there are genuine occult or satanic motives at play here, we'll find out about it. We will use whatever information we can to solve these murders and to find Patty Howard.

GRANTHAM: If I may, I want to review some popular cases and then get your opinion, Detective Basso. I have in front of me a copy of the memoir *Michelle Remembers*, which chronicles, in explicit detail, the satanic ritual abuse of a woman named Michelle Smith. Among some of her more monstrous claims: a satanic cult forced her to participate in the sacrifice of a baby. She was fed on by beetles, spiders, and feral cats. Bathed in the blood of a goat. Made to eat worms and bugs. And today, in sunny Southern California, we have the McMartin case: a well-liked family, owners of a popular pre-school, charged with the most depraved acts imaginable, including the sexual abuse of children and witchery. In your investigative experience, is there such a thing as satanic ritual abuse, otherwise known as SRA? And could Jeannette Conway and Viola Arrendondo be the victims of such abuse?

BASSO: I've heard of *Michelle Remembers*, but I've never read it, nor am I aware of any official police investigation that resulted from its publication. The McMartin case is another matter; I've been following that story closely. Now, a proper investigation is informed by the evidence—and from what I've read in the papers and seen on TV, there is little proof that any type of crime occurred at that pre-school, let alone satanic or occult activity. Unless the prosecutors have some sort of "smoking gun" that they're hiding from the rest of us, I predict there will be acquittals for all the defendants in that case.

GRANTHAM: Fair enough. Now, Detective Basso, let's talk about heavy metal music. It was "Metalhead Night" at the bar in Pacifica on the night Jeannette vanished. What do you know of this bar called the Seahorse Saloon?

BASSO: It's a popular dive bar. It attracts bikers, locals, and the occasional surfer passing through. They have theme nights, you see— disco night, heavy metal night—but we are not necessarily linking any type of music to Jeannette's murder.

GRANTHAM: But there *was* a seedy element at the bar the night she disappeared and there *was* a tape recording of metal music found at the dump site. It stands to reason that Jeannette met her killer at the bar, and that he was into the same kind of music she was. Maybe the tape belonged to him. Maybe it fell out of his pocket or got dragged out from his car. And Viola Arrendondo attended a heavy metal show on the night she was murdered. I don't need to tell you, Detective, that heavy metal music has become synonymous with the occult and with Satanism. I have a list of bands here—Black Sabbath, AC/DC, Iron Maiden, just to name a few—that have come under fire for their disturbing lyrics, onstage theatrics, and associations with the devil.

BASSO: I'm not sure I follow you, Ron.

GRANTHAM: Connect the dots, sir! I have a cross-country report here from the FBI. You might be surprised to learn that in the hundreds of cult-oriented murders committed each year, the killers always have some kind of heavy metal paraphernalia among their personal belongings. Records, tapes, pendants, patches, shirts—the list goes on and on. I don't think it's a coincidence that Jeannette and Viola were around the types of creeps who listen to this music when they were murdered. Detective, you have a killer on your hands, possibly a serial killer, who may be using heavy metal music as an inspiration to murder!

BASSO: At this time, the Pacifica Police Department is holding off on labeling these slayings as those of a serial killer. That's about all I can say right now about your theory. Let me also add that fans of heavy metal may put "satanic" or occult patches onto their clothes, but that doesn't necessarily mean they're making a philosophical statement or declaring a sacrilegious war against humanity. They might just be identifying themselves as fans of a certain genre of music.

GRANTHAM: Okay, Detective Basso, I sense the reservation in your voice. I understand you have an investigation to run.

I would like to hear from Moses Howard now—he is Patty Howard's father, and my producer is getting him on the line. Folks, you're seeing up on your screen a picture of Patty, a runaway from Northern California who is currently missing. Like our two murder victims, Patty is young and pretty—and may have been prostituting herself to make a living on the streets. Mr. Howard, are you there? Sir, thank you for joining the program during what must be a very frightening time.

MOSES HOWARD, PATTY HOWARD'S FATHER: Thanks for having me and for doing this show.

GRANTHAM: You're welcome. We're doing this for Patty, to get her back home. Tell me about her. What do you want people to know?

HOWARD: First, I want to make something clear to your audience. Patty would never prostitute herself. I know police found her purse with money in it, I know she was last seen in a bad neighborhood, but there's got to be another explanation. I want your audience to know that.

GRANTHAM: We understand, Mr. Howard. We hear you loud and clear.

HOWARD: Now, we've had our share of troubles, like all families do, but Patty is a very special young lady. She loves to sing. She sings for our church choir. She's smart and friendly—she never has a bad word to say about anyone. Whatever you need, if you need someone to listen to you or be your friend, you go to Patty.

GRANTHAM: I don't know if you have your set on, Mr. Howard, but we have pictures of Patty up right now. Thousands of people across the country are getting a good look at her. It's not just the police who are looking for your daughter. We've got the entire nation on this. Can you tell the audience—when was the last time you saw Patty?

HOWARD: We had a big fight on Halloween night, so that was almost a month ago. She wanted to go to a party, a costume party with some friends, but I didn't trust the people she was hanging around with. Suspicious folk. Kids with no direction. I told her so. We got in a huge blow-up.

GRANTHAM: And is that the night she ran away?

HOWARD: That's right. Just gone in the night. She called me about a week later, told me she was going to come home soon. But she wouldn't give me the address of the spot she was staying. I think she was bumming around from place to place. I haven't seen or heard from her now in over two weeks.

GRANTHAM: These so-called friends Patty was staying with. You said you thought they were "suspicious." Who are they and have you told police about them?

HOWARD: They sell drugs. They tag. They like weird music and books and scary movies. Patty's a good girl, a Christian girl. I brought her up right. I don't know why she wants to run with a dangerous crowd like that. I've spoken to police and told them what I know about these guys.

GRANTHAM: We will do everything we can to get your daughter back home, Mr. Howard. Let's repeat this on the airwaves right now. We have Jeannette Conway and Viola Arrendondo, two young women murdered, their bodies dumped most likely by someone with occult or satanic interests. Currently missing is Patty Howard, 18-years-old, a runaway, her purse found discarded by the side of the road.

To wrap up here in our final moments, I want to check in with a regular on *American Investigation*, psychoanalyst Elizabeth Shelton, joining us from Los Angeles via satellite. Elizabeth, you've listened to tonight's coverage, you've read the newspaper articles and are aware of the horrendous nature of these crimes. Why would you dismember a body? Why would you cut off its head and arms, or its fingers?

ELIZABETH SHELTON, PSYCHOANALYST: Obviously, the assailant has a serious disturbance of some kind, a lot of anger and rage against women. He is most likely the victim of abuse himself, which probably began when he was a small child. He probably comes from a broken home, and he may see himself as ugly or freakish, a mirror image of the suffering he puts his victims through. But the violent removal of extremities, the beheading, signifies a much deeper mental imbalance. Sure, he might have done this just so the bodies would be harder to identify, but there are psychological factors to consider as well. When a killer dismembers another human being, the victim ceases to be a person. In the psychopath's diseased mind, Jeannette Conway and Viola Arrendondo were no longer human; they were animals, like something you would hunt down and slaughter in the woods.

GRANTHAM: These poor women were tracked down, targeted by this killer.

SHELTON: The fact they were prostitutes adds to the dehumanizing way the killer saw them. It's not hard to sacrifice something that you don't value.

GRANTHAM: You used that word "sacrifice," Elizabeth. I'm already disgusted by these crimes, but I worry that there are darker forces at work here. Those body parts are going to turn up somewhere, unless they've been burned or buried deep in the ground. I want to urge the public to come forward if they know anything about these murders, and if you're a woman on the streets tonight, down on your luck, if you're somehow watching this show—please, please be careful.

I want to offer a special thank you to both Darlene Conway and Moses Howard, who bravely came forward to tell their stories tonight.

And thanks to our other guests as well. I'm Ronald Grantham, and this has been *American Investigation*—your only source for the latest telenews. I'll be back next week with updates to this disturbing story, along with a recent police corruption case out of California that might just shock you. Goodnight.

"Satanic Shocker: The Youth Behind *Blood Songs*" by Penelope Marks (originally published in *Silver Screams*, December, 1985, p. 5-6):

When they were kids, best friends Debra Morrow and Charlene Worsley wandered the bustling streets of Berkeley and Oakland with a beat-up Super-8 camera in their hands, filming anything that caught their creative eye. When jittery shots of moving cars and busy storefronts began to bore them, they ventured into the macabre world of horror cinema, turning a roly-poly bug into a flesh-eating mutant or a bicycling clown into a vision of terror. Their movies even had titles, including *Clown College Murders* and *Satan's Birthday Party*, which they wrote in black Magic Marker on posterboard and held up before the camera.

Most of us "horror nerds," especially those raised on Universal Monsters and *Creature Features*, have fond memories like these, but it's rare when our filmmaking dreams stretched beyond, say, the fifth grade. We never stopped going to the movies, of course, and we snuck into every R-rated splatter-party we could (yes, even us girls), but the clunky Super-8 wound up in a drawer somewhere and rarely saw the light of day.

But Debra and Charlene never stopped making movies. In the sixth grade they paid homage to Romero's *Night of the Living Dead*, casting their relatives and friends as zombies in a film called *Brain-Eating Creatures from Saturn*. In the summer of 1980, as both girls turned 13, they ventured into the slasher genre with *Claw*, the tragic story of a disfigured orphan who dispatches his victims with a sledgehammer.

As time passed, the girls honed their craft. While Debra took over directing duties, Charlene sparkled in front of the camera as arguably the youngest scream queen in the history of horror. They made more movies, including the gross-out *Monsters in Your Pants*, in which Charlene played a young girl with a sausage-like creature living inside her womb. Today, these guerrilla filmmakers hope to take the bull by the horns with their most ambitious project yet: a horror film about a home invasion and its terrible consequences.

Blood Songs takes place in a quiet town of farmhouses, horse pastures, and endless amber waves of grain. That picturesque setting is ripped apart during an explosive night of terror and violence. While out on a date, teenage Danielle (Worsley) and her boyfriend get into an argument, which forces Danielle to be late for her curfew.

Meanwhile, her mother, Melody (Beatrice Cooper), waits nervously for her young daughter to return home. This universal conflict provides the gateway into several shocking scenes of occult horror when an intruder breaks into their home, demanding a sacrifice worse than death.

While the storylines of Morrow and Worsley's earlier films were borrowed liberally from the horror movies they watched and studied growing up, *Blood Songs* is unlike anything the pair have produced before. Without giving away too much of the plot, the home intruder is one of the most frightening villains to grace the indie horror screen as of late. His methods of attack are unforgiving and sadistic, a fact made more startling when one considers that the entire project—from its script to its production and distribution to film festivals—has been spearheaded by two young women. But it is during the wild climax of *Blood Songs* that the artistic merits of Morrow and Worsley shine the brightest; at that pivotal moment, the movie becomes relentless in its depiction of violence and the corrupted nature of revenge.

Morrow and Worsley have also expanded their crew to include a team of novice but talented actors and artist-technicians, all of whom happily agreed to work for free on the movie. In addition to Worsley and Cooper in the starring roles, Darren Rivera portrays the home intruder with menacing relish, while Brad Payton expertly plays Eddie, the pony-tailed boyfriend who discovers Jesus at precisely the wrong moment. There is another character in the film who makes an unexpected "appearance" at the climax, but saying anything more will ruin the fiendish surprise.

As producer and director, Morrow capitalizes on her miniscule budget, keeping the suspense and tension at an all-time high before pulling out all the gory stops during an FX-heavy grand finale. Unlike other youthful auteurs who try to combine their horror with bits of comedy or even slapstick, Morrow keeps the tone serious and, dare I say it, existential. *Blood Songs* is that rare horror film that tackles a number of mature motifs—including religion and underage sex—while also ramping up the gore factor. By the time the end credits roll, the audience will have had its fair share of stranglings, disembowelments, skull-crushings, and other forms of carnage. Added to this insane mix is a wickedly sinister soundtrack, which, as the title of the movie implies, plays a critical role in the plot.

Equally powerful in the film is the smooth glide of the camera, manned by Billy Lee, who met Morrow and Worsley in a scriptwriting class at East Bay Community College in California. Though a newcomer to the world of cinematography, Lee colors *Blood Songs* in wispy shadows and flickering lights; in the house where most of the story takes place, we see *just* enough to elicit feelings of unease and fear. Though the darkness does become overwhelming at times (especially during the film's outdoor scenes), Lee understands how to manipulate the audience's sense of (dis)comfort with unusual angles and unbroken tracking shots. Owing much to films like *Rosemary's Baby* and *The Shining*, Lee's stunning camera work is an impressive compliment to Morrow's taut direction.

And the direction in *Blood Songs* is top-notch. Charlene Worsley and Beatrice Cooper are truly put through the horror wringer in the film, while Darren Rivera is so convincing as the intruder that I was truly afraid for the fate of the two female leads. While all of the actors are outstanding in the picture, Worsley provides the wow factor that most low-budget movies lack these days. Again, saying more will spoil the climax, but let's just say that a little blood and guts can't keep this brave girl down. A heady mix of beauty and brawn, Worsley immerses herself in the role of Danielle—and it is this level of commitment that makes everything in *Blood Songs* click. The actors in the film trust their director, and they trust that Morrow can make the heavy-duty violence and somber themes work. And, at just 18-years-old, Morrow does indeed make it work. Clocking in at 9 minutes and 33 seconds, *Blood Songs* is a triumph of a short film, and it goes without saying that I can't wait for the first feature-length project from this team of talented individuals.

While *Blood Songs* is far from perfect (along with the lighting issues, there are many out-of-sync overdubs and audio glitches), the strength of the film lies in its bone-chilling plot, dedicated crew, and a director-actor duo who has been turning out the skin-crawling goods since they were in pigtails. I hope you'll keep Debra Morrow, Charlene Worsley, and the rest of the gruesome gang behind *Blood Songs* on your radar. If these kids are the future of horror, then our beloved genre just got a whole lot brighter.

BLOOD SONGS

STORY TREATMENT, 1984-1985

ACT ONE – NIGHT FALLS IN HOLLISTER

A desolate road in a quiet agricultural town. A blood-red moon hangs high above barren trees while farmhouses dot the landscape in every direction.

The road is empty except for an OLDSMOBILE DELTA 88 parked in a muddy ditch, the windows blacked out with grime.

Inside the vehicle, the dashboard is littered with cigarette boxes, fast-food wrappers, and mildewed copies of *Screw* and *Hustler* magazine. A PENTAGRAM PENDANT dangles from the rearview mirror.

The PROWLER reclines in the driver's seat, his HEAVY BREATHING the only sound in the dark. His leather-gloved hands grip the steering wheel.

Meanwhile, inside a nearby farmhouse, MELODY ARMSTRONG, 45, is hanging up COLOR PRINTS to dry inside a darkroom.

The photos are of her daughter, DANIELLE ARMSTRONG, 16 and beautiful, with flowing brown hair and almond-brown eyes.

Melody uses a clothespin to hang another photo—this one of Danielle looking radiant in an ankle-length SUMMER DRESS.

Back inside the Oldsmobile, the Prowler takes the pentagram from the mirror and drapes it around his neck. He picks up a WALKMAN and a CASSETTE TAPE from the passenger seat.

Onto the cassette, someone has scratched the words BLOOD SONGS.

The Prowler inserts the tape into the Walkman and then hits PLAY. A DEATH METAL SONG erupts with sonic fury. The Prowler puts on headphones, and the song becomes muffled and eerily distorted.

Cut to a GREEN CAMARO parked alongside a remote field. In the backseat, intertwined like a pretzel, are Danielle and EDDIE, 18, having sex.

The two lovers reach an explosive climax. In the afterglow, they cling to each other with great passion just as...

The Prowler gets out of his car. He denim jacket is covered in patches of metal bands and Nazi imagery. He secures the Walkman to his belt.

Through the headphones, the metal song is a distant cacophony of rage as the Prowler begins walking toward the farmhouse.

ACT TWO – BROKEN HEARTS

In the back of the Camaro, Eddie tells Danielle that he has reached a decision about college. Instead of going to a nearby state school so he can be close to her, Eddie reveals that he will be attending seminary school in North Carolina. "I want to do missionary work," he informs Danielle, "and devote my life to Christ."

Though more sad than angry, Danielle can't help but point out the bitter irony of Eddie's decision. "I wonder what Jesus would think of what we just did," she says, throwing on her clothes. "Take me home. I'm past curfew anyway."

Inside the house, Melody has just climbed into bed. She checks the clock with a look of concern. The time is 12:30 AM. She glimpses the phone on her bed stand, worried that Danielle hasn't called to say she's going to be late.

CLICK. The sound, like an opening window latch, causes Melody to sit up in bed. She calls out her daughter's name. No answer.

CLICK. Nervously, Melody throws back the covers and walks on tip-toes to the bedroom door.

VROOM! The Camaro tearing down a dark stretch of country road. Inside the vehicle, Eddie and Danielle sit in silence before Danielle erupts. She reminds Eddie that she was a virgin before they met, and that she never would have allowed their relationship to go that far had she known he was going to move to North Carolina.

Eddie desperately attempts to explain himself, but he only makes the situation worse. "I've known for a long time that I was leaving," he says, "but we were having too much fun and I didn't want to ruin it." Furious, Danielle stares out the window, the bleak landscape passing before her eyes, the moon a bloody thumbprint in the sky above.

C-R-E-A-K. The hardwood floor groans under Melody's feet as she enters the living room. She then hears another noise—a hushed and faraway thrum, like the sound of the ocean through a seashell.

Melody freezes. Listens. And hears the low-tuned rumble of the death metal song, muffled as if being played through a pair of headphones.

She hurries into the kitchen and reaches for the phone, but the line is dead. Panicked now, she draws a butcher knife from the block on the counter and returns to the living room.

Melody crosses the floor and nears the darkroom down the hall. The distorted music FADES in volume. She backs away, turning to the bathroom. As she inches her way forward, the volume of the song begins to RISE.

Meanwhile, Eddie's Camaro rips into a corner too fast, spraying dust and gravel. Danielle orders him to slow down, but Eddie ignores her and punches the accelerator. Danielle demands to be let out of the car.

Eddie careens the car to a halt at the side of the road. He reaches over Danielle, opens the passenger door, and tells her to get out. Danielle climbs out of the car, her face streaked with tears.

"I'll pray for you," Eddie says just before Danielle slams the car door. The Camaro burns rubber down the road. Danielle wipes away her tears and turns toward her home on the near horizon.

Inside the house, Melody inches toward the bathroom, her body humming with fear. The death metal has grown louder, the words just audible: "Black magic prom queen / Satan's pain princess / Only sweet sixteen / Join us, join us."

Clutching the butcher knife, Melody nudges open the bathroom door and hits the light. The room is empty.

She peeks into Danielle's bedroom. Also empty. The moon casts an ominous red glow on the bed, which is neatly-made and adorned with a teddy bear in a leather jacket.

Melody notices her daughter's transistor radio on the nightstand and breathes a sigh of relief. But when she picks up the radio she realizes that it's turned OFF...

Just then, the hall closet SWINGS OPEN and the metal song becomes a ROAR OF TERROR as...

Danielle hops a fence and cuts through someone's backyard, trying to make it home as quickly as she can.

Back in the hall, the Prowler BURSTS from the closet. Before Melody can wield her knife or even scream, he pins her against the wall of Danielle's bedroom. The metal song provides a horrific soundtrack to the brutality of the scene, as the Prowler beats Melody to within an inch of her life.

He then drags Melody into the living room, arranges her on the floor like some grisly museum display, and removes a large hunting knife from inside his jacket.

Working in rhythmic tandem with the song, the Prowler cuts out Melody's heart and disembowels her.

ACT THREE – VENGEANCE IS MINE

Danielle ducks under a wire fence and enters her backyard. She takes her keyring from her pocket and begins searching for the right key by the light of the moon.

Inside the house, the Prowler has placed Melody's heart on the floor. Then he stops the Walkman and fast-forwards the tape, searching for a certain tune. He hits play and a battering-ram of a song begins, filled with savage growls, frenzied riffs, and violent lyrics.

As the Prowler adjusts his headphones, we see his face for the first time. It is a spidery face, gaunt, jaundiced, cratered with acne scars. The lips are smeared in blood, the hair a mess of long greasy strings.

While the song grows with raw fury, the Prowler kneels down beside Melody's body. He cups his hands and plunges them into her gutted abdomen. The Prowler delivers this chalice of blood to his mouth and drinks.

He swallows, dips, and drinks again, blood streaming down his chin and neck in red zippers. As the song enters a surreal and ghostly meditative bridge, the Prowler begins a SATANIC CHANT, his voice guttural and raspy. As he raises his arms to the ceiling in demonic prayer...

THWONK! The Prowler topples onto his side, the Walkman and headphones skidding across the floor.

Standing above him, fresh tears streaming down her face, is Danielle, her hands gripping an ALUMINUM BASEBALL BAT. As the Prowler attempts to move, Danielle steps over the body of her mother and approaches the deranged killer.

The Prowler glares up at Danielle with roiling black eyes. "I can give you power," he says. As he talks, blood pools around his head and bubbles up from his mouth. "With Lucifer as your Lord, you can do things you never thought possible, if only you would *listen*."

Before the Prowler can utter another syllable, Danielle SMASHES the bat down onto his head. And again. And again. The final hit rips open the killer's skull, exposing the rippled gray meat of the brain. Satisfied the man is dead, Danielle drops the bat and turns toward her mother.

Holding the broken body in her arms, Danielle sobs hysterically. Grief and shock come in crashing waves. As the abomination of the night overwhelms her, the Prowler's words echo in her mind: "...you can do things you never thought possible, if only you would *listen*." These words repeat like a mantra inside her head.

Danielle spots the Walkman across the room. Fighting back tears, she gently places a blanket over her mother's body. Then she picks up the cassette player. With great disgust, she puts the headphones on and presses PLAY.

The weird, ethereal bridge of the metal song gives way to a chugging guitar, over which a DISTORTED VOICE speaks. Danielle cranks the volume of the Walkman to HIGH and the song becomes the booming soundtrack to the film.

Danielle grows spellbound by the voice as it begins to recite lyrics that sound like an invocation: "Free me from the bull-god's lair / and all the evil inside my head / Moloch, hear this deliverance prayer / possess the child instead."

The house turns freezing cold; windows fling open and curtains billow like sheeted ghosts in the sudden wind. Though terrified, Danielle can't stop listening to the song.

As the haunting verses continue, books fall off the shelves, a painting floats in the air, a vase shatters, and a lamp shade shrivels like burned skin and drips with blood.

In a trance, Danielle sits by her mother's body. The song continues to play, returning to its violent lyrics and thrashing riffs. Danielle closes her eyes, waiting for the phonic horror to stop.

The song ends. Danielle opens her eyes. The wind has stopped raging. The windows no longer bang about.

And there, cast as a pitiless and deformed shadow on the wall, is the DEVIL himself.

Danielle takes off the headphones and stops the cassette player. Now all she can hear is the Devil's labored BREATH, its distended belly rising and falling in unholy gasps.

A BOOMING VOICE suddenly reverberates throughout the house, loud enough to shake the foundation. "PLEDGE YOUR LIFE TO ME, SURRENDER YOUR PERVERTED SOUL, AND YOU SHALL BE GRANTED AS MANY WISHES AS YOU DESIRE."

Danielle tries to clear her head, unsure if she is actually hearing the voice of the Devil or if she has lost her mind. But the voice rocks the house again: "YOU HAVE ALREADY SURRENDERED TO THE LIBIDINOUS PLEASURES OF THE FLESH. NOW IMAGINE A WORLD OF EVEN GREATER LUST AND SUCCULENCE, A WORLD FULFILLED OF ALL YOUR DREAMS. SWEAR YOUR LOYALTY TO ME AND IT WILL ALL BE YOURS."

Danielle looks from the shadow on the wall to her mother's body. Her eyes fill with tears. But when she looks at the Prowler's crushed skull, her expression turns angry and defiant.

She locks eyes on the shadow, gathering all her courage. "I swear," she says. Outside, a torrential RAIN begins to fall and THUNDER rolls across the hinterland.

"Good pet. You have pleased the Ancient Serpent with your black allegiance, and now you shall be rewarded," the Devil says, the voice softer now. "Confess to me your first desire."

Danielle reaches for her mother's hand as the screen goes BLACK.

EPILOGUE

Nighttime in Hollister.

Inside the house, Danielle is sleeping on the couch. The room is perfectly neat. No broken glass or fallen books. No blood. No dead bodies.

In the darkroom, Melody uses clothespins to hang up prints of her daughter. She smiles at one of them: Danielle looking radiant in an ankle-length SUMMER DRESS. The camera lingers on the picture before cutting to...

"Danielle, it's time to get up," Melody says, waking her daughter.

Danielle rises from the couch. "What time is it?" she asks.

Walking into the kitchen, Melody answers, "Almost eight. You better hurry up. You're going to be late for your date with Eddie."

Danielle stands and stretches. She tells Melody that the house smells like chemicals. "I was developing pictures," Melody explains. "There's some real beauties of you in the darkroom."

Confused by what must have been a horrific dream, Danielle walks to the darkroom. She steps inside and closes the door behind her. She is now enveloped in the red glow caused by the room's safelights.

She gazes at the pictures of herself, each one reminding her of some pleasant memory. She reaches the last photo on the clothesline—her in the summer dress. She is beautiful here, skin glowing, brown hair perfectly layered, eyes almond-brown.

And then the picture CHANGES. Her skin erupts into craters, her hair becomes a nest of hissing snakes, her eyes turn a smoldering black.

And inside the darkroom, the real Danielle GRINS. She hears Melody call out for her. "Dani! Honey! I think Eddie's car just pulled up!"

Danielle turns toward a shelving unit in the corner of the room. She finds a JUNK BOX and begins rummaging through it, casting aside wrenches, batteries, and rolls of film.

Then she finds it: a BOX CUTTER. She pops the blade and tests it with her finger. Nice and sharp.

HONK! HONK! The BLASTING of the Camaro's horn.

"Coming, Eddie," the new Danielle says.

"That's a Wrap: Facing the Music of *Blood Songs*" by Chrissy Garland (originally published in the *East Bay Experience*, Jan., 1986, p. 2-3):

Two weeks after completing her first major short film, a gruesome tale called *Blood Songs*, writer and director Debra Morrow, a first-year student at our college, spoke with the *East Bay Experience* about the challenges of making micro-budget horror, the struggles the crew went through to get that "perfect shot," and why an ambulance was called to the set on the final day of shooting.

On Wednesday morning, in between her American History and Creative Writing classes, Debra joined me for a hot chocolate in the Lower Lounge. She surprised me with some promotional items for the movie, including two stickers and a black scoop-neck tee emblazoned with the words "Death Rock Never Dies." Already I'm impressed!

"We're doing our best to get the word out there," Debra says, but her enthusiasm fails to mask the fatigue in her voice. Setting her hot chocolate aside to cool, she tells me that *Blood Songs* took seven straight days of filming to complete, with many of the shoots lasting deep into the night. "I didn't always know what I was doing," she says. "It's my first serious film and I made a lot of mistakes. I worked the actors hard and kept them up way too late. Still, we're all pretty stoked with the results!"

Among the cast and crew, Debra lists Charlene Worsley and Billy Lee—also students at East Bay—as two of the most valuable. Charlene plays the lead in the film, a teenager tormented by satanic evil and forced to make a terrible choice, while Billy shot the scenes with a camera he rented from the college.

"They're my friends, but they're also professionals determined to make their mark in the industry," Debra says. "They didn't get paid to be in the film. They just love making movies, especially the bloody ones! There's no other reason you would put yourself through this kind of hell."

Speaking of hell, Debra describes one of the more laborious moments during the making of the horror picture. The world's most ancient evil makes a sudden and surprise cameo in the final minutes of *Blood Songs*, and the camera shots that Debra wanted in order to convey this apocalyptic arrival seemed impossible to get.

"I yelled at Billy a lot on that day of shooting. I was kind of a bitch," a contrite Debra explains. "But Billy, who's older than me and has a passion for the horror genre, understood what I was trying to achieve. He was patient beyond belief and I owe the spooky look of *Blood Songs* entirely to him."

But as Debra spoons a dollop of whipped cream from her hot cocoa into her mouth, her delightful smile returns, and she is quick to explain that making the film wasn't all doom and gloom. She has been best friends with the star of the show, the stunning Charlene Worsley, for many years. The two had a killer time crafting the grisly flick, which includes scenes of disembowelment, blood-drinking, and one very barbaric attack with an aluminum baseball bat. As Debra tells me, "Charlene plays such a kick-ass heroine! She's just a hurricane-force of rage in the film, totally committed to the role," Debra enthuses. "When the one person her character loves is taken from her in an act of savagery, the character must fight back, or die trying. Charlene understands that conflict. She's a very instinctive and intuitive actress."

During our interview, Debra does take the time to address an unfounded rumor that began floating around the campus gossip-mill after production on the film ended. Allegedly, paramedics had been called to the set on the last day of shooting because Charlene Worsley had a "meltdown" and was lashing out at members of the cast and crew.

"An ambulance was called, yes," Debra admits. "The last day of shooting was the most stressful. For continuity, Charlene had to wear the same costume for several days—her hair and clothes streaked with the sticky red syrup that we used for blood, her muscles aching from the physical demands of the role. She started hearing strange noises— loud knocking and scraping sounds on the walls of the set—but no one else could hear them. Then she collapsed on the floor from nervous exhaustion.

"Paramedics came, and they treated her while everyone broke for dinner or a cigarette. Two or three hours later and we had finished the movie," Debra says. "I've heard rumors around school that people thought Charlene had gone crazy, and that she attacked one of the crew. That's absurd. Charlene's a lot tougher than people give her credit for. It was just fatigue and stress. Everybody knows that."

Now that production on *Blood Songs* has wrapped, Debra is most excited about the next step: getting audiences to see the film.

"We hope to do a screening here at East Bay, with t-shirt and sticker giveaways and some other fun things, and then to get the movie into some horror film festivals," Debra says excitedly. "We'll probably take some time off after that before moving on with the next project."

"College Filmmakers Get Gory: An Interview with Debra Morrow and Billy Lee" by Paul Leonard (originally published in *Monsters & Mayhem*, February, 1986, p. 20-22):

In December of 1973, on the day after Christmas, wunderkind film director William Friedkin (*The French Connection, Cruising*) released upon the world the most terrifying film ever made. Based on the international bestselling novel by William Peter Blatty, Friedkin's *The Exorcist* told the tale of a young girl's horrific ordeal with Satan himself—who, in the movie, manifests as a perverse and malevolent demon named Pazuzu. The rest is horror-cinema history as *The Exorcist* shocked and thrilled audiences around the world with disturbing scenes of projectile vomiting, rotating heads, and crotch-plunging crucifixes. And though many believe it impossible to surpass Friedkin's masterpiece of demonic possession, such an argument has not discouraged filmmakers from giving it the old college try—usually to the dismay of critics and horror fans alike (see "Another Devil, Another Dollar," *Monsters & Mayhem # 34*).

Enter Debra Morrow, 18, and Billy Lee, 20, the energetic and baby-faced team behind last year's short-film shocker of murder and satanic rock, *Blood Songs*. Still grappling with the imagery and themes of that project, the duo vows to pump fresh blood into the devil-possession genre with a new script as terrifying and fiendish as they come. While promoting *Blood Songs* at Sacramento's Skin and Bones Horror Festival, college students Morrow and Lee visited with *Monsters & Mayhem* to chew the fat about all things evil, including Satanism, Spanish demons, and the imminent arrival of the Anti-Christ himself...

MONSTERS & MAYHEM: The two of you are certainly working double-duty these days, trekking *Blood Songs* around California while spreading the word about your new screenplay. Let's start with *Blood Songs*. Can you tell us about the origins of the project, and what the production of the film was like?

DEBRA MORROW (director and screenwriter): The idea for the movie started with this beat-up paperback I checked out of my high school library. It was a corny little book, filled with gossip about rock 'n' roll bands from the 60s and 70s, but it also provided a glimpse into songs with satanic messages in them. I love Led Zeppelin, the Beatles, and Black Sabbath, all groups that were examined in the book, and I became drawn to the idea of subliminal messages in art, film, and music. I thought the topic could make for a very scary movie.

M&M: Debra, you started out as a documentary filmmaker, correct? Why did you make the transition into fictional films, and the horror genre in particular?

MORROW: I took a photography class in high school, and one of our assignments was to make a video documentary about any living photographer in the Bay Area. Charlene Worsley, who plays the daughter in *Blood Songs*, has been my best friend for years, and her mother, Ruth, is a professional photographer. Her work, especially her early architectural series, captures the historic aspects of Oakland and San Francisco in a way that I found very poetic. So I ended up making a film about Ruth and her work, and it won an award. I had already been dabbling in horror for a while—growing up, Charlene and I made a few short films about killer clowns and monsters—but it was actually Ruth who encouraged me to pursue the horror genre. Her photographs are deeply personal and show a genuine affection for her subject matter, and they remind me to do what I love no matter what anyone in the mainstream thinks.

M&M: In *Blood Songs*, the mother, Melody, is a photographer who gets viciously attacked by a home intruder. Was Ruth Worsley the inspiration behind that character?

MORROW: Melody Armstrong is an amalgam of the two most important women in my life: my own mother, who died when I was in high school; and Ruth, who was recently diagnosed with dementia. These two women are the motivation behind the film. It's a horror movie and audiences seem to be having a blast watching it, but there are deep layers underneath, including messages about death and dying, and the way we treat and care for others. And, for me, those themes were intentional. On the day my mom died—she was in palliative care and the nurse had given her morphine—she was holding my hand, and she was talking about taking an airplane flight. She was whispering, "Debra...I'm ready to go...there's a plane on the lake, a water plane..." She told me not to get on the flight—she said there would "be other flights to take." I think this was my mother's way of telling me to go to college, that I have a long life ahead of me, that I have amazing things to accomplish. The way Melody Armstrong worries about her daughter in *Blood Songs*, the way she loves her child above all else—that was inspired by my mother all the way.

M&M: Danielle, the teenage protagonist of *Blood Songs*, is such a powerful character, fearless in the face of extreme terror and brave enough to venture to the dark side to get what she wants. How did Charlene Worsley win the role and how did you manage to get her to such dark places when filming the movie?

MORROW: We didn't have that solid of a script for *Blood Songs*. I had written a treatment and some signature lines, and I knew I wanted the plot to take place on just one night, but that was about it. Charlene and Beatrice Cooper, who plays Melody, really brought the story and characters to life. From the start, I had every intention of casting Charlene for the role of Danielle. Charlene is a terrific actress, but she's also close to her own mother, so I thought she could really feed off the dynamic between Melody and Danielle in the treatment. That's actually why Charlene couldn't be here today—she's at home with Ruth, taking care of her. The power of *Blood Songs* doesn't come from the story, and it doesn't come from my treatment; it comes from all the energy and life experiences that Charlene and Beatrice brought to their roles.

BILLY LEE (cinematographer): I agree. There are some shots of Charlene in the film that I'm really proud of, where we seemed to capture both her physical beauty and the power of her performance in a single image. Though it wasn't always possible with *Blood Songs*, I'd like to one day shoot Charlene in more natural light to see what that brings out in her features. Beatrice Cooper was also incredible—a beautiful, sexy, older woman who used her extensive theater background to heighten her character's fear of the unknown.

M&M: Without revealing too much of the story, *Blood Songs* boasts a scorching soundtrack that is essential to the plot of the film. What can you tell us about the music and the group behind it?

MORROW: There are three songs in the film, and they were all written and performed by the same band, Carnal Season, who I met through a metal fanzine. The first song plays during the opening scene, and the last one plays during the closing credits. But it's the middle song, which plays during the climax of the movie, that everyone asks about. The title of that song is "Transfer of Spirits," and it's a stomping, dangerous little number. But, per their request, that's all I can really tell you about the song or the band. I don't mean to be mysterious, but my best recommendation would be to seek them out yourself. Try to score an interview—if you dare!

M&M: Our readers are notoriously obsessive about horror films and horror entertainment in general, usually to the exclusion of all other genres. Is it the same for the two of you and, if so, did that obsession fuel your desire to shoot horror? Or were there other factors that motivated you to explore darker material?

MORROW: I'm a horror nerd! What got me hooked were all those VHS box-covers in the video rental stores. Now that Blockbuster has opened, it's a little different, but before the big corporations took over, I could spend hours perusing the horror aisles of some little Mom and Pop rental place. Two covers that terrified me were for *The Texas Chain Saw Massacre* and for this monster movie called *The Beast Within*. I was scared to rent it because the cover said something like, "We dare you to sit through the last 30 minutes of this film without screaming and running from the room!" I eventually found the courage to see the movie, and I didn't scream—but it was still pretty good!

LEE: As community college students, we're under this stigmatic kind of microscope—you know, people will say things like, "As soon as you graduate you'll be able to do this and that," or "When you get to film school then you'll find out if you really have what it takes." I was always into horror and wanted to make splatter movies, but the genre is also very accessible for clever filmmakers who don't have big crews, fancy effects, and a bundle of cash just sitting around. You can slap a decent script together in a couple days, grab a camera and your best buds, promise them burgers and beer, and head off to the forest or somebody's basement and make your damn movie.

MORROW: (laughing) Okay, just for the record, I want readers of *Monsters & Mayhem* to know that I didn't slap my new screenplay together in a couple of days!

M&M: Billy, you mentioned that you're both college students. I presume that in between writing screenplays and making movies, you're hitting the books and attending classes. Has it been difficult striking that balance between your schoolwork and your various projects, and how has the college contributed to your efforts?

LEE: East Bay is an awesome school with great film classes and instructors. I'm in my third year here, but only because I don't want to leave! The thing I appreciate the most is that the professors in the Film and Television department give you credit for projects you take up and complete on your own. If you're into the arts and you're self-motivated, it's a great place to be.

MORROW: For our new movie, which is our first feature length, we're going to be relying on the college a lot—for actors, equipment, props, and anything else the school will be willing to loan us. Students in the Fashion Design department have agreed to make t-shirts to advertise the film, and I have a few artist-friends who want to help out creating other promotional items. The environment at East Bay is very supportive and I'll be sad to leave it behind when I transfer next year.

M&M: So let's hear more about this new film, which you've been talking up here at the festival in addition to *Blood Songs*. You have the script done and a rough production schedule in place. What can you reveal about the storyline?

MORROW: We've got two working titles for the project: *Inside Violet McCoy* and *The Devil and My Daughter*. The influences for the script are too many to list, but the obvious ones include *The Exorcist*, *The Sentinel*, and *The Omen*. But I also went beyond these choices to more unusual fare, the biggest one being 1975's *Demon Witch Child*, a Spanish film from Amando de Ossorio. It's a devil-possession movie, and I've only seen it in Spanish, but the girl who gets possessed in it is really creepy and effective. And Spanish demons are far more violent than American ones! It's quite a shocking film; along with all the devil stuff, it has infanticide and castration scenes and just a general sense of unease and psychedelic weirdness. Our new script owes a lot to it.

LEE: Debra's script—what I've seen of it so far—is brutal. It's not nearly as sentimental as *Blood Songs*, which came from a deeply personal place. As she finishes [the script], we're going to take a lot of road trips throughout Nor Cal to get inspired. We plan to visit some spooky places like the Winchester Mystery House and the old mission where *Vertigo* was filmed, but I also want to venture off the beaten path...*way off*, actually.

M&M: That sounds intriguing. Where exactly?

LEE: Well, that's a professional secret!

M&M: So would you say that there are elements of truth to your story, as in *The Zodiac Killer*, *The Entity*, or *The Amityville Horror*?

MORROW: (laughing) Oh, no, it's definitely fiction. If somehow we manage to shoot even half of what's in the script, you'll see that it's make-believe right away.

LEE: I'm not as quick to answer that question. I think that how we live outside our art always works its way *into* our art. If you write a novel while holed up in a motel where someone was killed, or if you record an album inside a haunted house or some abandoned asylum for the criminally insane, there's a strong possibility that whatever residual energy has been left behind, for better or worse, is going to creep its way into the material. The plot might not be based on a true story, but reality always has a way of showing its ugly face.

M&M: In 1974, in a sermon about "warlocks" and "sacrifices to the devil," the televangelist Billy Graham said that a terrible demonic force actually existed within the celluloid of *The Exorcist* itself. And we've all heard rumors about that film being cursed, the set catching on fire, and people who were close to the film dying during or after the production. Do you believe that Satan, or some other evil entity, is behind such events? Did anything like this occur during the making of *Blood Songs*?

LEE: We shot the film in Hollister, which is this small farming town in Northern California that is supposedly filled with haunted roads and buildings, and Charlene Worsley claimed to hear strange noises while we were filming, but nothing supernatural happened! However, the film does address some serious issues about spiritual warfare and the transference of evil. I could easily imagine a project like *Blood Songs* giving rise to some kind of sinister force in the world.

M&M: Debra, do you think horror movies have the power to invite evil feelings into our lives?

MORROW: No, I don't think so. I suppose that if a very simple-minded person, or a weak or deeply troubled person, watched a really scary or gruesome horror movie, then they could possibly go out and commit violent acts themselves, or consider themselves possessed by a demon or whatever. But, in the end, a movie is just a movie, nothing more and nothing less.

M&M: *Blood Songs* is a horror movie shot on 16mm black and white film stock, and features impressive camerawork. Will you take a similar approach in your first feature film?

LEE: We're actually shooting on video this time around, which has its advantages and disadvantages. On the plus side, it's going to enable us to shoot as much as we want, to free up our actors and give them more time to explore their characters and the script, and it's just cheaper. We plan to shoot in chronological order and edit in-camera, which should be interesting! On the minus side, video *looks* cheap—and that's what we definitely want to avoid. I want the movie to look less electronic and homegrown, so I'll be experimenting with different cameras, diffusing filters, and lighting until I find the look that I want.

MORROW: We also intend to get actual distribution for the new movie, unlike *Blood Songs*, which has only screened at festivals.

M&M: *Terror in the Aisles*, Andrew J. Kuehn's documentary on the horror genre, was just released on VHS. Part of the doc is devoted to films on the occult and "our oldest fear—the devil himself." What is it about the mythology of demonic possession that keeps filmmakers and audiences returning to the genre?

MORROW: No matter your spiritual or religious beliefs, most of us have a lingering fear of evil in the world. Call it whatever you want—Satan, Lucifer, or just demons in general—but it's that invisible presence in our lives that keeps us looking over our shoulder, turning all the lights on when we get scared, or, for some of us, praying and running to religious tools like crucifixes and rosaries for comfort and security. One of the movies that Charlene and I made when we were younger was called *Monsters in Your Pants*, and it was about a girl who had a parasitic creature living inside her urethra. The creature only came out when the girl had to pee. But there wasn't any rationale to that story, no explanation for the girl's condition. It just *was*. I think our fear of the demonic is like that. We have no tangible proof of Satan's existence, no concrete reason to believe in him, and yet we do—and he scares the hell out of us. It's that fear that drives us into the theater seats to see movies like this—fear that demonic possession could really happen to us or to someone we love.

LEE: I agree with everything Debra said, but the draw to the demonic and the occult reaches miles beyond the movie theater or the local drive-in. It reaches deep into our world history. Hitler dedicated *Mein Kampf* to an occultist and practitioner of black magic. The Bible speaks of the Anti-Christ and gives clues to the timing of his arrival. I'm not going to get into all of this now, but it's a terrifying threat that involves nuclear attacks, city riots, spree killings, ghettoes turned into concentration camps, and other demonstrations of occult power. So, on a conscious or subconscious level, we are captivated by this genre, and as artists we are compelled to explore it, because we know this crisis is coming in some form or another.

MORROW: (laughing) You can see why Billy designs our press kits—he's just trying to scare you!

Keep your zombified eyes glued to the grim and ghastly pages of *Monsters & Mayhem* as we continue to bring you the latest news on

Morrow and Lee's upcoming projects…and check out *Blood Songs* at a horror film festival near you!

"Carnal Knowledge: The Devil Comes to San Francisco" by Gustavo Carillo (originally published in *Monsters & Mayhem*, June, 1986, p. 4-6):

In June of 1985, at a dingy music venue in San Francisco called Necropolis, an 18-year-old woman stabbed her best friend to death in the restroom, then turned the 6-inch blade on herself and committed suicide in front of several stunned onlookers. As that grisly scene unfolded, death metal band Carnal Season was just finishing its set for the night, violating the eardrums of the crowd with tunes like "Infestation," "Moloch's Virgins," and a thundering encore of their most notorious track, "Transfer of Spirits," a rip-roaring onslaught of ritual murder and demonic possession that political activist "Tipper" Gore and the Parents Music Resource Center (PMRC) called the most "vile, reprehensible, and soul-crushing song we have ever heard."

The music press tore into Carnal Season and its controversial lyricist and singer Abaddon (Hebrew for "The Destroyer"), blaming the group for the two deaths that occurred and demanding that music venues no longer book the shock rockers. Angering critics even more, Abaddon told music 'zine *The Sadistic* that he was "overjoyed" when he heard the tragic news and "hopes even more teenage blood will be spilled during Carnal Season shows."

How much of Carnal Season's macabre and misogynistic lyrics and onstage theatrics (which include bloodletting and simulated sex) are merely an act to garner attention (and perhaps a record deal—the band is currently unsigned) is still up for debate. The members of the group refuse to reveal their real names to the public, perform in black ceremonial hoods adorned with skulls and inverted crosses, and claim to summon demonic entities while playing onstage and "attaching" them onto unsuspecting members of the audience.

Their music itself is the stuff of nightmares, filled with distorted and detuned guitars, blistering percussion, dark basslines, gore-laden lyrics, and the most disturbing sound and vocal effects ever put to splatter-platter (screaming children, dying animals, and the Catholic mass spoken in reverse, just to name a few). Abaddon has described the band's collection of songs as a "murder soundtrack" and their live shows the "sonic equivalent of a Black Mass." Adding to their growing repertoire, Carnal Season has also infiltrated the world of indie horror cinema, having provided three tunes for director Debra Morrow's malicious tale of satanic revenge, *Blood Songs*.

After a month-long correspondence of handwritten letters and one slightly creepy game of phone tag, Abaddon agreed to meet this *Monsters & Mayhem* scribe inside the lobby of the Hotel Majestic, San Francisco's premiere haunted locale, for a chat that was anything but ordinary…

MONSTERS & MAYHEM: This hotel is rumored to be haunted by several ghosts, the guests report hearing strange clanging noises at night, and in one of the rooms the bathtub fills with water on its own. Your music and lyrics would suggest that you believe in paranormal activity. Is that true?

ABADDON: While I believe in ghosts, they're much too benign for my tastes. Making tapping noises, rattling the cupboards, turning off the lights—none of that scares or even interests me. I much prefer demons, who have never inhabited this earth and whose methods of attack are far more cunning and cruel than any ghost's. Demons are supernatural tricksters, and their intent is to ruin your life, turn you against the people you love, and possibly even kill you. I can relate to these murderous feelings, that immoral longing to *destroy*, which was the motivating factor in forming Carnal Season. Now, if the bathtubs at the Majestic filled with blood instead of water, that would be an entirely different matter!

M&M: I definitely want to talk about Carnal Season's music and your recent foray into horror soundtracks. But first—I have to ask you about Lynne Parrish and Sheila Downing, who died during the band's set at Necropolis in June of last year. Would you be willing to discuss your feelings about what happened?

ABADDON: I'm going to say something that was never revealed to the press at the time of their deaths. Shortly after the events that occurred, all five members of Carnal Season wrote personal letters to the parents of the two girls, expressing our condolences and offering whatever support we could. What the media never told you was that the parents had no beef with us; they knew, just as any logical person knew, that we could never be blamed for what happened, and that we had nothing to do with Lynne Parrish's depression and anger issues, or her suicidal ideations, or her history of mental illness. Now let me be clear—I'm not denying that our music, or any art form that deals with satanic power, does not have the capability to exert catastrophic influence over another person. Carnal Season gives birth to evil and destruction whenever someone listens to our songs. But this fact does not make us responsible for the deaths of Lynne Parrish and Sheila Downing. What happened to them was a tragedy of the highest order. But rather than raise awareness about mental health issues or suicide prevention, the media decides to target some death metal band from San Francisco. Makes no sense to me.

M&M: But aren't you on record for saying you were "overjoyed" by what happened and that you hoped it would happen again?

ABADDON: What some people fail to understand about Carnal Season is that we're playing *characters*—and when I uttered those words, I was playing Abaddon, the destroyer, the angel of the bottomless pit. I was angry, I was sickened by what had happened, and I wanted to vent. In hindsight, it was insensitive and stupid, but it's not the first in a long line of horribly scripted lines for horribly tragic situations. I apologized to the parents and moved on.

M&M: Does this mean you'll tell us your real name?

ABADDON: Abaddon may be a character I play, but that doesn't mean he isn't shaped by my own personal beliefs and philosophies. In other words—*no.*

M&M: Though Carnal Season doesn't have a record deal and has never released an official album, you have given your current collection of songs the title of THE SATANIC AGE. Can you explain the origins of that title?

ABADDON: It sums up perfectly our society today. It's 1986, so you would think we'd be living in more sophisticated times. But there are massacres and war crimes taking place all over the world. Gang-related shootings, riots, and the threat of nuclear war are now a part of daily life. You can get shot point-blank in the back of the head just by eating at McDonald's or Kentucky Fried Chicken! Calling our songs THE SATANIC AGE is our declaration that the world is a vile, terrible place, and it reflects our insistence that we need to indulge in as many vices possible before the universe explodes.

M&M: The themes that underlie the lyrics of death metal bands seem to be universal—horror, violence, death, decay. Have you always been interested in morbid subject matter, and do you have any ideas as to where your penchant for the gloomy and macabre comes from?

ABADDON: Let me stop you right there. It is true that the lyrics to some of our songs examine archetypal themes. It is also true that I have been a rabid horror fan ever since I first sucked on my mother's teat. At 12-years-old, while most of my friends were riding BMX and trading baseball cards, I had a *Texas Chain Saw Massacre* one-sheet on my wall and a bookshelf full of *Monster & Mayhem* magazines and pulp horror novels. But Carnal Season is no carnival sideshow act. We are practicing Satanists and each of us holds active membership in the Church of Satan. We have broken bread inside the Black House. We are the only band in existence whose songs and live performances feature satanic sermons, summoning rituals and spells, and elements of the Black Mass. We have nothing against other death metal bands, but I urge you not to lump us into the same category as everyone else.

M&M: Can you talk to me about the other members of the group and how you work together?

ABADDON: [Guitarist] Judas Grimm and I grew up together in Pacifica and we co-founded Carnal Season. People often look to the frontman as the leader of the band, but Judas is the heart and soul of this group. He's the most wicked, most screwed-up, most talented guy I've ever known. The kid had a messy childhood. His old man beat him up a lot, whipped him with a belt, that kind of cowardly shit. Judas got in trouble at school. The other kids thought he was a weirdo, a punk. They called him "pizza face" and "crater face" because of his acne. Then his old man got gored to death by a *fucking bull*, if you can believe that. The thing bored a hole right through his perineum—right between the balls and ass! Talk about karma! But look at Judas now. Look at how far he's come. The kid's a survivor, a killer guitarist, and my best friend.

We met [bassist] Nox Dagon through an ad we placed in some music rag; he was the first bass player we auditioned and we knew we wanted him because his girlfriend was this smoking hot blonde who was always bopping around the garage with her titties out. [Guitarist] Mitrik Skinner is the most diabolical member of the band; as a little kid he would torture and skin cats and birds alive, and that's how he got his surname. [Drummer] Auntie Christian is just a crazy beast, a steroid junkie and musclehead who hits the skins with the force of an atom bomb.

M&M: Let's talk more about your songs, which you describe as "murder soundtracks." Do you have any favorites? Which ones do you enjoy playing live the most?

ABADDON: "Moloch's Virgins" is probably my favorite. Moloch was an Old Testament god, half-man and half-bull, to whom the Jews would sacrifice children. He is often referred to as the "fire god" or "sun god" because children were usually set on fire as part of this cult ritual. In more modern times, SS officers in Nazi Germany claimed to see visions of Moloch in the crematoria smoke rising from the ovens and fire pits at Auschwitz. They believed the beast would help deliver Hitler to the heights of his power. Even Winston Churchill referred to the Führer as an "all-devouring Moloch," a universal symbol for human sacrifice and death.

When Judas Grimm was 13, he wrote a pop-punk song about Moloch called "Rise, Demon, Rise." The tune was a Ramones-style stomper—pretty cool for a kid of his age. "Moloch's Virgins" is an extension of that track, with darker lyrics and an added guitar solo.

We open all our shows with "Moloch's Virgins," calling forth the great fire god to watch over us—and perhaps even to choose a few virgins from the crowd for his own personal defilement.

But "Transfer of Spirits" is the song that really gets the audience roaring. Judas wrote it especially for *Blood Songs*, at a time when he was going through some deeply emotional shit. It's got ferocious riffs and thundering percussion that sounds like machine-gun bullets on concrete. Judas added a spoken-word section at the bridge that deals with entity clearing and demonic transference. You see, this is leagues beyond death metal or performance art. The track is called "Transfer of Spirits" for a reason! You might become possessed by a demon as you listen to it, or you might meet the Father of Lies himself. That's the risk you take when you buy a ticket to one of our shows.

You can hear three of our tracks in *Blood Songs*, which I think contributed greatly to the demonic forces behind that film. Debra Morrow, the director, is not just a hot piece of ass; that girl is quite a nasty little filmmaker and she knows how to get the most out of her actors. I don't know the name of that little brunette chick who played the teenager in the movie, but she was forced to listen to our songs on a loop while they made the picture. Talk about your instant Satanic conversion right there. Come to think of it, the brunette was sexy as hell too—Moloch, no doubt, was very pleased!

M&M: How did the collaboration between Carnal Season and Debra Morrow come about?

ABADDON: She got a hold of me through some metal fanzine; I can't even remember the name of it. She had also been to one of our shows in S.F. and liked our sound. She mailed me a treatment for the movie and I thought it was pure exploitation trash. In other words, the perfect film for Carnal Season to make its start in horror cinema!

M&M: What is next on the agenda for Carnal Season?

ABADDON: Black magic. Orgies. Mass murder. Who knows? But we also hope to get a record deal by the start of the new year. We have a bunch of new songs we'd like to officially record, including one called "The Birth of Moloch" that serves as a prequel to "Moloch's Virgins." We'll continue to tour the country as much as possible, packing all our gear up in Judas Grimm's van and spreading the proud word of Satan to the masses. You can also book us for house parties, by the way. As long as there's free booze, hot chicks, and the *possibility* of something evil happening, we'll be there.

"Special Exhibit to Honor Oakland Photographer" by Franny Douglas (originally published in the *Oakland Tribune*, August, 1986, p. 10-11):

OAKLAND - The Oakland Museum will host a month-long exhibit featuring the photography of Ruth Worsley. The exhibit marks one of the last public showings of her work, as the Bay Area native has decided to retire after a 30-year career in the arts.

The exhibit will be on display in the Personal Archives gallery in December, with an invite-only reception to be held on New Year's Eve for Worsley's family, friends, and other guests of the museum.

Titled "At the End: Pictures of a Forgotten Memory," the exhibit features photographs that depict Worsley's life now that she has been diagnosed with frontotemporal dementia, an illness that reduces the brain's ability to function and impairs both language and motor skills.

At age 53, Worsley could never have expected to be battling such a disease, but it has taken a devastating toll on her work and personal relationships.

The exhibit includes moving and fragile images of Worsley trying to complete simple tasks in her home in Oakland, intimate moments with her daughter Charlene, and haunting close-ups that underscore the artist's sense of loss and confusion.

The photographs, taken on a timer, will be displayed in unique collages and jarring organizational patterns that reflect Worsley's state of mind during the past several months.

From the beginning of Worsley's career, her work has captured the historic elegance of Bay Area landmarks while paving the way for the many female photographers who have followed in her wake.

As a student at San Francisco's Academy of Art College between 1957 and 1959, Worsley photographed unusual and sometimes radical community events, including protest marches and underground book clubs and concerts. In the late 1960s, she chose Oakland architecture as her primary subject, capturing the aesthetic soul of neighborhoods like the Lower Bottoms and "Dogtown."

"I want to tell a gripping story with every photograph, and to get the viewer involved in that story," Worsley has said. "With my Oakland portraits, you bring your own experiences into the photos, but you're also seeing the history and beauty of a culturally-significant city."

Currently, Worsley lives with her daughter Charlene, an 18-year-old college student and actress, who is helping to oversee the sales of the countless photographs, paintings, and sculptures that her mother has created over the years. The earnings from these sales will contribute toward Worsley's health care.

"There's a lot to do around the house, tax papers, school tuition, bills and things like that, but the most important thing is making sure my mom is comfortable and doing okay," Charlene says.

Charlene hopes the exhibit will honor her mother, but also shine a light on those suffering from debilitating illnesses like frontotemporal dementia.

"Right now, there is no way to slow, stop, or reverse FTD, so the more people who learn about it the better," Charlene says. "I want the photographs in the exhibit to help communicate that message."

Charlene, who has appeared in a number of student films and local stage productions, credits her mother for always encouraging her and supporting her career as an actress.

"After my parents divorced, my mother and I were on our own. My father left the state, and he refused to pay child support or alimony, but Mom insisted that I earn my college degree because she understands the value of education and the knowledge it provides," Charlene says. "But, just as much, she encourages me to be an artist and to take chances with my work. Now it's my turn to give something in return to her. She's going to stay at home and I will be her caregiver, and I'm not going to let her down."

"Open Auditions for Local Horror Flick" by Larry Crenshaw (originally published in the *East Bay Experience*, September, 1986, p. 1-2):

East Bay College sophomore and fledgling filmmaker Debra Morrow is making a horror movie so shocking that it will surely have audiences squirming and screaming in their seats.

Titled *The Devil and My Daughter*, the film tells the terrifying story of a young girl's battle with the angry spirit of an evil witch. Keep reading to learn more about the movie and how you can land a starring role!

The plot of *The Devil and My Daughter* resembles horror classics like *The Exorcist* and *The Omen*, but with far more diabolical twists. The story follows 16-year-old Violet McCoy and her father, a hardboiled cop who sets the cruel witch's plan for revenge in motion. Though the script features some common tropes to the horror genre, Morrow promises that copious blood will flow and the body count will be high.

For this producer and director, horror movies should always be bold, creative, and even outrageous.

"There are so many amazing movies and directors out there—geniuses like Wes Craven and Tobe Hooper. If you want to make it, you have to take your project to the next level and get to heart of what really frightens people," she says. "You need to do everything right—the script, the actors and crew, and especially the effects."

Morrow explained how this film will be different from her past cinematic endeavors. *The Devil and My Daughter* is her first feature-length movie, and it will be shot entirely on video. This approach will inevitably give the movie a less polished look, but the young director hopes to make up for the lack by telling a compelling story and having characters the audience can actually care about.

"Hopefully, the plot and characters will drive the film forward and make audiences feel connected to the story," Morrow says. "And the theme—well, it's a very powerful one. We all have different beliefs about religion and we come from different faiths, but I find the notion that there are demons out to get us very scary. It's been more than 10 years since *The Exorcist* came out, and that movie still scares the hell out of me."

The topics of religion, faith, and demonic possession are already familiar to Morrow; her short film, *Blood Songs*, dealt with similar themes and showed a horrific vision of what could happen if one were to enter into a pact with evil. While she had a great time shooting that movie and views it as a tremendous learning experience, Morrow is insistent that making films of this nature is not all fun and games.

"It's crazy expensive—most of the crew have part-time jobs, but we still rely on our parents to help us out financially. It's exhausting too, and the end results are never the way you imagined them in your head," she says. "But then there's also the subject matter—when so many of your thoughts are devoted to the 'dark arts,' so to speak, you have to not let it seep into your real life outside of the movies.

"My point is, you can't lose yourself," Morrow emphasizes. "You can't forget that even fiction can have just as powerful of an effect as real-life events."

Though the lead role in *The Devil and My Daughter* has already been cast (Violet McCoy will be played by second-year student Charlene Worsley, a long-time collaborator with Morrow), there are many parts still available, as well as spots on the crew. Here is where Morrow is relying on the talent and expertise of the East Bay Community College student body.

"We'll be holding auditions in the next few weeks, and there will be an announcement in the paper and flyers with dates and times posted in the student lounge," Morrow says. "The auditions will take place here on campus, inside the Film and TV building."

Fred Rice, an adjunct professor in the Film and TV Production department, is enthusiastic about the project, hoping it will encourage more young people to get involved in the visual arts. "It's very exciting to have students like Debra and Charlene out there, following their dreams, making creative choices, and utilizing all the resources at the college."

Morrow plans to turn the auditions into a sort of horror-themed party, with Halloween music, food, and free promotional items for the film, including stickers and postcards designed by the talented pupils of East Bay Community College.

"We want to find the right people for the roles in the movie, but we want to network and have fun too," she explains.

As an East Bay student, Morrow recognizes just how much the school and its faculty have contributed to her success. "I hope that all of the creative departments here will continue to get the necessary funding to be able to provide for students," Morrow says. "*The Devil and My Daughter* won't happen without the support and guidance of the strong community at East Bay."

If everything goes according to Morrow's plan, the Film and TV Production department will host a screening of her movie as soon as it is released.

"We have a hard road ahead, but we don't intend to let anything stand in our way," Morrow says.

"Community College Attacked by Satanic Thugs" by Marsha Polzin (originally published in the *Island City Times*, October, 1986, p. 3-4):

ALAMEDA - Police are currently investigating a disturbing incident of vandalism that occurred over the weekend on the campus of East Bay Community College. When a professor entered the school's film studio on Monday morning, he discovered satanic messages scrawled on the walls and windows. He also found a small statue of the Virgin Mary that had been desecrated with a protruding horn made out of clay. The statue was hanging from a rope tied to a light fixture on the ceiling.

"We've had instances of vandalism in the past at the college," said the professor, who asked not to be named in this article. "But I've never seen anything of this nature before."

The campus studio is for students and teachers in the Film and TV Production department to edit their media projects and to receive hands-on training on how to operate the expensive equipment.

Fortunately, none of the studio's cameras or editing machines were damaged in the incident.

After calling the police and campus security, the film professor photographed the vandalism that had taken place. Spray-painted in dripping red across the walls were the words "Rise," "Hail Satan," and "Feast of the Beast."

A pentagram, the traditional symbol of satanic cults across the world, was painted on one of the studio's windows.

Police are concerned because the word "Rise" was also found at the Manson Murders crime scene in 1969—only then the word was written in the blood of the victims.

"We can clean up the studio in a day—that's not a problem," the professor said. "But who did this, and why? That's what I want to know."

Investigators have also concluded that one of the other phrases written on the wall, "Feast of the Beast," comes from the controversial memoir *Michelle Remembers*, an allegedly true account of torture, murder, and satanic ritual abuse.

But of all the sinister vandalism that occurred, investigators are focusing the most on the statue of the Virgin Mary. They are hoping the culprit was careless enough to leave his or her fingerprints on the religious icon, which will enable investigators to track down their suspect and will hopefully lead to an arrest.

"We don't want to rush to conclusions," said Alameda County Police Chief Curtis Stephenson. "But we take this crime seriously and we intend to find out if this is actually a sign of devil worship or occult activity.

"I've done a considerable amount of research and even taught a classes on satanic cults, so I know how dangerous this can be," added Chief Stephenson.

"All you have to do is look at the McMartin case to see the evil we're up against," the chief went on to say, referring to the court case out of Los Angeles County that involves devil worship, strange rituals, and child abuse.

"The desecration of a sacred place or religious item like the statue of the Holy Mary—that's a sign of a witch coven or weird religious cult. The fact that the vandalism took place on a college campus is also disconcerting because cults tend to target young people who are too naïve to know what they're getting into." Chief Stephenson said he would not be surprised if there were other signs of occult activity around campus or in towns nearby, including sacrificed animals or more satanic writing.

"Usually, when you hear about these kinds of crimes, it's in the towns in the middle of nowhere, where groups of like-minded people can gather without drawing suspicion. Trust me—these groups exist, and if you come into contact with them, you need to be very careful," the chief warned. "But this recent incident might be a sign that devil worship is moving with terrifying vigor into the suburbs, which is troubling to law enforcement.

"We're going to scour the grounds and the classrooms, leaving no stone unturned," he emphasized.

The vandalism at East Bay is not the only sign in recent months that pagans, witches, and black-magic cults might be thriving on the peninsula.

"We've found pentagrams, animal horns, and the lyrics to heavy metal songs painted on abandoned houses, and we've come across detailed sites that include candles and voodoo paraphernalia. My colleagues in other counties have reported similar discoveries. Again, it might be just another cock and bull story, but we have to remain vigilant on this issue," Chief Stephenson stressed.

Young people can be enticed, sometimes unknowingly, into the occult through hard rock music, horror movies, and television shows like *Tales from the Darkside*. The artwork on a recent album by metal band Iron Maiden features subliminal satanic images and messages, while films like *Children of the Corn* and *The Oracle* encourage their audiences to commit immoral or sacrilegious deeds.

"Scary movies, heavy metal music, TV, *especially* if it's cable—they function like links on a chain, each one leading toward more depraved and violent acts," cautioned Chief Stephenson. "Strung together, they have a negative cumulative effect on the youth of today, and that's a very frightening thing."

Campus security at East Bay Community College will be on high alert over the next several days as law enforcement continues the investigation. Anyone with knowledge of the vandalism incident is asked to contact the Alameda County Police Department.

"Carnal Season Guitarist Leaves Band" by Teddy Gilmore (originally published in *Thunderknot*, December 1986, p. 7-8):

Guitarist and songwriter Judas Grimm has left Carnal Season, providing "deeply existential" and "emotional" reasons for his departure from the extreme metal group.

In a statement released exclusively to *Thunderknot* and written to fans of the band, Grimm explained his surprising decision to leave and essentially dismantle the group: "I've made a lot of mistakes in my life. Hurt a lot of people. Betrayed them. Deceived them. Though I love my bandmates, I can no longer participate in and endorse Carnal Season's central message of violence, morbidity, and death. It is with great sorrow that I must break away from the fold, but I'm looking forward to my new life, one that will hopefully be marked by peace and good will," said Grimm in a handwritten letter.

In the statement, the heavily-tattooed songwriter, who has been accused of everything from anti-Semitism to domestic violence, noted that he is no longer a member of the Church of Satan. He stated that he had always intended that his most recent project, the soundtrack for the horror movie *Blood Songs*, would be his last, writing in his letter that "*Blood Songs* was the last thing I had to do, the deliverance of the demon from my soul, the final transition."

To industry insiders, Grimm's departure comes as no surprise. The musician, known for his disturbing lyrics and thunderous guitar-playing, has had his fair share of trouble with the law in the past few years. In addition to charges of vandalism and petty theft, Grimm has been arrested for solicitation of prostitution and assault.

"He's had some girlfriends, mostly hookers, bag bitches, and runaways. He treats them like shit and they all come running back for more because he plays in a fuckin' rock band," a source close to Carnal Season says. "But there's a rumor going around that he's gone in with the cops somehow—maybe as an informant or supplier. That's why they can't take him down. But I think the heat was getting to Judas, and that's why he's pulling this disappearing act."

Not surprisingly, Grimm did not address any legal problems in the letter, nor did he indicate whether he would continue to pursue a career in music. The troubled musician did allude to taking a lengthy break from songwriting and playing concerts.

"Evil was all I'd ever known and it almost destroyed me. It was only through the music of my band that I was able to stick around for so long," the letter read. "I didn't want to die, but suicide was the last box of my life's experiences I had to tick, and my poison pen was hovering like a fly…but now I am finally free."

In response to his bandmate's departure from the group, Carnal Season singer Abaddon, who grew up with Judas Grimm in Northern California, spoke exclusively with *Thunderknot*: "I'm sorry to see him go, as he was my best friend and his leaving means an end to the group as we know it. We're not going to call ourselves Carnal Season anymore, but that doesn't mean that me and the boys are going to stop making killer music. After all, why should the devil have all the good tunes?"

"Police Blotter for Oakland" compiled by Murray Fauchner (originally published in the *Oakland Tribune*, January, 1987, p. 11):

The following information was provided by employees of the Oakland Police Department unless otherwise noted.

Between downtown Oakland and Lake Merritt

Gallery dust-up: Around 9 p.m. on Saturday, police responded to a disturbance call from an event at the Oakland Museum on Pine Street. The museum was hosting a private New Year's Eve reception for the photographer whose work was on display in the gallery. The 19-year-old daughter of the photographer began complaining of a rotten odor coming from somewhere in the building. When the young woman became violently ill, she struck another patron who was trying to offer aid and police were called to the scene. The report indicated that the daughter was feeling "strange and unstable." The daughter was escorted safely from the building and no arrests were made.

Near MacArthur Boulevard and Fruitvale Avenue

Book vandal: A police officer was patrolling the 800 block of Fruitvale Avenue when he received a call from dispatch concerning a frightened librarian at the Oakland City Public Library. Upon arrival, the officer was led to several books that had been vandalized on the second floor. The books, on topics ranging from the paranormal to witchcraft, were ripped apart, drawn on with black Magic Markers, and graffitied with graphic messages of violence and murder. The investigation into who committed the vandalism is ongoing.

On Midcrest Road between Allendale Avenue and Park Road

Midnight raid: Detectives from the Property Crime and Burglary Unit were called to Crocker Highlands Parish School on Thursday morning after the severed heads of two religious statues were found propped up outside the school church steps. According to the police report, the vandals must have hit the church during the overnight hours and may have used a steel pipe or hacksaw to break the heads off the statues. Investigators are in the process of reviewing the surveillance camera footage of the school grounds in the hope of identifying the suspects. The investigation is ongoing.

In the "Lower Bottoms" between West Grand Avenue and 7th Street

Satanic strike: A drive-through nativity scene at a Catholic church was destroyed during the last week of December. After a priest discovered the scene, in which vandals carved satanic symbols into the wooden figures and scratched vulgarities on the props, police were dispatched to photograph and document the crime. Investigators reported that a pocketknife or other small blade was most likely used to commit the vandalism. The case remains open.

In the Oakland Hills

Mountainside mutilation: Oakland police and animal control officials were called to a hiking path in the Oakland hills where a resident had found scattered candles and a sack filled with headless chickens. Authorities are requesting help from the public, encouraging anyone with information to contact the City of Oakland Animal Care Services.

Sonic witchcraft: A young woman was arrested inside her home after attacking her husband with a claw hammer. According to the officer's report, the woman claimed to be under the psychological influence of *Seduction Through Witchcraft*, a spoken-word music album recorded by a "witch" from Southern California. The husband was treated for his injuries at the scene and intends to press charges against his wife.

In Bushrod Park

Daycare terror: Police arrested an elderly couple operating a daycare center on accusations involving animal cruelty, cannibalism, and the abuse of a corpse, according to an Oakland Police Department statement released on Tuesday afternoon. The statement alleged that the couple was using the popular daycare center as a front for a "cult house" that catered to the needs of a local underground satanic network.

MORROW PRODUCTIONS PRESENTS

CHARLENE WORSLEY
KEVIN MILLER
MICHAEL CALLAWAY

in

"THE DEVIL AND MY DAUGHTER"

Also Starring

CAROLE WARNER
GRACE SMITH
CHERIE LYNN DUNN

BASED ON "DEMON WITCH CHILD" BY AMANDO DE
OSSORIO
PRODUCED BY DEBRA MORROW and BILLY LEE
WRITTEN and DIRECTED BY DEBRA MORROW

CAST

Violet McCoy.................................CHARLENE WORSLEY
John McCoy.......................................KEVIN MILLER
Father Gregory................................MICHAEL CALLAWAY
Roberta...CAROLE WARNER
Sarah..GRACE SMITH
Mave..CHERIE LYNN DUNN
David...THOMAS RANDALL
Jackie Keenan....................................MALLORY TROTTER
Amber Keenan.....................................THERESA WEISERT

CREDITS

Written, Produced, and Directed by.....................DEBRA MORROW
Director of Photography..BILLY LEE
Sound and Music...GINGER STEVENS
Edited by...DEBRA MORROW

Costumes/Make-up by...SHAUNA NICKELS
Special Effects by..TODD WHEELER
Production Coordinator...............................MATTHEW BENOWITZ
Still Photography...JULIE MITCHELL
Production Assistant...HANNA FORD
Production Assistant..JESSICA LAMPERT

"THE DEVIL AND MY DAUGHTER" PRODUCTION NOTES

In 1975, Spanish movie director Amando de Ossorio released a disturbing and controversial film of satanic savagery, *Demon Witch Child*, to disenchanted European audiences already familiar with the motifs of demonic possession films. William Friedkin's *The Exorcist* had captured the world's attention two years before, and de Ossorio's low-budget masterpiece, despite its scenes of sexually-charged horror and outrageous violence, came and went with little fanfare.

Today, 19-year-old writer and director Debra Morrow has reimagined de Ossorio's grisly nightmare into one of the most horrifying movie experiences you will have this year.

With a script penned by Morrow, *The Devil and My Daughter* is a wickedly inventive, feature-length, and independently-produced horror film. Shot on video to take advantage of the latest commercial technology, the movie features stunning special effects, pulse-pounding sound design, and performances that burn like hellfire right through the silver screen.

The always-courageous Charlene Worsley takes on the part of Violet McCoy, a teenager who becomes possessed by the spirit of a vengeful witch. Kevin Miller plays Violet's father, flawed police detective John McCoy, while accomplished stage actor Michael Callaway portrays a brooding priest who attempts to rescue Violet while battling his own symbolic demons.

The film is directed by Debra Morrow, whose previous work, a 16mm horror short titled *Blood Songs*, was a smash hit at festivals in California. The director of photography is Billy Lee, who lensed *Blood Songs* and is the prolific scribe behind the unproduced scripts *Bone Altar* and *Monte Rio Massacre*. Inspired by the work of Tom Savini, Todd Wheeler helms the movie's special effects, creating jaw-dropping sequences and props on a less-than-shoestring budget.

Shot mostly on location throughout scenic Northern California, *The Devil and My Daughter* capitalizes on the vibrant local color of the Bay Area and some of its morbid locales, delivering to audiences everywhere a tale of demonic possession so shocking it has to be seen to be believed.

THE STORY

16-year-old Violent McCoy is a tender-hearted young girl, devoted to her father and curious about the world around her. Recovering from the tragic death of her mother, she spends most of her time with her older cousin, Sarah, a college student having an affair with one of her professors. John McCoy, Violet's father, is a lonely and embittered police detective, struggling to solve the kidnapping of two teen girls while trying to keep Violet safe in a city rife with crimes and perversions.

When a troubled priest, Father Gregory, warns McCoy that the kidnapping case has trappings of the occult, the detective knows he must solve the crime before other women are abducted and possibly killed. He brings in an elderly witch named Roberta, hoping she can provide him with clues about the kidnapping of the teenage girls. But during an ensuing struggle, McCoy's gun goes off, killing the witch and sending her demonic spirit on a quest for brutal revenge.

The demon targets the innocent Violet McCoy, manipulating her body and corrupting her mind with deviant thoughts. One night, Violet is led to a secret coven on the outskirts of town. There, she participates in a horrific ceremony in which she commits unspeakable acts, casting the possessed girl into the darkest and sickest depths of satanic despair and mind-numbing terror.

John McCoy, Father Gregory, and Sarah join forces in a frantic attempt to expunge the demon from Violet's doomed soul, but not before being forced to confront their own dark secrets. What results is a powerhouse climax of murder and cult horror that pits good against evil and man against devil.

CASTING AND PRE-PRODUCTION

In writing the script for *The Devil and My Daughter*, Debra Morrow already had long-time friend and collaborator Charlene Worsley in mind for the part of Violet McCoy, but it was not nepotism that won the talented actress the pivotal role. "Charlene is a fearless performer," Morrow says. "She's not afraid to question my directing choices when she feels I'm making a mistake, but she also trusts me to push the material in the right direction." Other actors in the film, including Kevin Miller and Cherie Lynn Dunn, gave auditions and were selected for their roles based on those performances.

Well-aware of the conventions of the horror genre, the actors knew they were in for a fun but challenging project. Grace Smith, who plays Sarah in the film, had a particularly disturbing scene with Charlene Worsley that tried her patience and made her question the value of becoming overly attached to a fictional role. "It was a very primal moment, and Charlene played her role to the hilt," Grace says. "When I see the scene now, I love it, but at the time we were all very wound up and scared."

Morrow, Worsley, and cinematographer Billy Lee held many pre-production meetings in which they discussed how to ground the film's grotesque moments in reality. They all agreed that they needed a devoted team of actors to bring *The Devil and My Daughter* to life. Once all of the parts were filled, the actors rehearsed for several weeks on the campus of East Bay Community College in California. Every Friday night the entire cast and crew gathered for pizza, beer, and screenings of direct-to-video classics like *Boardinghouse, Blood Cult,* and *The Long Island Cannibal Massacre.* "Out of the entire experience of making the film, those were my favorite moments. It was just a bunch of friends hanging out and watching horror movies," Worsley recalls. "We felt like we could accomplish anything, as long as we worked cohesively as a group."

During pre-production, Morrow and Lee scheduled equipment rentals from the college and scouted filming locations throughout the Bay Area. One morning, to blow off steam, the filmmakers took a road trip along the Russian River to a place called Monte Rio. There, in the mysterious town nestled among the woods, they had several strange experiences that enabled them to embrace the lurid oddity of the film they were about to make. "My experience with horror had always been in the fictional universe of slasher and thriller movies. But now I know where evil hides in the real world," Billy Lee says.

PRODUCTION

Though the setting of the movie is never stated in the script, *The Devil and My Daughter* was filmed on locations throughout the San Francisco Bay Area, including Oakland, Burlingame, and the Golden Gate City itself. Some of the filming spots are allegedly haunted by ghosts both playful and demonic, which added to the spooky tone on set. While writing the screenplay, Debra Morrow used a number of sources for inspiration; in particular, she and Charlene Worsley wandered through St. James Presbyterian Church in San Francisco, a centuries-old Gothic refuge with a history of paranormal activity.

To finance the film, Morrow relied on her own savings, as well as the personal investments of Billy Lee, Charlene Worsley, Todd Wheeler (FX), and Shauna Nickels (costumes/makeup). The parents of the cast and crew also donated extensively to the cause. In addition, East Bay Community College, where the most of the team were students during the production, contributed lights, microphones, sound recorders, and the shoulder-mount Super-VHS camcorder that was used to shoot the movie. Considering the micro-budget of the project, Morrow relied on sharp dialogue rather than big action set-pieces to drive the film, saving as much funds as she could for the bloody FX sequences. Editing in-camera whenever possible and working with a small crew enabled the filmmakers to complete the entire movie in just 11 days.

Along with *The Exorcist*, more recent films like *The Entity* and *Amityville II: The Possession* reflect the continued interest in stories of demonic possession. Morrow set out to pay tribute to the genre, but also to push its boundaries by having her female protagonist commit the most grisly deeds imaginable. The actors were encouraged to ad-lib their dialogue, and one scene between the possessed Violet McCoy and Father Gregory was entirely improvised based on a handful of scribbled notes that Morrow gave privately to the actors.

Post-production of *The Devil and My Daughter* was completed inside the film studio at East Bay Community College, where Ginger Stevens perfected the eerie sound design and Morrow whittled hours of footage into a nail-biting 82-minute film. Faculty from the TV and Film Production department often stopped by to check on the project, offering their own insights and advice. A collaborative effort and an uplifting group experience for all involved, *The Devil and My Daughter* will hopefully find distribution after what is sure to be a successful film festival run.

CAST NOTES

Charlene Worsley (Violet McCoy): Born in Marin and raised in the Upper Laurel district in Oakland, Charlene has loved horror and science fiction films ever since she was a kid (her favorites include *Xtro*, *The Changeling*, and *Rosemary's Baby*). Growing up, she developed an interest in the arts, citing her mother, photographer Ruth Worsley, as her biggest influence. "Ever since I can remember, my mom was taking pictures or making art, documenting city life and architecture through photographs and paintings," Charlene says. "She's not into horror—though she loves Alfred Hitchcock and has a strange fascination with Bigfoot—but I still get much of my inspiration from the sublime beauty in her work."

Prior to starring as the ravaged Violet McCoy in *The Devil and My Daughter*, Charlene played the lead role in Debra Morrow's tale of supernatural revenge, *Blood Songs* (1985), in addition to parts in the student films *My Teacher is a Sexy Alien* (1982) and *Whisper Me Dead* (1984). Charlene has also tackled a number of tragic stage roles, including the conflicted Mary Warren in *The Crucible* and the suicidal Ophelia in *Hamlet*.

Charlene is well-known for inhabiting her parts with a passion and commitment that would make Stanislavski proud. "It's my goal to become my character, but also a living and breathing *person*, and to give everything I can to support my director's vision," Charlene says. She dedicates her chilling portrayal of Violet McCoy in *The Devil and My Daughter* to her mother.

Kevin Miller (John McCoy): The versatile and always dynamic Kevin Miller can be seen this winter in the indie horror films *The Cannibals of Bridgewater Triangle* and *Ghost Janitor: Ernie's Resurrection*. On stage, he has starred in community theater productions of *West Side Story*, *The Odd Couple*, and *Dracula*.

Michael Callaway (Father Gregory): Though new to the world of horror, theater actor and acting teacher Michael Callaway displays a commanding presence onstage and onscreen. With a broad range, commitment to his craft, and over 25 years of work experience in both Hollywood and New York, Michael has starred in countless repertory company productions, including *Aresenic and Old Lace*, *Fiddler on the Roof*, *The Whiz*, and *Deathtrap*. In a twist of fate, Michael first learned of Morrow's film when he served as a guest lecturer in an acting class at East Bay Community College. Intrigued by the role of Father Gregory but unaccustomed to working in low-budget films, Michael confesses that it was Morrow's "ambition and stubbornness" that made him sign on for the part.

Carole Warner (Roberta): Raised and educated in the German city of Osnabrück, Carole Warner is thrilled to make not only her film debut in *The Devil and My Daughter*, but to play such a critical role in the story. The 67-year-old actress had no hesitation when performing in the movie's more explicit moments, including a scene of full-frontal nudity. In 1955, Carole starred in an episode of the CBS soap opera *The Guiding Light*, playing a legal secretary accused of murdering her womanizing boss. She left show business in 1956, got married, had three children, and went on to earn degrees in World Literature and Latin.

Grace Smith (Sarah): Now in her final year at East Bay Community College, Grace had a speaking role in the thriller *Whisper Me Dead* (1984) and has appeared in several theater productions on campus.

Cherie Lynn Dunn (Mave): Cherie is an actress, swimwear model, and brand spokesperson with an impressive list of performances to her name. She has appeared in the direct-to-video horror movies *Slasher FBI Academy* (1981), *Paranormal Coin-Operated Sex Booth* (1981), and *Cherie and the Salt Lake City Mutant* (1982). Known for her full-sleeve tattoos and her uninhibited style of acting, Cherie wishes to thank Debra Morrow for challenging her on the set of *The Devil and My Daughter* and for writing the ultimate "killer script." Cheri can next be seen alongside adult film star Tracey Adams in *The Curse of the Double D Zombies*, coming to select adult theaters in 1987.

Thomas Randall (David): Thomas joins the cast of *The Devil and My Daughter* as one of the busiest actors in the San Francisco Bay Area. His recent credits include roles in repertory company productions of *Death of a Salesman*, *The Tempest*, and *The House by the Lake*, a thriller stage play that led to his fateful audition for Debra's film.

Mallory Trotter (Jackie Keenan): *The Devil and My Daughter* is Mallory's first film. Shortly after the production ended, she graduated from East Bay Community College and has gone on to pursue her undergraduate degree somewhere in the Pacific Northwest.

Theresa Weisert (Amber Keenan): After her memorable performance in *The Devil and My Daughter*, Theresa moved to Reno, Nevada to attend Truckee Meadows Community College.

ABOUT THE FILMMAKERS

Debra Morrow (writer/director): After years of writing, producing, and directing short films, including *Portraits of My City* (1983) and *Blood Songs* (1985), Debra Morrow has just completed her first feature: the grim and gutsy *The Devil and My Daughter*. Debra partnered with longtime friends and collaborators Charlene Worsley and Billy Lee to create a harrowing piece of Mephistophelean horror that will challenge everything you know about low-budget cinema.

Debra had this to say about the process of making *The Devil and My Daughter*:

"I have always loved horror movies. My earliest memories include late-night viewings of John Stanley's *Creature Features*, reading Joe Bob Briggs' drive-in reviews in the newspaper ("Eleven dead bodies. Eighteen breasts. Death by bone saw. Joe Bob says check it out"), and searching my local library for the latest Stephen King masterpiece. I also recall, with great fondness, my mother's bookcase, where, on the top shelf, she tried to hide her copy of William Peter Blatty's *The Exorcist*. The book terrified me. It gave me nightmares. It made me believe that the Devil was a force to be reckoned with in my young life. When William Friedkin's film version came out in 1973, I found myself praying to God more than ever before, begging Him to protect my soul from the threat of Satan. When I got older, I dreamed about making a horror movie that captured the sheer power of both the book and the film.

"When I discovered the Spanish version of Amando de Ossorio's *Demon Witch Child* years later on VHS, I saw a unique opportunity to improve upon a movie I loved and to put my own creative spin on the demonic-possession genre. The end result of all this introspection is *The Devil and My Daughter*, a thought-provoking and sleazy movie made by the best people I know.

"During production, I spent what little free time I had at the public library, researching cases about demonic possession in order to jazz up the script. I came across the case of Arne Cheyenne Johnson, a 19-year-old man who stabbed his landlord to death with a knife in 1981,

During the trial, Johnson's defense team argued that their client was suffering from demonic possession at the time of the killing and was not responsible for the crime. Johnson claimed that a friend had undergone an exorcism and that he, Johnson, asked that the demon enter his body instead. Months later, Johnson murdered a man he barely knew, claiming that a demon had taken possession of his soul and forced him to commit the grisly deed. Not surprisingly, Johnson was found guilty of first-degree manslaughter and sentenced to 20 years in prison.

"The case deeply impacted me while we made *The Devil and My Daughter*. Do demons and evil spirits really exist? If they do, can they take control of our souls? Are they able to 'body jump' between their victims, selecting them at will?

"The world of *The Devil and My Daughter* is savage and unforgiving, filled with fear, doubt, paranoia, and the loss of religious faith. And at the root of the film is my own loss of faith—not in religion or God, but in my abilities as an artist. I want to be a good filmmaker. I want to give my actors a chance to showcase their talents. I want to push them to be their best, but I don't want them to get hurt in the process. I hope, in the coming months or even years, I will learn that I have achieved these goals through the making of this movie."

Billy Lee (directory of photography): Billy Lee first became interested in cinematography by studying the music videos of his favorite bands, including Bauhaus, Christian Death, and Alien Sex Fiend. Though he acknowledges the impact that horror authors like Stephen King and Dean Koontz had on him as a child, he credits much darker works, including Anton LaVey's *The Satanic Bible* and Aleister Crowley's *The Book of Lies*, as having the most influence on his world view. In high school Billy developed an interest in the Biblical paintings of William Blake and the surreal films of Kenneth Anger. He first collaborated with Debra Morrow on the horror short *Blood Songs*, creating a haunting black-and-white palette that matched the somber tones of the film. Billy said this about the experience of shooting *The Devil and My Daughter*: "With sixteen bottles of karo syrup, a lo-fi camera, and the resources of our college, Debra and I have expanded the universe of our previous movie and created something truly scary."

Todd Wheeler (special effects): Hailing from the scenic fishing village of Bodega Bay, California, Todd worked on a number of student films and theatrical performances before moving to the Bay

Area to study Film and TV Production at East Bay Community College. His role models include Dick Smith (*The Exorcist*), Tom Savini (*Dawn of the Dead*), and Michael Westmore (*Raging Bull*).

PRESS KIT

Fearless determination: **Debra Morrow**, the director of *The Devil and My Daughter*, on the campus of East Bay College. Debra has directed a number of other horror films, including *Clown College Murders* (1979), *Satan's Birthday Party* (1980), *Monsters in Your Pants* (1983), and *Blood Songs* (1985).

Goofing around: Debra Morrow makes a new friend during auditions for T*he Devil and My Daughter.*

Angelic actress: **Charlene Worsley**, the star of *The Devil and My Daughter*, Debra Morrow's frightening adaptation of Amando de Ossorio's *Demon Witch Child*. A "scream queen" on the rise, Charlene has also appeared in *Monsters in Your Pants* (1983) and *Blood Songs* (1985), both of which were directed by Morrow.

Devilish daughter: Demonic possession takes terrifying hold of Violet McCoy (Charlene Worsley) in Debra Morrow's satanic shocker, *The Devil and My Daughter*. Makeup by Todd Wheeler and Shauna Nickels.

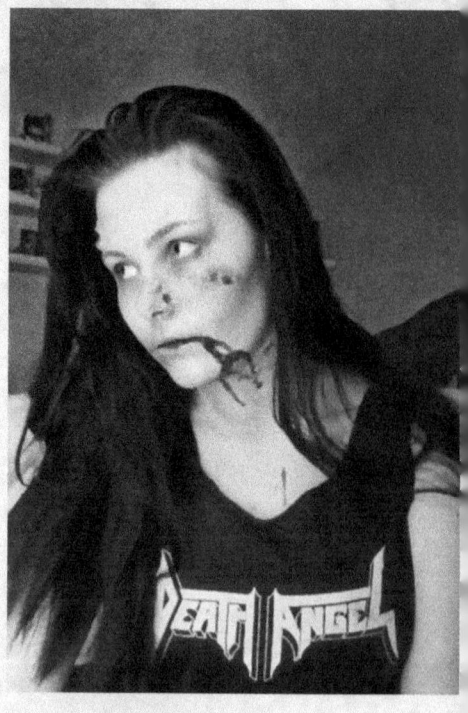

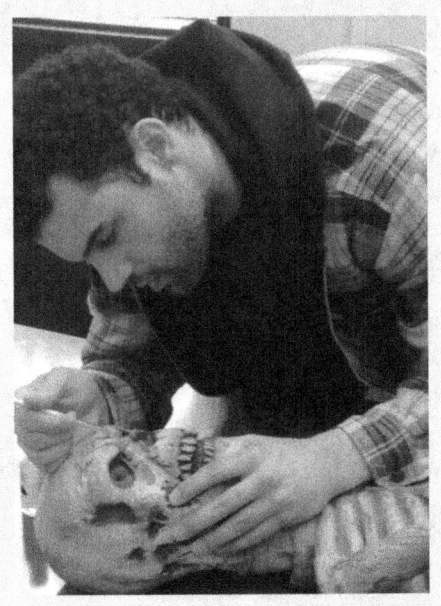

F/X whiz: Working on a shoestring budget, **Todd Wheeler** created all of the special effects and gruesome props in *The Devil and My Daughter*. His role models include Tom Savini (*Friday the 13th*) and Dick Smith (*The Exorcist*).

Seeking inspiration: Director of photography **Billy Lee** discovers an underground world of horror while location scouting for *The Devil and My Daughter*. An accomplished cinematographer and full-time college student, Billy has written several screenplays, including *Monte Rio Massacre*, which tells the chilling story of a satanic cult lurking in the forests of Northern California.

"Demonic Possession and the Art of No-Budget Filmmaking: An Analysis of *The Devil and My Daughter*" by Matt Porter (originally published in *Cult Films Exploitation Edition: Vol. 3*, December 1987, p. 15-35):

Debra Morrow's *The Devil and My Daughter*[1] begins inside a folk medicine shop, a claustrophobic space of kettle drums, amulets, and hand-crafted runes. The shelves are stocked with elixirs, oils, and prayer candles, the walls decorated with tapestries of Catholic saints. In emulation of William Friedkin's *The Exorcist* (1973),[2] the title of the film appears onscreen in oversized red-block letters; after it fades, spectral yellow light flickers from above, casting an electric glow over the opening credit sequence.

The looming shadows of this first scene portend the horrors to come—both in the film and in the far more disturbing events that took place beyond the screen. Though this essay will reference the real-life atrocities that occurred this past summer—commonly known as the Mercy Care Murders—its main purpose is to analyze the plot, cinematic techniques, and production of one of the most discussed (and disparaged) exploitation films of all time.

When the film proper begins, an elderly witch named Roberta (Carole Warner) appears inside the medicine shop. She is dressed in a black nightgown and slippers. Crouching on spindly legs, she urinates onto the floor, then selects a medicinal jar from the shelf, tucks it into the folds of her gown, and hurries from the shop. Moving to the right, the camera discovers an unfocused image of Moloch,[3] the bull-headed deity of the ancient Middle East, projected as if out of thin air onto the wall. How Moloch appears in the shop is never explained, but the diaphanous image sets the stage for the spiritual warfare between God and the devil that serves as the film's primary theme.

---

[1] Modeled after Amando de Ossorio's *Demon Witch Child* (1975), also known as *The Possessed*.
[2] Adapted from William Peter Blatty's international bestseller, published by Harper and Row in 1971.
[3] A pagan Ammonite god, often appearing as an enormous bull, to whom followers would sacrifice their children by setting them on fire; also a prominent fallen angel in John Milton's *Paradise Lost* (1667) and a symbol of Adolf Hitler and the Third Reich.

The next day, in the home office of police detective John McCoy (Kevin Miller), a milddle-aged priest named Father Gregory (Michael Callaway) expresses confusion over the crimes committed inside the medicine shop, his concerns rooted in fears of the occult. "The stealing of the rare elixir, the crude disposal of human waste—this is witchcraft!" the priest argues. But the hardboiled McCoy dismisses the theory that the perpetrator is involved in the dark arts. "He was probably stoned on angel dust and wet himself," he says. Gregory seems unimpressed with McCoy's analysis of the scene and remains convinced that black magic is afoot.

Though Morrow's script has been bashed by some critics for its banal dialogue, the disagreement between the two friends establishes a powerful dichotomy in the film. Gregory insists that the world is falling apart due to "ritual killing and supernatural murder," while McCoy argues that evil exists in humans—not in ghosts or demons. This debate will grow in significance once 16-year-old Violet McCoy (Charlene Worsley) begins exhibiting strange behavior that none of the other characters in the film can rationally explain.[4]

Gregory asks McCoy about Jackie and Amber Keenan, two teenage sisters recently kidnapped from town. Gregory suggests that there may be a connection between the kidnapping and the theft in the medicine shop, but McCoy warns against such rumors: "The last thing we need is kids thinking Satan runs the show. They're already hooked on sex, pills, and heavy metal—what the Christ is next?" Here, McCoy alludes to the vulnerability of his own young daughter, but also to a subtext in the narrative. The impending demonization of Violet McCoy reduces her to a stereotype: she is either a hapless virgin in desperate need of adult protection, or a preternatural force that needs to be destroyed by those in positions of power. Gregory understands the danger of such unchecked authority; when McCoy mentions bringing in a local "witch" for questioning, the priest worries she will suffer at the hands of a violent and judgmental police force.[5] "My methods are cruel,"

---

[4] Charlene Worsley was 19-years-old when the film was shot. According to Morrow, Worsley had "not only an angelic face, but an innocence that made her believable in the role of a younger Violet McCoy" (*Monsters & Mayhem*, 1987).

[5] Reflected in a number of American films with police corruption as a motif, including *The Killing* (1956), *Touch of Evil* (1958), *Dirty Harry* (1971), *The Sting*

McCoy snaps, "but I have kept this town safe." At this moment, Violet strolls into the office, a subtle portent of the shift in power to come.

Dressed smartly in corduroy pants and a form-fitting black sweater, Violet approaches the camera from behind her father, hinting at her future predatory behavior. Before going to the park with her cousin, a college student named Sarah (Grace Smith), Violet gives her father a kiss, a platonic gesture that underscores her fleeting innocence. Fresh-faced, with a playful bounce to her step, Violet is one of many teens in a slew of horror films whose good-natured demeanor and familial bond become inverted and corrupt.[6]

Once Violet and Sarah leave the room, McCoy reflects on the passing of his wife, Margaret, who died of cancer less than a year before. McCoy tells Gregory, "Violet was very close to her mother, and I'm worried about her. Her cousin is staying at the house for a while, cooking dinners, keeping an eye on Violet, but I don't know if it will do any good." The somewhat generic plot device of McCoy losing his wife to cancer resonated deeply with Morrow, whose own mother passed away from the disease when the director was in her early teens. Speaking with *Cinema Escapes* in 1987, Morrow said,

"I was by her side when she passed, holding her hand, telling her I loved her, but the nurse has pumped her with so much morphine that I don't think Mom really knew I was there. I told her it was okay for her to go, and that I was going to be all right. And then the color of her skin just faded. The way watercolor fades. She died right there in front of me. And my father—he was standing in the corner, his arms folded across his chest. He was trying to be strong. But then his face scrunched up and he started to cry..."

"I'm telling you this because the character I relate to the most in *The Devil and My Daughter* is John McCoy. He's not the best dad. He ignores Gregory's warnings, he lets Violet do whatever she wants, he's a bit of a jerk and a bigot...but I feel sorry for him. I understand his feelings of pain and helplessness after the death of his wife."

The scene between McCoy and Gregory ends with a jarring cut that takes us to a darkened room inside Roberta's house. The camera pans

---

(1973), and *First Blood* (1982).
[6] Including *The Bad Seed* (1956), *The Village of the Damned* (1960), *The Other* (1972), *The Exorcist* (1973), *The Omen* (1976), *The Brood* (1979), and *Children of the Corn* (1984).

across a record player, a Gothic candelabra, and a table covered with tarot cards and mugwort leaves.[7] Wearing a diaphanous white gown, 18-year-old witch Mave (Cherie Lynn Dunn) stands in the center of the room. Roberta enters, naked, her frail body riddled with warts. She puts a record on the turntable. A crackling voice recording begins to play, the unintelligible sound evoking some sort of magic ritual.[8] Roberta turns to Mave and starts to remove the young witch's gown. Just then, McCoy can be heard banging on the door, interrupting the ceremony and forcing the two women to change into house clothes.

In one brief but chilling sequence, Morrow unites two motifs in the film: Gregory's fear of the occult, substantiated by the mystical trinkets in the house and the ambiguous ceremony about to unfold; and the transgressive sexuality of the witches, a foreshadowing of the carnal awakening of Violet McCoy. Of her explicit nudity, 67-year-old Carole Warner told *Silver Screams*, "Roberta is a libidinous creature, and her desire for sex or intimacy is no different than yours or mine. It was a challenging scene, and it's true that Debra could be pushy on set, but I was more than willing to shoot [the scene] the way she wrote it. I wasn't embarrassed by the material."

While Mave hides in the house, McCoy demands that Roberta come to the police station for questioning. When he attempts to take her by the arm, the witch delivers a speech that sounds like an invocation, mocking the detective's masculinity while binding herself to Satan: "Needle-dicked pig…there is no law, no authority, no justice. There is only darkness and slime, and the Angel of the Bottomless Pit, and all his loyal followers!"

Though somewhat contrived, the speech sets up the scandalous nature of the next scene: Violet's discovery of Sarah's affair with her professor, a married man named David (Thomas Randall). While drawing in her sketchpad, Violet wanders alone through the park. There, she discovers the illicit lovers groping each other underneath a

---

[7] A nod to Roman Polanski's *Rosemary's Baby* (1968), in which a pair of elderly satanic witches uses the fictional tannis root, a herb infused with magical powers, to control Rosemary Woodhouse and the devil's spawn inside her womb.
[8] For the ceremonial record inside the witch's house, Morrow used recordings of bells, gongs, chimes, and "devil chasers," a percussion instrument made from bamboo.

tree. "Not here," Sarah mildly protests as David tries to fondle her breasts through her sweater. "We don't want Violet to see us." In a voyeuristic moment not uncommon in slasher films,[9] Violet's sexual curiosity becomes aroused. For the adolescent, however, the moment spells trouble, as she learns that the trip to the park was merely a ruse for Sarah to frolic with her professor. In this fragile balance of hurt feelings and sexual awakening, Morrow suggests that a certain transformation of Violet McCoy has already begun. Violet is not supposed to "see" Sarah and David, and yet she does, steered by hormonal desires that are only beginning to manifest themselves.

Despite his earlier doubts about the occult, McCoy attempts to force Roberta to confess to the theft at the medicine shop and to the kidnapping of the Keenan sisters. He employs several tactics inside the interrogation room—including striking the woman and calling her a "filthy lesbian"—before displaying his gun and threatening her with it. In presenting McCoy as ruthless and amoral as the criminals he puts in jail, Morrow aligns the detective with evil and presents him as a worthy successor to the father-villains of earlier horror films.[10] In a sickly voice, Roberta growls, "Degenerate scum! I am your tormentor, your scourge! I am the cancer that rotted the bones of your cheating wife! That conniving bitch Margaret!" Here, Roberta's psychic ability provides an understated link to the previous scene in which Violet saw Sarah and David at the park. While the witch has knowledge of Margaret's adultery and tragic death, Violet is now aware of her cousin's sexual relationship with a married man. This parallel establishes a perverse bond between Violet and Roberta, not unlike the bond between Regan and Captain Howdy in *The Exorcist*.

McCoy's furious reaction to the mention of his deceased wife sets up the film's first special-effects sequence. After McCoy threatens Roberta with his gun, the pair begins struggling for possession of the weapon. During the fight, the gun goes off, killing Roberta and spraying her blood against a corkboard of "missing child" flyers on the

---

[9] Including *Black Christmas* (1974), *Halloween* (1976), *Friday the 13th* (1980), *Happy Birthday to Me* (1981), *My Bloody Valentine* (1981), *The House on Sorority Row* (1983), and *Sleepaway Camp* (1983).

[10] Including *Eyes Without a Face* (1960), *The Amityville Horror* (1979), *The Shining* (1980), and *Creepshow* (1982).

wall. As Carole Warner told *Silver Screams*, the gory effect was achieved using the crudest of tools:

"Todd [Wheeler, the special-effects technician] used a bang snap for the blast, then we cut and Billy [Lee, the cinematographer] set up the next shot. I got on the floor and played dead, while Todd threw a small balloon filled with stage blood, oatmeal, and mashed-up banana at the wall as hard as he could. It worked perfectly, just this huge explosion of mushy red glop on top of all those pictures of little kids. I'm not sure why flyers of missing children would be hung up in the interrogation room, but it was a dirty little effect..."

After a grainy shot of blood dripping from the wall, the film cuts to Violet McCoy asleep in bed. A hallway light casts a warm glow on her face before a low-angle shot from the floor disrupts the solemnity of the scene. Dressed in a nightshirt decorated with a cartoon snake,[11] the girl sits up slowly, as if in a somnambulistic trance, then swings her legs off the bed and stands up. In a succession of quick edits, Violet takes off her clothes and glides, wraith-like, into the hallway as the camera tracks her bare feet on the floor. In the implied nudity of a teenage girl, Morrow's careful editing presents Violet as a vulnerable figure on the eve of corruption. But in her only published interview after the release of the movie in 1987, Charlene Worsley revealed that Billy Lee, the film's 22-year-old cinematographer, had wanted a much more explicit scene:

"An earlier version of the script called for Violet to be nude onscreen at this point in the film—to show that Roberta's demonic spirit wanted to control her, and turn her into this aberrant sexual figure. I got where Debra was going with the idea and I had agreed to do it initially—but during pre-production I changed my mind. Violet is 16, barely a teenager, and I didn't feel comfortable with the implications of a girl that young appearing naked onscreen. Besides, what she does next, getting into her father's bed, was enough to show that the demon had gained the upper hand. Debra understood and cut the nude scene out of the screenplay.

---

11 Though it was a snake who tempted Adam and Eve into sin, and not Satan himself, the serpent quickly became the quintessential symbol of evil and the fall of mankind.

Before we shot that scene, Billy approached me inside the school library.[12] I remember because I was looking for resources on nursing homes for my mom,[13] and he came up right behind me, and I actually thought he was following me. Right there in the stacks, he said he wanted to see me naked in the film. He was very crude, and confrontational. 'Debra and I are partners now, it's our movie and you need to do what we say,' and all that. I ran out of the library, but when I got on set that night, he acted like nothing happened, so I let it drop and focused on doing my job. I wasn't going to let him ruin the movie or come between me and my best friend.

"If you look carefully at the undressing scene at just the right moment, you can see the flesh-colored bands I was wearing around my chest and lower body. I had Todd make them for me—I wasn't taking any chances! In the end, the scene works fine, but it caused a major rift between me and Billy. We had never seen eye to eye before, but after that we basically avoided each other."

Whatever disharmony existed between Worsley and Lee seemed to coincide with the next several scenes in the film, each one pushing the boundaries of what was expected in a low-budget, shot-on-video horror movie.[14] After Violet undresses, she drifts into the dark of her father's bedroom, the pallor of her skin rendering her a ghost. Here, the film suggests that the young girl's body has become a vessel through which the demonic spirit of Roberta can act out her most perverse fantasies and ritual acts.

---

[12] On the campus of East Bay Community College, opened in 1965 and the smallest community college in the San Francisco Bay Area. Morrow, Worsley, Lee, and Wheeler were all students there during the filming of The Devil and My Daughter.

[13] It was in the early stages of filming The Devil and My Daughter that Ruth Worsley, Charlene's mother, began residing at the Mercy Care Medical Center in Oakland, California. She was suffering from frontotemporal dementia, a neurological disorder that attacks the frontal lobe of the brain.

[14] According to Morrow, the production budget for the film, which took 11 days to shoot, was around $4000, which included the cost of videotapes, stock footage, music and audio effects, festival submission fees, and promotional items.

Violet slips into her father's empty bed, pulls up the covers, and falls asleep. Later, McCoy enters the bedroom, discovers his daughter, and carries her back to her room and puts her to bed. That he never attempts to clothe her has led critics to question the incestuous tone of the scene. Writing for *Monsters & Mayhem*, Paul Leonard noted feeling "creeped out by the bedroom scene between Violet and her father," but also indicated "that's the whole point, to show that old Lucifer had won." Morrow herself downplayed the significance of the scene, saying, "We shot in sequence, and it was late at night. Charlene was dead on her feet, and she and Kevin were having a hard time communicating. We shot it quickly, just so we could all go to bed." Nevertheless, the discomfort of the scene is palpable, adding a layer of unease and menace to what might normally be a moment of tender paternal care.

The movie moves swiftly along as Violet nears her confrontation with evil. Sarah awakens the girl in the morning to find her pale and feverish, dressed in an open pajama top. When Sarah scolds her for staying up too late, Violet hisses back, "That's nothing compared to all the fucking you do, you self-righteous cunt!" As Sarah recoils, Violet throws back her head and cackles, gloating laughter pouring from her throat. Sarah flees the bedroom, runs to the phone, and calls McCoy at the police station. "There's something wrong with Violet!"[15] she cries into his answering machine. "Come home right away!"

Speaking in hushed tones with Father Gregory, McCoy misses the call. In the script, Morrow emphasized McCoy's feelings of guilt over the death of the witch, including a monologue in which the detective sees parallels between her demise and the loss of his wife to cancer. "I was negligent, cowardly, and people died as a result," McCoy says in a scene that resembles a confession. He reveals that Margaret *did* have an affair, but that he never blamed her for it; his unpredictable hours, "obsession with this shitty job," and his tendency to ignore his family forced his wife into the arms of another man.

Though the monologue was filmed, Morrow excised many of the lines from the final cut, focusing instead on McCoy's anxiety over the witch's psychic ability: "How could she have known? Did she glimpse inside my soul? And is that why she died? I was angry and confused. Could I have pulled the trigger intentionally and killed her?" Though Gregory insists that the shooting was an accident, the possibility that

---

[15] Which became the tagline for the film.

McCoy murdered Roberta becomes the focal point of the scene, and explains why Morrow edited it so tightly. As the scene stands, the exchange between McCoy and Gregory makes the reason for Violet's possession clear. "One of the original titles for the movie was *The Vengeful Possession of Violet McCoy*,"[16] Morrow revealed to *Cinema Escapes*. "Roberta's evil spirit, in the form of a murderous demon, invades Violet because Violet's father was responsible for her death. In this way, the movie is not only about Violet's suffering, but about the consequences of her father's actions."

That night, after checking on his sleeping daughter, McCoy tries to contain the situation by telling Sarah, "Violet is a teenager. That's what teenagers do." Despite Sarah's insistence that something is wrong with the girl, McCoy dismisses the thought. As McCoy settles in for the evening with a glass of gin and a record of Hawaiian music (a comedic mirroring of the witch's demonic recording earlier in the movie), Morrow emphasizes that it is the father's continued negligence that widens the scope of Violet's possession. As midnight falls and the film cuts to a terrifying ceremony in the cellar of the witch house, the story takes a turn for the truly grotesque and bizarre.

When one considers all of the horrors that transpired after the release of *The Devil and My Daughter*, it is impossible not to weigh heavily the role of the next scene in the shocking chain of events that occurred. When asked about the scene in the cellar, Morrow explained to *Cinema Escapes* that she based it on real cases of devil worship and occult-related crime:

"I had this book[17] that was like an encyclopedia of killers and murders throughout the world. For people who thought the scene was too extreme or unrealistic, all I could tell them was that this is where the script comes from, this is the world I read about, as sick and depraved as it may be. The sacrifice scene is one of the most honest scenes in the film, but no one wants to believe that the society we live in might be this scary and messed up."

---

[16] Other possible titles included *Inside Violet McCoy, Satan's Bitch, Witch's Revenge*, and *This Evil House*.
[17] According to Billy Lee, the book was Daniel Bracewell's *The Devil's Playground: An Illustrated History of Satanic Ritual Abuse and Other Occult-related Crimes*, published by Gauntlet Press in 1985.

Buzzing with flies, the cellar of the dead witch is decorated with chicken feathers, human skulls, and animal skins[18] that hang like the tapestries of Catholic saints inside the medicine shop at the start of the movie. Mave stands before a small coven of witches. They are all wearing black dressing gowns and clutching knives. As the witches make the sign of the inverted cross, Mave asks that Roberta's soul, "in the name of Satan, his demons and legions," return to them in "the fresh and unblemished body of our new disciple."

The film dissolves to a shot of Violet sleeping in her bed. Suddenly, she bolts upright and stands on the floor. She puts a coat on over her nightgown, tucks her bare feet into a pair of bunny slippers, and walks out of the room. In this sequence, the black robes of the witches provide a disquieting contrast to Violet's virgin-white nightgown, while her bunny slippers—with their evangelical connotations of Easter and the resurrection of Christ—serve as a blasphemous affront to the hellish cult she is forced to join. The solarizing dissolve[19] that concludes the scene suggests that the audience is about to enter some aberrant dimension beyond the scope of human understanding.

At this moment, the film leaps clumsily forward. Mave points to the foot of the cellar stairs, announcing, "The chosen one has arrived." The camera swoops dramatically to find Violet standing before the coven, her complexion ghostly white, a creeping smile on her face. A sudden low-angle shot gives the young girl the physical qualities of a monster. Mave instructs Violet to renounce her two fathers—"God and the dirty swine whose foul seed led to your birth." She then asks just how far the possessed girl is willing to go to demonstrate her commitment to "Satan and all the demons of hell." A wild yet pained look in her eyes, Violet picks up a nearby butcher knife and digs the blade into her arm. The Keenan sisters (Mallory Trotter and Theresa Weisert)[20] are then dragged into the cellar. Dressed in rags, the

---

[18] An emulation of scenes from Tobe Hooper's tale of cannibalistic horror, *The Texas Chain Saw Massacre*, released in 1974.
[19] Morrow has said that the psychedelica of this sequence was inspired by the truly bizarre short film *Winter of the Witch* (1969), which depicts the quirky relationship between a pancake-making witch and a curious boy who intrudes upon her home.
[20] In the tragic commotion of the Mercy Care Murders, it has been overlooked that, shortly after the

kidnapped girls are forced to kneel at Violet's feet while Mave and the rest of the coven look on approvingly.

At Mave's command, Violet ferociously stabs the sisters with the butcher knife, mutilating and killing them. In a discontinuous shot that adds to the apalling horror of the scene, their blood pools into a large cauldron that Mave begins stirring with a wooden spoon. The blood-caked bodies are then dragged offscreen by members of the coven. Of the sequence, which had audiences gasping during festival showings of the film, Charlene Worsley told *Silver Screams*,

"It freaking sucked. We shot that in an actual cellar in mid-afternoon, and it was *burning* hot. Mallory and Theresa looked like they were dying of dehydration or something, and Debra had this strange recording playing the whole time that gave me bad vibes.[21] A lot of us, after that day, got physically ill, throwing up, diarrhea, cramps…you could tell Debra was concerned, but she didn't want to hold the production back. She made us keep going. That terrible day was like an endless game of tug of war between the actors and Debra."

Another dissolve signals the passing of time. The coven returns with the broken bodies of the two sisters, their severed skulls and limbs arranged on a rolling table. The remains are dumped into the boiling cauldron. An unnatural cacophony of sounds begins—screeching whistles, scrambled orchestral passages, and bits of John McCoy's Hawaiian theme played in reverse—as Mave produces the medicinal jar that Roberta stole from the medicine shop. She pours the contents

filming of *The Devil and My Daughter*, 21-year-old Theresa Weisert was arrested for indecent exposure and assault on a police officer at a Best Western Motel in Reno, Nevada in February of 1987. According to the police report: "The suspect was acting deranged, knocking down one of the housekeepers and running out of the motel room fully naked. Suspect was observed trying to break into a vending machine when the officer approached. Suspect charged the officer and was forcibly detained at the scene."

[21] A 44-minute cassette recording of the "Jonestown Death Tape," made by Reverend Jim Jones on November 18, 1978 as he directed his followers to kill themselves with cyanide-laced Flavor-Aid. Of the 914 people who died at Jonestown, nearly 300 of them were children under the age of 18, whose death cries can be heard on the tape.

of the jar, a black gelantinous glop,[22] into the cauldron while ordering Violet to "tend to the sacrificial lambs." The possessed teen begins stirring the ghastly soup, all while maintaining a deadened, artificial expression that Morrow later used as one of the central images in the film's press kit.

When removed from the cauldron, the skulls have been stripped to the bone, the glop in the jar having acted as some kind of corrosive acid. Mave gives one of the skulls, now dripping with steaming blood, to Violet. After Violet laps up several drops from the jawbone—a monstrous inversion of the Christian chalice—Mave outlines the next task while animals moan on the film's soundtrack. "The slaughter of this night provides our Dark Lord two gifts for his consumption," she says. "But we must procure a third, for such is the true number of the beast."[23] Mave tells Violet that she must fulfill this sacrifice herself if she truly wants to join the coven. The clattering soundtrack increases in volume as the coven begins to chant. The camera zooms in on Violet's deranged smile until the image blurs, distorting her features. "Cast aside your holy water, priest, and your litanies of blind faith," she intones, summoning Father Gregory and pre-echoing the ritual scene that comes later in the film. "You must understand—Satan does not retreat!"[24]

The murder and blood-drinking sequence in the cellar has become a source of great contention among those who condemn and blame *The Devil and My Daughter* for the horrific murders that took place in the summer following the movie's release. The brunt of this public outcry has fallen on Debra Morrow, who initially remained unwavering

---

[22] Actually pulverized black JELL-O, made by combining grape and orange flavors of JELL-O gelatin.

[23] Occultists have often used the number 333 as a cloaked reference to the more notorious 666, which refers to a term in the Book of Revelation and, in modern culture, has come to be known as the Devil's mark and a mockery of the Holy Trinity. These associations were popularized by *The Omen* (1976), in which the number 666 appears as a birthmark on the scalp of the Anti-Christ Damien Thorn.

[24] These lines are based on the translation of "Selected Verse of Giosue Carducci" by Leslie Warner, taken from *The Agnellutti Anthology of Italian Poems— 13th to 19th Century*, published by Albert and Sons Inc., 1966.

in her defense of the picture and its most disturbing scene. In April of 1987, just four months before the fictional horrors of the film would become shocking reality, she told *Cinema Escapes,*

"When these types of crimes happen in real life, the killers don't hold anything back—so, in my attempt to reflect at least some of the real world, why should I hold anything back? I live near San Francisco, and just a few years ago, the police found this homeless man's body in Golden Gate Park. His head and arms were chopped off and replaced with chicken bones and ears of corn, and a few yards away from the corpse was a box filled with mutilated chickens.[25] The police were convinced it was a ritual murder, and they even brought in a cult expert to investigate the crime scene. It was a gross, ugly, sickening thing, and so are some of the scenes from my film. I wrote them, I directed them, and I stand by them."

Charlene Worsley, on the other hand, was not as quick to defend the controversial sequence. Her comments to *Silver Screams* would later take on a chilling double-meaning in light of the terrible events that transpired:

"The sacrifice scene looks almost too real. There's no grace to it, no subtlety, no aesthetic style. It's like a punch in the face. It stayed with me for a long time after the production was over. It haunted me. Kept me awake at night. And when I could finally fall asleep, I had nightmares about all that cutting and chopping and blood."

As the audience recoils from the graphic realism of the sacrifice scene, Morrow ratchets up the unease in the next scene by uniting death, sex, and female bodily emissions. Inside a motel room, the camera discovers David and Sarah, clothed, kissing and fondling each other in bed. But as David positions himself on top of his mistress, the young woman becomes stiff and uncomfortable. "What's with you?" David asks. "You're acting like a corpse." When Sarah reveals that she is menstruating and not in the mood for sex, David flinches and pulls

---

[25] Morrow is most likely referring to the ritual homicide of transient Leroy Carter, whose dismembered body was found in San Francisco's Golden Gate Park in 1981. The killer placed chicken wings and ears of corn where Carter's missing head should have been, and police found mutilated chickens and rats in a cardboard box close to the crime scene. Carter's murder has never been solved.

away.[26] Here, the professor's knee-jerk reaction points to his fear of women's sexuality and, more specifically, his menophobia (fear of menstruation). Whether Morrow intended such interpretations is debatable, but the subtext of the scene is worth nothing in view of Violet McCoy's sexual awakening. While Sarah retreats into a nervous shell, Violet grows more perversely liberated. Morrow emphasizes this role-reversal by bringing Violet into the conversation between the two lovers, as Sarah tells David, "I can't spend the night tonight. I need to take Violet to school in the morning." When David tries to persuade Sarah to give him oral sex before she leaves, she storms out of the room in anger. This last exchange highlights David's misogyny and foreshadows the explosive encounter between Violet and the professor that will fuel one of the climaxes of the film.

Back at the McCoy residence, Morrow disrupts the expectations of the genre by amplifying the horror in the glare of broad daylight. In the morning, Sarah enters Violet's bedroom to wake her for school. The bed is empty, the sheets spotted with blood in a symbolic parallel of Sarah's menstruation. Violet's coat and nightgown, smeared with blood, lay rumpled on the carpet. As Sarah walks slowly around the bed, thinking Violet is hiding from her, the camera cuts back and forth between her fearful expression and her hesitant footsteps. Here, Morrow uses another ground-level tracking shot of walking feet—only this time to communicate dread and suspense in the narrative.

The bloody spectacle of the next shot—Violet skittering out from underneath the bed to sink her teeth into Sarah's ankle—required Worsley to wear a pair of prosthetic "rotted" teeth[27] that caused a

---

[26] Morrow and Worsley also used menstrual blood as a secondary motif in the body-horror short film *Monsters in My Pants*, which they wrote and produced in their early teens.

[27] "What terrified me more than anything else about *The Exorcist* was the physical transformation that Regan MacNeil went through as the demon took over her body," Morrow has said. "It was the complete disregard for hygiene, the savage violation of her privacy, that I found totally unnerving. We tried to capture these same themes in *The Devil and My Daughter*, but obviously on a much smaller scale" (*Monsters & Mayhem*, 1987).

number of problems on set. Todd Wheeler explained to *Monsters & Mayhem* magazine,

"I didn't fit the damn things right. They dug into Charlene's gumline and caused her mouth to bleed, and I think she had an allergic reaction to the polishing paste. To make matters worse, Debra wanted it to be really gory, so Charlene had to stuff her mouth with blood capsules and chew them up. But the powder capsules were cheap, and the blood was more pink than red. Charlene tried being gentle with Grace, but she was supposed to be acting all possessed and crazy, so the biting got pretty rough. In the movie the blood has this frothy, pulpy quality to it that I like, almost cartoonish…but it was just another pain-in-the-ass day on set, especially for the actors."

Grace Smith added to Wheeler's description of the sequence by revealing that her scream, which carries over into the next scene, was genuine. "Charlene really bit with me those things, and they were sharp!" Smith told *Cinema Escapes*. "It wasn't enough to draw a lot of blood, but by the third or fourth take, she was getting really ferocious." Fully immersed in her character by this point in the shoot, Worsley would increase the intensity of her performance in the upcoming hospital scene.

A sedated Violet sleeps in a hospital bed (careful viewers will note that the scene was shot in the same room used for John McCoy's office). Her lips are cracked and raw, and she has a bandage on her neck and another around the wrist of her arm. Vampire-brown circles hang under her eyelids. "We couldn't afford anything like the medical scenes in *The Exorcist*,[28] so we used the bandages and the dialogue to show a jump forward in time," Morrow explained. "Violet has already been through a series of medical exams by the time the scene starts."

Morrow presents the dialogue between McCoy and the doctor in a contrived voiceover while the camera drifts along the left side of Violet's face. The moment is surprisingly tender, an antidote to the shocking horror of the previous scenes. "First—the good news," the doctor says to McCoy. "Blood and urine tests came back negative. Same with the bone scan. The CT scan shows no signs of a brain

---

[28] A reference to the arteriogram sequence in *The Exorcist*, arguably the film's most disturbing scene, in which Regan's doctor uses a needle to inject dye into the child's carotid artery in order to detect abnormalities inside her body.

tumor, and no sign of swelling or bleeding." But when the doctor delivers the bad news—"We have no idea what's wrong with her"—Violet's eyes open wide to the sound of a screeching synthesized stinger, a moment on the soundtrack that Morrow described as "a telepathic response from the demon inside her." The director drives forward this point in the next sequence, as Violet climbs out of bed and wanders the lonely corridors of the hospital,[29] eventually making her way to the geriatric ward. Though the movie never explains how Violet can walk around without drawing the attention of hospital staff, the scene has a soft, meditative quality that suspends disbelief; the feeling is enhanced by the unearthly and tuneless piano notes that play while Violet glides along the corridor.

Most likely the result of the film's limited budget, the ward is eerily desolate. As Violet drifts down the hall, she sees only one other patient: an elderly Native American woman sitting in a wheelchair by the window. As Violet approaches, we see a pile of medicine cards[30] in the woman's lap, and we are symbolically transported back to the witch's house of haunted artifacts and ritual tools. The old woman's appearance—her thinning gray hair, sagging skin, and sunken eyes—seems to touch something deep inside Violet, something beyond the reaches of the demon. Her expression softens; the gentle look of the young girl within her returns, and her gaze is that of a daughter looking into the loving eyes of her mother. When the film had its festival run in the spring of 1987, audiences could not have been aware of the impact this brief moment of calm had on Charlene Worsley, who revealed to *Silver Screams*,

---

[29] The hospital scenes were shot at Lowell High School in San Francisco, where Charlene Worsley's mother, Ruth Worsley, was once a student. Opened in 1856, Lowell remains one of the oldest public high schools in the country.

[30] More fad than genuine Native American custom, medicine cards draw upon ancient wisdom and the natural ways of animals in order to divine truths about how to live a more powerful and spiritual life. The three medicine cards used in this scene each have their own meaning based on the events in the film and the demon's attempt to control and ultimately kill Violet McCoy: the Rabbit (fear), the Coyote (trickery), and the Snake (transmutation).

"My mother is in a nursing home, so this scene really affected me. Off-camera, I barely talked with the woman who played the Indian lady, but it was like looking at my mom. The rumor on set was that the actress was a real Indian medicine woman, and she could cure you of your ills just by touching her hand to your face. I once asked Debra how she cast her, but she never told me.[31] Still, it was so strange to look at her, to be that close to her...she had a warm quality, and yet there was this primitive darkness in her eyes."

The scene is layered with subtle moments of terror before chaos erupts. Without saying a word, the elderly woman shuffles the pile of medicine cards, then places three of them in her lap in front of Violet. She then motions for Violet to turn each of the cards over. The rapid-fire editing dramatizes the moment as the faces of the cards—the Rabbit, the Coyote, and the Snake—stare at Violet with mocking derision. "The rabbit will multiply your fears, while the coyote will trick you into sacrifice," the woman says, indicating the first two cards. "And, unless you seek help, the serpent will take your life," she warns, pointing a wrinkled finger at the Snake card. At that moment, a shrieking whistle from the soundtrack spurs Violet into action. She lunges for the old woman's throat, teeth gnashing, eyes burning with rage. As the camera jostles about the scene, losing focus and at one point spinning upside-down, we hear doctors prying Violet loose and restraining her. The Native American woman survives the attack, the scene fading out to the sound of her heaving sobs.

Though some reviewers panned *The Devil and My Daughter* for being another exploitative rip-off of *The Exorcist*,[32] Morrow remained stubbornly optimistic about what she and her crew had accomplished with the film:

"Movies like *The Exorcist* and *The Omen*[33] had enormous budgets, famous actors, big sets, and knock-out special effects. But those films,

---

[31] And to this day no one knows the identity of the actress. Her name is nowhere to be found in the press kit or closing credits of the film. In interviews, Morrow has remained notoriously mute on the subject.
[32] Along with *Beyond the Door* (1974), *Seytan* (1974), and *Exorcismo* (1975).
[33] Richard Donner's 1976 tale of a cherubic Anti-Christ, the first in a trilogy that also includes Don Taylor's *Damien: Omen II* (1978) and Graham Baker's *Omen III: The Final Conflict* (1981).

as great as they are, never showed the possessed child actually killing anyone. It's *implied* that Regan kills Burke Dennings, it's *implied* that Damien tries to kill his mother. With *The Devil and My Daughter*, I didn't want the audience to have to infer much. I wanted to show Violet trying to hurt and kill people. She wants to rip out the woman's throat because that's what the demon wants, that's the human sacrifice it demands. It's not a better film than *The Exorcist*—it's not even in the same stratosphere! But it's *different*, and that's what we had hoped to achieve."

The warning of the old woman catalyzes the next scene, as John McCoy paces in his home office, gin in hand, awaiting the arrival of Father Gregory. After Sarah escorts him into the room, the priest sits across from McCoy, a parallel to their earlier meeting—only now with higher stakes. Featuring one of the longer sequences of dialogue in the film, the scene ties up loose ends in the narrative. The death of the witch was ruled a suicide; the bones of the missing sisters were discovered half-buried in the woods; and Violet, now on sedatives and sleeping in her room, has become increasingly abnormal: "It's not just that she's violent and unstable," McCoy explains. "She *knows* things. Things about my police work. Things about me and my wife we never told her. Our arguments, our sexual indiscretions…"

Retro-cognitive ability appears repeatedly throughout the film, which separates, in some ways, *The Devil and My Daughter* from its predecessors. Violet never levitates, rotates her head, or speaks in a foreign language (*The Exorcist*); no one in the movie gives birth to the anti-Christ (*Rosemary's Baby* and *The Omen*); and demons never drag Violet into hell (*The Sentinel*).[34] Aware of her dwindling budget and the technological limitations of shooting on video, Morrow relied on expository dialogue rather than action and costly special-effects to drive the story forward. Setting the movie apart even further, when McCoy asks Gregory to attempt to "cure" Violet through prayer, neither the detective nor the priest ever uses the word "exorcism." Morrow told *Monsters & Mayhem*,

---

[34] Based on the horror novel by Jeffrey Konvitz, Michael Winner's 1977 film concerns a fashion model whose NYC apartment building is a portal to hell. Most famous for its controversial climax, in which a horde of lurching demons, played by real-life deformed and disfigured people, attacks the protagonist.

"I wanted to surpass the rigmarole of Father Gregory having to get approval for an exorcism from the Catholic Church. That scene has been done before, and [avoiding] it suggested something sinister about Gregory, that he would perform a religious or spiritual rite on Violet without getting permission or asking for assistance..."

Gregory agrees to see Violet and perform a ritual prayer in her name, though he warns McCoy, "For the priest to be truly powerful, he must believe," an ominous line that suggests the conflict of faith about to unfold in the house. The priest goes to the rectory to gather some religious items, including holy water, a rosary, and a St. Nicholas prayer card.[35] The vibrant colors of the card, as shown in the image of St. Nicholas in red and gold robes, parallel the colors of the medicine cards from the hospital scene and serve as a visual cue of the supernatural powers at work in the story. As Gregory leaves the rectory, the distant clanging of church bells marks the time, but also acts as a summoning of the internal power and faith the priest must discover within himself in order to vanquish a sacrilegious evil. Charlene Worsley understood the symbolism of the bells in simpler terms, explaining, "It's like the bell before a boxing match, the signal that a bloody fight is about to begin."

In altering Worsley's angelic features for one of the more volatile scenes in the film, Todd Wheeler relied on several disparate sources of inspiration, including photographs of Anneliese Michel,[36] a young German woman who believed she was possessed by demons (including Judas Iscariot and Adolf Hitler) and who died of extreme malnutrition in 1976. In addition to Wheeler's on-the-fly makeup effects, Billy Lee's effective blending of light and shadow adds to the monstrosity of the scene, turning the sight of Violet into a disturbing

---

[35] Though primarily known as the patron saint of sailors and merchants, St. Nicholas was also known as the protector of children and others in need, which explains why Father Gregory would bring the prayer card to the residence.

[36] To capture the demonic transformation of Violet McCoy, Wheeler studied photographs from Felecitas D. Goodman's *The Exorcism of Anneliese Michel* (1981). In a 1988, radio interview, Billy Lee claimed to have seen Charlene Worsley with the book on multiple occasions. "She carried the book around with her, reading it between takes," Lee said.

source of abject horror. Indeed, when Gregory enters the room to begin the ritual, he takes one look at Violet writhing in bed and mutters under his breath, "My God, my God…what have you done?"

The possessed Violet wastes no time in attempting to assert her control over the priest. As Gregory drapes the rosary around his neck and recites the Hail Mary, the possessed girl spits out a number of vulgarities and insults: "You're sick in the head and cock, priest…you should be excommunicated. Impale yourself on a roasting fork! Kill yourself so you can rot down here with the rest of us!"

Next, Violet and Gregory engage in a vicious argument that the director says was unscripted. "We went off book. There was one major plot point that needed to come out of the ritual scene, and Charlene and Michael knew what it was," Morrow explained. "I let them take their time getting to that place, which built up their hate and distrust for each other's characters. They didn't know what the other was going to say, and that freedom scared them a little."

While Todd Wheeler and Billy Lee used this artistic freedom to add their own personal touches to the film, not everyone was pleased with the improvisation required during the ritual scene. Charlene Worsley told *Silver Screams*,

"It was very hard to let myself go during that scene. Debra had given me some 'satanic' lines to memorize and I knew I needed to accuse Father Gregory of these terrible things, but she had asked me to insult *Michael* himself. Listen, if you know Michael Callaway, then you know what a good guy he is. He's a very gentle and soft-spoken man, and he treated everyone on the set like they were his family. It was hard to pull off. I think, in the end, it was harder for Michael than it was for me, because he had a real fondness for me, for everyone on the set, and here Debra was telling him to abandon his character's spiritual decorum and really let me have it.

"The scary thing is…the words just *erupted* from my mouth. By this time we were close to being done with the movie, and it was like the possessed Violet had taken over. I was like, 'What are you doing inside my head? Get out of there!' It was a very surreal acting experience for me."

Though Violet and Gregory remain on mostly even ground during their verbal battle, the tone of the scene grows considerably darker when the demon inside the girl gains the upper hand. "The teenage sisters, the Whores of Babylon," Violet growls in a voice enhanced by husky vocal effects. "You knew those sluts well, didn't you, priest? They were your parishioners." Gregory briefly silences the teen by dousing her in holy water and thrusting the prayer card against her forehead, but Violet remains defiant, cursing and spitting a glob of saliva onto the priest's cassock. When Gregory asks who killed the Keenan sisters, Violet gleefully croaks, "We chopped them up into little pieces and drank their blood. But not before you fucked them, corrupt priest! Like the bull does the heifer, you fucked them!" The film then slips into what Paul Leonard describes as a "psychedelic softcore porn fever dream," in which Polaroids of naked women flash onscreen, the pictures backlit by garish neon gels. Gregory makes implicit his guilt when the movie returns to the horrors of Violet's bedroom. "Damn you—you can see inside my mind! You succubus! You witch!" he roars at the demon. "You burned the pictures, didn't you, priest?" the Violet-thing replies. "But not all of them, right? You still keep some of Amber under your bed because that pubescent bitch was your special favorite. Right next to your gun and your Bible! Kill yourself, Gregory! Kill yourself!" The priest flees the room to the sound of Violet's howlish laughter. He nearly collides in the hall with McCoy, who feeds his daughter another sedative to end the chaos.

While Lee described the shooting of the ritual scene as "a wild ride, and lots of fun," Worsley recalled being physically and emotionally drained after the day was over:

"It was a strain on my vocal chords, all that screaming. To tell the truth, I felt *scared* doing it…scared to say those vile things to a priest, even if he was just an actor. And this is going to sound a little weird, but knowing the scene was *recorded* on video, that the sounds were *recorded* on microphones, that there would be copy after copy of it. It was part of history now, and the camera had become my enemy. There was no erasing the film. No erasing *me*. That freaked me out. But I think that's why people were frightened by *The Devil and My Daughter*. They saw something in our eyes…they knew the actors were frightened too."

In the next scene, as McCoy falls asleep while keeping vigil in his daughter's bedroom, Violet slips away and creeps toward the phone in the hall. Crouching against the wall, her face mottled by flickering shadows, she calls the professor and pretends to be her cousin. After David arranges to meet "Sarah" inside their favorite motel room, Violet hangs up the phone just as Billy Lee indulges in another ill-advised zoom shot, squashing the actress's face into the frame to the sound of various audio signals in reverse.[37]

Guided by the instructions of Mave, who speaks in a haunting voiceover, Violet finds herself wandering the outdoor corridors of the motel in a slow-moving tracking shot (the film never makes clear how Mave knew the name or location of the motel, or how far Violet had to walk to get there). Flashing yellow and orange neon lights from the archway echo the earlier Polaroid sequence, forcing audiences to question if Gregory had ever brought the Keenan sisters to the same motel. As she reaches the end of the corridor Violet finds the correct room through Mave's hypnotic instructions: "He's waiting for you in the last room on the right. Waiting for you in the dark. Bring us his blood to drink, and bring the Prince of Darkness this final sacrifice." Violet opens the door and steps inside. The film then cuts to Gregory sitting on the floor inside the rectory, a bottle of whiskey in one hand, his rosary beads clutched in the other. Gregory gulps his whiskey, pulls at his hair and face, and smashes the rosary against the wall. The cross-cutting sequence that follows links the motifs of death and sex once again in the film. While Gregory picks up his gun, Violet crawls into bed next to David. She wakes him by unbuttoning his shirt and purring against his chest. Gregory then puts the gun in his mouth. As David recognizes Violet in a moment of bewildered terror, shrieking violin notes build to a crescendo.[38] Violet plunges a knife into David's throat and drags the blade across, spurting gouts of blood onto the bed. Inside the rectory, Gregory pulls the trigger. His body crumples to the floor, his face splashed with blood, a gruesome sight that ends the sequence.

Morrow told Todd Wheeler that she wanted the effects required for the murder-and-suicide scene to be as gory and as inexpensive as possible. Wheeler reported to *Monsters & Mayhem* that Gregory's suicide was a fairly standard effect—face putty, molding clay, makeup, and stage blood. But the throat-cutting sequence proved far more complicated and time-consuming. Wheeler recalled:

---

[37] The reversed audio clips were inspired by Morrow's short film, *Blood Songs* (1985), the story of a teenage girl who uses a satanic song to bring her slain mother back to life.
[38] Modeled after Bernard Herrmann's shrieking violins in Alfred Hitchcock's *Psycho* (1960), but with broken tuning pegs for hair-raising effect.

"We started early in the morning for once, which was good. The latex and the makeup all looked great and Thom Randall was so patient and understanding. We ran heat-shrink tubing into the appliance on his neck and we were ready to shoot. The problem was with the slits in the tubing. We used an old bike pump to run the blood through the slits, but the blood would pour out in some places and not in others. It looked like the blade didn't cut all the way across, and that was definitely not the way Debra wanted it.

"Then blood spurted into Charlene's eyes and mouth, and Debra said we had to start the scene all over again. That was when Charlene broke down. She started shouting at Debra and Billy, and crying. She cursed out Matthew Benowitz, our set coordinator, when he tried to help her clean up. They were standing next to each other, and she smashed her heel right onto his foot. Then she lunged at the *camera*, trying to smash the lens! It was crazy. Her eyes were swollen and red, her makeup was smeared—she was a mess. Debra had to shut everything down for the night. And then it was Billy's turn to go off half-cocked. He called Charlene a shit-stirring bitch and blamed her for ruining the movie, which got *Debra* pissed at Billy, and pretty soon everyone was screaming at each other."

Disguising the lackluster effect, the film cuts to a reaction shot of Violet, her mouth pulled wide in a lopsided grin. While running her fingers through the professor's blood, she hears Mave's voice in her head: "Now bring the adulterer to the coven and please your Eternal Father, the Prince of Dogs and Devils." These lines, borrowed partly from Matthew 9:34,[39] usher in the climax of the film.

In a shaky high angle shot, McCoy and Sarah dash from the McCoy house to the car in the driveway. With stilted dialogue dubbed during post-production, the two discuss a course of action to find the missing Violet. The car peels out and roars down the street to a synthesized drum beat, signaling the film's first and only action sequence. Shot from entirely inside the car, the scene lasts far too long, as McCoy tears down suburban streets looking for Violet. Sarah shouts directions to all the usual places—the school, the park, the mall—before McCoy announces, "I have an idea!" With screeching tires, the car barrels down an industrial road; moments later, McCoy spots Violet in the

---

[39] From the King James Bible, New International Version: "But the Pharisees said, He casteth out devils through the prince of the devils."

shadows, lugging David's corpse over her shoulder. A static shot of the witch house, backed by the ominous drone of a didgeridoo,[40] reveals Violet's destination. McCoy's car roars up to the curb. Violet, aware that she is being pursued, lurches toward the house, struggling to maintain her balance. Sarah leaps from the car and runs toward Violet. Nimbly, Violet drops the body and turns on Sarah, snarling and flashing rotted teeth. In one deft motion she slices her fingernails across her cousin's throat.

"I based that sequence off the climax in *Marathon Man*,[41] when the Nazi dentist uses a spring-loaded knife to slit the old man's neck," Morrow said. "It's a shock because Violet becomes this killing machine by the end." As Sarah falls to the ground and dies, Violet rushes into the house. Realizing he can do nothing for his niece, McCoy draws his weapon and chases after his daughter.

Mirroring images from *The Texas Chain Saw Massacre* (1974), the search sequence inside the witch house finds McCoy stepping over animal bones, discovering a nest of spiders, and finding a pentagram drawn on the floor with salt. As the tension mounts, Mave startles the detective by jumping out from behind a door and stabbing him with a large kitchen knife. McCoy stumbles into a corner, blood seeping from his arm as he struggles to maintain control of his gun and point it at the advancing witch. "It is useless to fight, McCoy, for the girl belongs to us," Mave says, brandishing the knife. "Would you care to join the devil's ranks as well? Swear to Satan and it shall be done. Swear your corrupted soul to Satan and become one of us!"[42] As Mave raises the

---

[40] Native to indigenous Australian culture, the didgeridoo is a long, conical-shaped wind instrument that produces a low-frequency droning sound. Historically, known for its use in ancient religious ceremonies and tribal rituals.

[41] "Is it safe?" The 1976 conspiracy thriller directed by John Schlesinger and based off the 1974 William Goldman bestseller. Laurence Olivier stars as Nazi madman Dr. Christian Szell, notorious for torturing his victims with sharp dental instruments.

[42] Not unlike the words of Richard Ramirez, or "The Night Stalker," the serial killer and satanist who terrorized the citizens of Southern California and the San Francisco Bay Area between 1984 and 1985. According to eyewitness reports, Ramirez told his victims to "Swear upon Satan that you won't scream

knife, McCoy fires twice, hitting her in the chest and shoulder and killing her. But, in an implausible twist, the second bullet exits Mave's body and strikes Violet in the neck just as she runs into the room. As somber piano notes play, McCoy cradles his daughter in his arms and weeps to God for forgiveness. In the superimposed shot that ends the film, Violet's ravaged facial features fade and she dies with the hint of a smile on her lips.

"The question that remains at the end has to do with Violet's loyalty," Morrow said in a radio interview in 1987. "Was she running to McCoy, or was she running to Mave? Her father's bullet prevents us from ever knowing the answer." Though critics were less than kind about the abrupt resolution of *The Devil and My Daughter*,[43] it was not until the fall of 1988, after the murders at the Mercy Care Medical Center in California, that Morrow revealed a surprising secret behind the conclusion of the film:

"By the time we finished the movie, Charlene was totally fried. Her skin was breaking out, she was exhausted, she hated Billy, and she was frustrated by what she called my "lack of direction." And, like most of the critics, she despised the ending of the movie. She said that Violet was the heart of the story, and that [the character] needed to play a bigger role in the climax. I argued we didn't have the time or budget for a different ending. We wrapped late on a Saturday, around midnight. Billy and I hauled all the equipment back to campus, locked it up, and I went home and crashed...

"Charlene showed up at my house around 3 that morning. She was still dressed like Violet, her clothes splattered in fake blood. She demanded we reshoot the ending. She wanted something not so bleak.

for help." Ramirez was arrested in 1985 and convicted of several brutal crimes, including murder and sexual assault. He is currently on death row in California's San Quentin State Prison.

[43] In her 1988 article "*The Devil and My Daughter* and the Mercy Care Murders," Dorothy Liverton called the ending of the film "a flimsy resolution that denies the viewer any kind of lasting bond with the protagonist—not that we wanted one in the first place"; Martine Parsons, writing for *Crimson Highway*, argued that the film's climax is "a clear example of the limitations of a shoestring budget and less-than-average script; it's the child's last opportunity to *do* something and she winds up doing nothing."

Something uplifting. I was exhausted and nearly shut the door in her face. And right then, it all came rushing back to me. Our childhood. Making brooches out of bottlecaps. Watching fireworks over Lake Merritt. Cranking Black Sabbath as loud as we could. And then how fast we grew up. How brave Charlene was, her father deserting her, her mother fading away, and there was nothing anybody could do about it. I thought of my own mother, my own failings—everything.

"I hugged Charlene. I told her I was sorry for pushing her too hard. For being selfish. For not recognizing how stressed out she had become on set. It all just came spilling out. Pretty soon we were both standing there, holding each other and sobbing like babies! Then she came inside and we washed all her makeup off in the bathroom.

"We spent the rest of the morning drinking coffee, eating leftover pizza, and talking about the reshoot. But no matter how convincing Charlene could be, I couldn't do it. I owed my dad money. I could barely afford gas or school books. I told Charlene no. She begged me, and I still said no. The movie was in the can, and that was it. She got really sick after that, throwing up pizza and coffee in the kitchen sink. I tried to help her and she cursed at me in this horrible, gurgly voice. She was bent over the sink, her shirt was riding up her waist...and she had a bunch of pustules on her lower back. These purple swollen knobs. Some of them were bleeding...it was terrible. And then she left. Ran right out the door. Her face ashen, her body so thin and white, just like a ghost. Her beat-up car turned the corner and sputtered away...

"And only later that day, as I tried to sleep, did it hit me: Charlene wanted Violet to heal. To return to her father. To be forgiven for all the killings. To *live*. But Violet couldn't live, or else her life from that point forward would have been hell. She would have gone to prison. Gotten the death penalty, or be sent to an insane asylum. I thought heaven was the answer, the gift, but Charlene disagreed.

"A reporter asked me recently whether I feel guilty about it, as if reshooting the end of movie, redeeming Violet in some way for the murders—the way Regan MacNeil was redeemed at the end of *The Exorcist*—was the clue to unlocking whatever mental problems Charlene was having. My answer is *of course I do*. Charlene and I had known each other since the first grade. She was my best friend. She was also a talented actress and her performance saved the movie. To think I could have put a stop to what happened, or could have gotten

Charlene some help…I should have seen the signs, and it kills me every day that I didn't. It rips my fucking heart out."

Morrow's refusal to reshoot the ending, and the tragic events that occurred following the release of the film notwithstanding, the conclusion to *The Devil and My Daughter* functions on two thematic levels that were touched upon at the start of the narrative. First, Violet's death, unintentionally committed by her father, returns the audience to the scene in which John McCoy admits to neglecting his daughter. Her death becomes his reckoning—the pain he must endure in order to make amends for his sins. In this symbolic analysis, Morrow's B-movie tale of demonic possession becomes a curious morality play in which the leading man must turn to God in order to find salvation.

Second, and more importantly, the resolution to the film means that Violet McCoy will never have to remember her time spent in the devil's grip; she will never have to suffer through the emotional and psychological torment of having murdered four innocent people, nor will she have to face the merciless hands of the law. Unlike Regan MacNeil, who still must live among Satan's playthings in *The Exorcist II: The Heretic* (1977),[44] or Damien Thorn, who possesses the DNA of a jackal and causes the death of countless people in *Damien: Omen II* (1978), Violet McCoy remains liberated, haunted neither by memory, justice, or the possibility of a tired sequel.

This last point—that the young Violet McCoy *had* to die in order to avoid her irredeemable guilt and an unforgiving judicial system—is worth considering in light of the murders in Oakland and the fate of Charlene Worsley. This essay was not written to draw extensive parallels between the fictional events in the film and the painful circumstances of Worsley's real life, or to analyze the murders in any way; at the same time, it seems negligent to not address the crimes to some degree and to recognize the lives lost on that tragic day. As Debra Morrow told *Rolling Stone* in this unedited interview excerpt from 1988:

"If I had even the faintest idea that Charlene was in serious trouble, or really sick, we never would have made *The Devil and My Daughter*. I

---

[44] Slow and psuedo-scientific 1977 sequel directed by John Boorman in which beleaguered Regan MacNeil undergoes weird psychological experiments in order to revive her memories of the exorcism in Georgetown. Avoid at all costs.

loved Charlene. I had also known her mother ever since I was a kid. Ruth was a brilliant woman who galvanized the Oakland art scene in the 60s and 70s, especially for female artists and photographers. No matter how you interpret what Charlene did, she loved her mother very much. There was no anger or hatred between them, at least none that I ever saw.

"No one deserved what happened that day. Not Ruth, not Charlene. Not the others. Some people blame the movie; they say all that demonic bullshit messed with Charlene's mind. If that's true, then that's on me, and I take responsibility for that. Some people say she must have been schizophrenic. But it's impossible to make sense of every detail. We're never going to have all the answers to why so many people died."

The Devil and My Daughter will always hold a firm but strange position in the world of exploitation and "cult" horror films. Since the movie's release, the low production value, hackneyed script, and at-times amateurish direction have only contributed to its popularity. As the horror genre evolves throughout the nineties and beyond, and as the citizens of Oakland continue to grieve their dead, it will be curious to see how the film perseveres and how critics and horror audiences will ultimately weigh the value of its unconventional legacy. As Violet McCoy bellows to Father Gregory during the ritual scene: "I am your immortal enemy, your ugliest fear, your most vile temptation…I am your *future*."

"The Devil in the Details: 19 Things You Never Knew about Debra Morrow's *The Devil and My Daughter*" by Scott Chambers (originally published in *Crimson Highway*, January, 1988, p. 3-4):

Issue # 26 of *Crimson Highway* featured a brief editorial about the low-brow artistic merits of Debra Morrow's horror movie *The Devil and My Daughter*. Though the shot-on-video story of a teen girl possessed by a witch had its share of critics, we appreciated the film's micro-budget approach, its willingness to explore mature themes like youthful sexuality and the horrific abuses of the Catholic church, and its copious amounts of bloodshed and gore. The audience response at horror festivals and conventions was generally positive, and it became clear that the creative team behind the indie effort had a bright and promising future in the world of horror cinema.

It's been five months since *The Devil and My Daughter* had its final public screening, and since that time, all hell has broken loose. The filmmakers have denied requests for interviews. Two members of the cast have fled the state, refusing to speak about the project. And, tragically, five people are now dead, possibly as a result of this film.

The murders at Mercy Care Medical Center have caused both audiences and critics to return to *The Devil and My Daughter* in an attempt to understand the senseless events that occurred. Joining the fray, *Crimson Highway* has compiled a list of 19 facts and tidbits that explores the controversies that surround the movie. We do not claim that anything on this list caused the murders in Oakland, and we readily admit that we included a small handful of throwaway items solely to inform and entertain (we're still a horror rag, folks). But it is impossible to ignore the ever-deepening symbolism behind many of the items presented below. We're not a tabloid magazine, nor do we publish articles strictly to stir the sensationalistic pot. But, like most people who are affected when innocent people are killed, we are still grappling with the *why*. Here's our attempt to put at least some of the pieces of this scattered puzzle together.

1.   Within the press kit for *The Devil and My Daughter*, director of photography Billy Lee interspersed phrases from Anton LaVey's *The Satanic Bible*.

2.   Todd Wheeler, who handled the special effects for the film, was raised in Bodega Bay, California, the charming oceanside

town where Alfred Hitchcock shot scenes for his ode to winged terror, *The Birds.*

3. On the sweltering afternoon that the sacrifice scene was filmed, Mallory Trotter, who plays one of the kidnapped sisters, became furious with director Debra Morrow, called her a "bitch," and stormed off the set. Trotter left for the Pacific Northwest shortly after production ended and refused to do any press for the film.

4. Charlene Worsley divided her time between shooting *The Devil and My Daughter* and visiting her mother at the Mercy Care Medical Center in Oakland. A nurse at the center said that at times it seemed like Charlene had no control over her facial expressions. "Her mouth would bend and droop as if it was made out of rubber. Other times, her face would become stiff, withered and cracked," the nurse described. "It was like she was wearing a different mask every time she visited."

5. Sources close to the film have suggested that the vandalism that occurred at East Bay Community College during the pre-production stage (a figurine of the Virgin Mary, caked in blood, was discovered inside the editing studio, and the windows were graffitied with satanic symbols) was an attempt by the filmmakers to drum up publicity for the movie.

6. Carole Warner, who plays the part of the demonic witch in the film, was born and raised in Osnabrück, Germany, a city famous for witch-hunts and religious wars in the 16th century.

7. Throughout the filming of the movie, Charlene Worsley allegedly suffered from violent nightmares, obsessive thoughts about death and dying, and suicidal ideations.

8. During pre-production, Morrow and Lee spent weeks fine-tuning the script and scouting locations. Though Lee had filmed *Blood Songs,* he did not have a role in the planning of that film. *The Devil and My Daughter* marked the first time that Morrow had worked so closely with someone other than Charlene Worsley, and the situation caused animosity in the group. Cherie Lynn Dunn, who plays one of the witches in the film, said that Charlene was "insanely jealous of Billy's relationship with Debra," and that Charlene viewed Lee as "an outsider."

9. The nude pictures that Father Gregory keeps stashed away in his bedroom were actually cut-out photographs of women from *Hustler*'s "Beaver Hunt," a popular feature in the pornographic magazine devoted to amateur models. The photos were glued to white index cards in an effort to make them look like Polaroids.

10. During the film's short-lived festival run, Theresa Weisert, who appears in the sacrifice scene as Amber Keenan, was living in a motel in Reno, Nevada. After an altercation with another guest, Weisert was arrested for indecent exposure, assault on a police officer, and disturbing the peace. In the police report, Weisert blamed her behavior on the "psychological abuse" she endured during the filming of Morrow's movie.

11. Carnal Season rhythm guitarist Mitrik Skinner, whose music appears in Debra Morrow's *Blood Songs*, is penning a biography of the group titled *Satan's Henchmen*. According to an inside source, one chapter, "Curse of the Moloch," describes how the death-metal rockers would plant "spells, voodoo hexes, and satanic messages" in their songs with the intent of driving listeners insane or causing them to become possessed. Moloch, a pagan demon who delighted in human sacrifice, makes a brief appearance in *The Devil and My Daughter.*

12. During production, Morrow kept a director's notebook in which she jotted down events that occurred on set. Like many of the props and physical items associated with the movie (including costumes, videotapes, cassette recorders, and miscellaneous wires and cables), the notebook disappeared and has never been recovered.

13. To make the internal organs and intestines (including the semi-digested food) for the sacrifice scene in the witch's cellar, Todd Wheeler used popcorn Styrofoam soaked in fake blood, wet dog food, and sausage casings stuffed with boiled spaghetti.

14. The kidnapping in *The Devil and My Daughter* is loosely based on the real case of Barbara and Patricia Grimes, teenage sisters who disappeared from Chicago in 1957 and whose bodies were found dumped by the side of the road a short time later.

15. To establish a frightening tone on set, Morrow played excerpts of the Jonestown "suicide tape," which included the eerily soothing voice of cult leader Jim Jones as he demanded his

followers to "step over," "hasten the medication," and "die with a degree of dignity."

16. Though in interviews she made light of the famous ankle-biting scene, Grace Smith was genuinely frightened by Charlene Worsley's behavior at the time. In the months following the murders, two entertainment magazines alleged that Charlene used her prosthetic teeth to intentionally bite Smith's ankle, causing the actress to bleed.

17. After facing a misdemeanor conviction for poisoning the family dog, Charlene Worsley's father, a former college professor and drug addict, abandoned his wife and daughter and fled the state. His whereabouts are currently unknown.

18. All the exterior motel scenes were shot at an Easy-8 Motel that stands just off the freeway in South San Francisco. One week after filming ended, a 45-year-old man was found stabbed to death in one of the rooms on the second floor.

19. During the throat-cutting sequence, stage blood shot into Charlene Worsley's eyes and caused the actress to have a meltdown on set. According to Todd Wheeler, Charlene's erratic behavior forced the director to rush through the last shots of the movie. "It's a credit to Debra, because she cared more about the well-being of her friend than she did the end of the film," Wheeler has said.

"The Long Goodbye: Living with Frontotemporal Dementia" by Rose Graham (originally published in *Health and Family*, February, 1987, p. 5-8):

Though he had been a well-respected Biology teacher for nearly 28 years, Steve Iverson did something strange one afternoon: in front of a class full of high school students, he flipped over a desk and wrote the F-word on the board. Two weeks later, after locking his keys in his car, Steve tried punching out the glass in one of the vehicle windows. Students reported these incidents to the school principal, wondering what was wrong with their favorite teacher.

Around that same time, Steve began treating his wife, Bonnie, differently. He made insensitive comments about her weight and hair. They stopped going out for dinner and to the movies together. Steve began spending most of his time wandering the neighborhood in his sandals, driving to the all-night market, or trying to fix the sprinklers.

"But the sprinklers weren't broken," Bonnie says. "And when he returned from the store, he came back with nothing, or with things we didn't need—like eggs. Neither of us eats eggs."

These problems lasted for four months before Bonnie convinced her husband to see his doctor. After conducting some tests, the doctor referred Steve to a neurologist. Two weeks later, the couple, who have been married for 35 years, learned what was wrong.

"I thought of all those times I had yelled at him for his behavior or his crappy attitude," Bonnie says. "I even thought he was having an affair, he was acting so strange and mean. At the hospital, I couldn't stop crying, but Steve took my hand and said he loved me. I had never felt so guilty in my entire life."

At 61, Steve Iverson has frontotemporal dementia—a group of brain disorders that causes a progressive decline in both behavior and language. Within as little as two years, those diagnosed with FTD can be entirely dependent on caregivers to help them with everyday tasks. Though there is no cure for FTD, researchers are trying to determine the most effective treatment options for the disease, including speech therapy, anti-depressants, and exercise.

Never one to run away from a fight, Steve Iverson is determined to regain control over his life and maintain his dignity in the process. He and Bonnie have established a daily routine of memory games, brain teasers, and nonaerobic stretching and toning exercises to ward off the effects of his illness. Their objective is to keep Steve's cognitive abilities strong while they stay on top of the latest advancements in FTD research. "We were lucky to get the news early, and we want to do all we can to take advantage of the time we have," Bonnie says.

Unlike Steve, not all people with FTD are diagnosed correctly or so soon after they show symptoms of the disease; this delay can cause confusion, undue suffering, and added expense.

"The first step is for patients to get the right diagnosis," says Dr. Keshav Fardi, a professor of neurology and an attending physician at Georgetown University Medical Center. "There are some similarities, but FTD is not the same as Alzheimer's. Symptoms for Alzheimer's appear in most patients after the age of 65, whereas FTD often strikes people at a younger age, and can result in personality changes that are both tragic and startling."

Although they often occur gradually, these personality changes can still be dangerous. In 1984, Ruth Worsley, an artist and photographer, learned that she had FTD. Prior to her diagnosis, the single mother had crashed her car into a sand barrel, scorched her arm with an iron, and cut up several of her favorite photographs.

"When the car accident happened, I was scared for my mother's safety, but I didn't connect it to anything wrong with her health," says Ruth's daughter, Charlene, who was 16-years-old when her mother was diagnosed. "My mom was only 53, and neither of us are good drivers, so I just chalked it up to family genes and bad luck."

But on the night she found her mother on the floor, kneeling over a pile of photographs with a pair of scissors in her hand, Charlene realized something needed to be done.

Ruth visited several doctors before consulting a neurologist. On the same day she received her diagnosis, she discovered that she had trouble speaking; her words came out as nonsense, or they remained lodged in her throat, uncommunicable forever.

"Don't worry—you don't have a mental illness, and you didn't have a stroke," her doctor told her. "But we do need to come up with a caregiving plan to get you through this."

Charlene did all she could for her mother. A junior in high school at the time, the brunette teen prepared home cooked meals. She marked important spots in the house with glow-in-the-dark tape so that Ruth would not injure herself at night. She helped her mother get dressed in the morning and managed her medications. She listened patiently when Ruth became irritated over simple things, and she masked her anger when her mother said something hurtful or offensive.

But Charlene admits she had more than her share of tantrums. When she walked into the kitchen one afternoon and found a pot of stew burning on the stove, and Ruth standing idly by, Charlene lost her cool.

"I yelled and I screamed, and I dumped a whole bucket of water on the stove and made a big mess of everything," she says. "Later that night, when my mom and I were getting ready for bed, I told her I was sorry—that I was reacting out of fear and anger. And for a brief moment our roles had returned to normal. She hugged me like I was her daughter, and I held onto her for dear life."

But after Charlene graduated from high school and began taking classes at community college, the special moments that she and Ruth shared became few and far between. Most painful for Charlene was to see her mother turn her back on photography, an art form to which the 53-year-old had devoted over 30 years of her life.

"FTD is a silent killer. Like certain types of cancer, it can appear without warning. There may be early signs, but you might not automatically connect them with a disease. Researchers are currently looking into how much family history and a healthy lifestyle play a role in the onset of the illness," says Dr. Fard.

"The personality changes, the changes in attitude or morals, the disregard for social cues—these are debilitating to sufferers and their spouses, children, and loved ones," Dr. Fard adds. "Even worse, these changes can fluctuate over time, affecting movement, language, and a host of other human behaviors."

In many patients diagnosed with FTD, including Steve Iverson and Ruth Worsley, MRI scans will detect tissue atrophy in the frontal and temporal lobes of the brain. Like cotton fabrics soaked in hot water, the frontal and temporal regions shink, affecting thinking and certain behaviors. Though a patient with FTD can live for up to 10 years after symptoms begin, it is currently impossible to predict just how long someone afflicted with the disease can survive.

"Researchers are understanding more about how the front lobes work, which then teaches them more about frontotemporal dementia and how to treat it," Dr. Fard explains. "But we still have a long way to go."

The behavioral effects of the disease are seemingly arbitrary and senseless, forcing sufferers to act out compulsively and often without warning. After taking a leave of absence from teaching, Steve Iverson began showering up to 10 times a day. He started collecting baseball cards, hundreds of them, though he had never before shown interest in the sport. Ruth Worsley began shoplifting from camera stores, filling her vintage handbag with rolls of film, until finally the store manager forbade her from entering the shop.

When Charlene discovered what her mother had been doing, she was devastated. "It was as if her brain was telling her, 'Do this, you used to take pictures,' but that was all she could comprehend. She couldn't do anything with the film she stole, even if she wanted to."

While struggling to give her mother the care she needed, Charlene sought different outlets to help her deal with her sorrow. An aspiring actress, she began working on a feature-length film with some friends from school. "Acting keeps my creative juices flowing, which is good, but it's also a distraction from everything going on at home," she says.

As time wore on, and as the physical and emotional demands on Charlene grew more severe, she realized there were two options: either hire a caregiver to come to the house, or put her mother in a nursing home. Once Ruth became incontinent, the two of them decided on the latter.

"It was the worst day of my life, something I told myself that we would never do," Charlene says. "But not only because of the pain I felt; it was also because I saw that same pain and fear in my mother's eyes, magnified by a thousand."

To offset the cost of her mother's care, Charlene and Ruth are working with a real estate agent to help sell the house where they spent so many memorable years. "That's going to be tough, saying goodbye to our old Victorian," Charlene says with a warm smile. "My mother has so many memories there—her photographs and art, her books and wooden treasure boxes, her clothes and jewelry and expensive furniture and silverware that's been in her family for generations. We're selling everything."

Despite these obstacles, Charlene, now 19, works hard at keeping positive. She knows she and her mother have an easier situation than others do. While her frontotemporal dementia can sometimes make her say angry or rude things, Ruth has retained most of the kindhearted spirit that she has had since she was a child. She has never become overtly hostile, a change that Charlene has observed in many of the elderly residents of the nursing home.

"Mostly I'm an upbeat person, but I get depressed sometimes. I worry about my mother constantly," Charlene says. "Does she want to live like this? Would she rather die? We communicate mostly through little handwritten notes, but we haven't written about the big questions like these."

Charlene tries to keep her mind uncluttered by existential thoughts. She visits Ruth at the nursing home almost every day, where they watch movies and read together. They play Bingo and memory games made up of marble tiles and puzzle pieces. They listen to music and flip through coffee-table books on photography and dance.

"I'm learning to be angry at the disease, not the person who has the disease," Charlene says. "The person I love, my mother, has not gone away."

From "On Satan's Trail in Monte Rio" by Harmony Allen (originally published in *Dark Roads*, April, 1987, p. 3-6):

A dozen men dressed in dark-colored hoods and jeans, a chalice filled with animal blood, a terrified woman forced to pose as a human altar, and orgiastic rites designed to conjure the spirit of a vile demon known as the "fire god": these are the shocking secrets of a terrified young filmmaker who warns of the satanic dangers lurking within his latest project.

When college student and cinematographer Billy Lee contacted this magazine and claimed he had a scary story to tell, we assumed he wanted to promote his new movie, a horror flick about devil worship, bloodthirsty witches, and demonic possession.

But the story Lee told us did not take place on the silver screen. No—these disturbing events occurred in real life—in a secluded forest that Lee says is the most depraved place he has ever seen, even in the often sickening world of horror fiction.

While seeking inspiration for the movie that became *The Devil and My Daughter*, Lee claims that he witnessed what may have been a satanic ritual—and he says that he experienced at least part of this surrealistic nightmare with the film's director, a bold young talent by the name of Debra Morrow.

"Debra didn't see everything—she got spooked and ran off—but I know what I saw and I'm telling the truth," Lee says today.

Lee's chilling story arrives on the heels of a fall-out between the two filmmakers, whose partnership has had its share of turbulence over the years. Though *The Devil and My Daughter* was an audience favorite on the film festival circuit, the shot-on-video production was ridiculed by some critics and has since failed to find a distributor. In the horror press, Morrow blamed the failure on their limited experience making movies, while Lee criticized the director for her "tendency toward nepotism."

Now, the cinematographer is urging horror fans not to see the film at all, telling anyone who will listen that there may be a curse on the entire project.

Written and directed by 19-year-old Morrow, *The Devil and My Daughter* features bludgeonings, throat-slashings, shootings, and stabbings. That the gruesome violence transpires while characters grapple with their religious faith makes the movie even more disturbing.

Billy Lee worked hard on the project, spending countless hours collaborating with Morrow and the actors, storyboarding, and filming the movie—all while taking college courses and studying for exams.

Now, for the first time, Lee reveals the startling backstory of the project, explains why he believes Morrow has not been able to find a company to distribute the movie on VHS, and exposes the reality that may be lurking behind the film's fictional plot.

Lee, 21, explains how all the trouble started: "Debra was seeking inspiration while writing the script, so I decided to take her to a bunch of spooky places in the Bay Area. We toured the Winchester Mystery House, visited the USS Hornet, and wandered around a Toys 'R' Us that is haunted by the ghost of an old preacher.

"But Debra wanted to find a place that had a more relevant connection to the motifs in our movie. So, on a cold Saturday morning in October, we woke up early and drove to a little town called Monte Rio, which sits just along the Russian River in the forests of Northern California."

Lee interrupts his narrative to provide some insight into his background: "I've always been a student of the macabre. I'm a big fan of *Dark Roads* magazine and horror books and esoteric texts and philosophers. My two favorite movies are *Cannibal Holocaust* and *I Spit on Your Grave*. But I'm no Satanist!

"When we were making *The Devil and My Daughter*, I talked a big game, trying to spook interviewers, generate buzz for our movie, and generally freak people out. I talked about Satanism and LaVey and Crowley. But when you see something like this, you realize it's not a joke. This shit is real. This shit actually happens."

Monte Rio—a sequestered haven of redwood groves, blue lakes, horses, and whitetail deer. Camping spots pepper the wooded terrain. Fishing and rafting are popular. The downtown area hosts an old-fashioned diner, a single-screen movie theater, and a few plant nurseries and coffee shops. With a population of around 900, the town exudes none of the menace and terror that Lee describes in his story.

But while talking with this interviewer, the man never breaks a smile; his face remains bone-white. "In the daytime, Monte Rio is like a picture postcard," the filmmaker describes. "But everybody knows that real monsters only come out at night."

Lee goes on to explain his reasons for bringing his friend to this isolated location. "At the edge of town, the woods stretch deep for about two miles—and then you come upon this big open area, like an outdoor concert hall. At the back stands an old abandoned farmhouse, nestled among these enormous black pines. And when you see the farmhouse for the first time—with its boarded-up windows staring down at you like the eye sockets of a skull—you just know that all the stories you've heard are true."

Lee is talking about one of the most secluded spots in Northern California—Highland Dell Grove, a forest and open amphitheater that visitors to Monte Rio wouldn't be able to locate on any map. And like all strange places in the middle of the woods, the Grove comes with its own eerie collection of horror stories and urban legends.

Lee explains: "I had heard so many wild tales about the place. Devil worshippers are supposed to hold rituals and sacrifices there, and hikers are always finding disemboweled animals and pentagrams burned into the grass nearby. I thought it would be cool to check out."

Lee and Morrow spent the day in Monte Rio, visiting the stores, exploring the museum, and taking photographs along the town's tree-lined streets and pleasant beachfront.

"But as we began hiking toward the Grove," Lee says, his voice growing more stern, "I couldn't shake the feeling that we were being followed."

Using Lee's hand-drawn map to guide them, the pair reached the amphitheater by nightfall. But they were disappointed by how little they found. There was no evidence of the occult anywhere—no animal bones, no black candles or satanic crosses, not even a single spray-painted pentagram.

"I was ticked off. I had grown tired of living in the fictional world of horror movies and Stephen King books. I wanted to *see* something, to *feel* something evil," Lee says as he tells of his decision to explore the creepy farmhouse.

"Debra wanted no part of it, but we had gone all that way and I refused to leave," Lee says. "Looking back on it now, I think a dark force took hold of me that night and made me do things that in the normal light of day I never would have done. I was a fool.

"So Debra split. She said she would follow the trail back to our motel in town. In her defense, she begged me to come with her, she really did, but I was being stubborn. I wouldn't listen."

Cheap flashlight in hand, Lee spent nearly thirty minutes wandering the outside of the property in the dark until he mustered enough courage to venture inside the farmhouse.

"It wasn't ghosts or witches I was afraid of," he says, describing the creaking floorboards, cobwebbed corners, and peeling wallpaper. "What scared me was the very real possibility that there were people inside that old house, waiting for me, wanting to know what the hell I was doing there."

On the first floor Lee saw things that took on a threatening aura in the gloomy darkness, including rustic candleholders, a row of tin buckets, and a black-lace dress hanging from a clothesline.

In the kitchen he found a dead cat in the sink; on the counter, a chalice that looked like it had blood in it.

When he heard noises coming from the basement, every fiber in his being told him to turn around and run.

But Lee stayed. And he fumbled his way toward the basement. And he began creeping down the stairs, treading as lightly as he could in his big hiking boots.

"It was like I was in a trance," Lee explains. "I had spent so long reading books and seeing movies about Satanism and devil cults that I had to know if the stories about Highland Dell Grove were real."

Once he reached the bottom step, Lee realized he had made a terrible mistake.

The basement reeked of blood and sweat and piss. And Lee saw right away that he had company in this awful house of horrors.

"There was a group of figures clustered together, dressed in black masks and jeans, and there was a taller man, skinny as your finger, standing in the middle. He had on a mask, and a purple gown that swept the floor as he rocked on his heels. He carried one of those metal censers that Catholic priests use in church…a thurible, I think it's called…and he was swinging it gently back and forth. Smoke filtered through the censer, and the room took on the smell of black licorice."

His voice trembling, Lee describes many other horrible sights in the room, among them a statue of the Virgin Mary with an erect penis jutting from between its legs, candles fashioned out of animal skulls, and a large mask with the face of a bull hanging on the wall.

"When the group parted in front of me to opposite sides of the basement, I realized what I was actually seeing. It wasn't just a ritual or some weird sex party. I was witnessing a Black Mass."

As the leader of the group began to recite the Catholic liturgy in reverse, Lee saw that one of the figures was holding a video camera, pivoting the lens toward the back of the dark room.

There, on all fours, crouched the figure of a woman, fully nude and ashy white, her face turned down to the floor. Small pillar candles lit a flickering trail along her protruding spine, and what appeared to be a severed hand, marbled with purplish veins, rested along her neck, the rigid fingers entwined with some strands of her hair.

"I should have run away. I should have called the cops. I should have done something," Lee now bemoans.

Heart thudding in his chest, Lee watched from the shadows as the cult leader took the bull mask off the wall and fastened it around the woman's face.

The hooded figures removed the candles from her back, and the leader placed the severed hand into the folds of his gown. He ended the satanic chant, held up his thurible, and began an invocation in jumbled Latin. Though Lee couldn't understand the words, the cult leader repeated a name that reverberated throughout the basement in demonic soundwaves:

Moloch.

Known for inspiring sexual madness in his followers, Moloch is an ancient Ammonite god to whom parents sacrificed their children. In literature and the arts, he is often depicted as an enormous bull, with phallic horns and bulging muscles. Other illustrations show the creature sitting on a chair of fire, cradling an infant in his enormous arms. According to *The Demonology Handbook*, historians have long associated the sacrificial desires of Moloch with those of Adolf Hitler and the Nazi regime.

"I don't have the words to describe what happened next, but as the ceremony went on, the girl began to *change*," Lee describes with mounting terror. "She began to snort and bellow and claw at the floor, butting the air with her head and thrusting her neck out. Her feet clattered like hooves, kicking up dust.

"And the men got excited by the sight. I think this is why no one noticed me; they were too aroused. They began circling the poor girl, clutching their lit candles. Some of them were laughing, nudging each other. It was a like a game to them. And the girl was so thin, so frail... like you could break her in two with a snap of your fingers.

"The leader picked up what looked like a communion wafer from the back ledge. He approached the girl from behind, holding the wafer up in the air with both hands...but then he stopped. He whirled around, gesturing angrily with his arms.

"And then I remembered seeing the chalice in the kitchen. I'm an atheist, but I know the implements for a Catholic mass. Someone had forgotten the chalice, and the leader was furious. He motioned to the stairs, commanding one of the followers to go get it.

"I just bolted. I ran up the steps and hit the first floor and kept running as hard as I could, through the clearing and back into the woods. By the time I reached our motel, I was sick, and I puked my guts out in the parking lot. I then ran into our room, woke up Debra, and told her we had to get the hell out of there. We drove all the way back to Oakland, and I didn't speak a word of what I saw to anyone. There was this deep, scratchy voice in my head, warning me not to go to the cops."

As Lee concludes this part of his tale, he takes a deep breath and buries his face in his hands. He then explains how his horrifying experience in the woods of Monte Rio helped shape *The Devil and My Daughter*.

"All throughout filming, I would think about what I saw in that house. I thought about the men and their black masks, the leader with his stick-man body and purple robe, and the girl...especially the girl.

"And it was strange because I felt like she was with me while we made the movie. Like her spirit, or even Moloch himself, had followed me back from the farmhouse," Lee says. "I'd be setting up a shot, and I'd hear that same scratchy voice in my ear, telling me what angles to shoot or what kind of lighting to add. By the end of production, it had pretty much driven me crazy. The guilt of doing nothing to help the girl, and this creepy voice in my head bossing me around."

And this is the reason why Billy Lee is now asking people not to see *The Devil and My Daughter*. He believes the movie is haunted or cursed—and that, by watching the film, audiences could possibly find themselves afflicted with the same terrifying mental condition.

"It's not like you can actually see anything demonic in the footage itself," he rationalizes. "It's more of a sinking feeling you get. A dark, dreary, oppressive feeling, like intense melancholy. Like the worst kind of heartbreak. You start thinking strange thoughts. I got really depressed when writing the press kit for the movie, and I only found out recently that I had put a bunch of subliminal messages in it, which I have no recollection of doing. All of us that worked on the film were affected by the curse in some way, especially the actresses. But I'm the only one who has the courage to talk about it."

Recently, Lee gathered this courage and contacted the Sonoma County Police Department. He gave one of the officers a detailed report on what he witnessed at the Grove that night. The cop said he would check it out, and that he would give Lee a call if he needed more information. But the call never came.

"He just shined me on," recalls Lee. "Like it was all just another spook story. Meanwhile, there's a girl out there—she's either being held captive by those creeps, or she's dead. And no one's doing a thing about it."

Lee believes that the curse on *The Devil and My Daughter* has negatively impacted its chances of success.

"Festival audiences seemed to enjoy the picture, but everything since then has crashed to the ground. Debra can't find anyone to release the film. She and I don't get along anymore. And from what I've heard, Charlene's gone nuts. She just sits around all day, writing weird stories about monsters, devils, and satanic plots. She and Debra haven't spoken in months!"

Lee means actress Charlene Worsley, the star of *The Devil and My Daughter* and Debra Morrow's best friend since the two were little kids.

"That's what demons do," Lee says as he leaves our office. "Like the jealous creatures they are, they destroy our relationships from the inside and turn loved ones against each other."

The team at *Dark Roads* conducted a cursory investigation, and we learned that the Sonoma County Police Department has no active cases that involve animal sacrifice, satanic vandalism, kidnapping, or ritual abuse.

A Sonoma County official told us there are plans to bulldoze the farmhouse in Highland Dell Grove and convert the open field into a true amphitheater for live music and other outdoor festivities.

For Billy Lee, the change would be inconsequential. He has no intention of ever returning to Monte Rio again.

"The Book of Revelations tells us that one day Satan will gather his demonic armies, return to Earth, and wreak havoc on us all," Lee warns. "That day has already come. That war has already started."

From "Satanism, Demons, and the Monte Rio Woods: An Interview with Barbara Crinkle" (originally broadcast on KUSF's Underground Horror Radio Program, May, 1987):

UNDERGROUND HORROR RADIO: Tonight, Underground Horror Radio is bringing you a special summer show—a one-hour program devoted entirely to the occult, demonology, and a mysterious town by the sea that you've probably never heard of. My name is Roger Creed, and I'm truly honored to have an old friend on the program tonight: Barbara Crinkle, former editor of *Dark Roads* magazine and author of *The Truth About Black Magic Cults and Secret Societies*. She's going to help us decide what we should and should not be afraid of when we are faced with satanic influence. Barbara, it's great to see you again. Welcome back to the show.

BARBARA CRINKLE: Thank you for having me, Roger.

UHR: Now, the last time you were on the program, we discussed the tragic stories of Jeannette Conway and Viola Arrendondo, two prostitutes who were killed in 1985 in Northern California. At the time their bodies were discovered, the media speculated that the murders might be the work of an underground satanic network. Tonight, I'd like to briefly revisit your opinion on these two cases, as I think it will set the tone for the rest of the show. Were these murders related to the occult?

CRINKLE: No, I don't think so. You see, we're told to be afraid of black magic and occult activity, but most of us really have no idea what these terms mean. We see *Satan's School for Girls* on TV, or *The Exorcist* in the movie theater, and we think that we're experts. And it's not just horror movies or television that has led to the myth-making behind Satanism and occult murder. Role-playing games, including *Dungeons & Dragons*, and supposedly non-fiction books like *Michelle Remembers*, have contributed to the moral hysteria that has taken over our country since the start of the decade.

UHR: But there is at least some cause for alarm, isn't there? I mean, Jeannette and Viola died horrific deaths, their bodies cut up and covered in all sorts of unusual wounds.

CRINKLE: Oh, absolutely—these were horrible crimes. Revolting crimes. But saying the prostitute murders were occult-related just because there was body dismemberment might not be accurate. It could just be the work of a psychopath.

UHR: Let's explore that tonight—what does "occult" really mean?

CRINKLE: Well, first—and I don't mean to take umbrage with fans of the show—we have to gather everything we've learned about the occult and Satanism from horror movies and chuck it out the window.

UHR: Be careful, Barbara. Our listeners are quite the volatile bunch. They love their horror flicks!

CRINKLE: And so do I! Sci-fi and horror are my favorite genres. I'm a big fan of *Rosemary's Baby* and *Audrey Rose*—movies that merge the theological and the supernatural. But I don't use these films to inform my knowledge about the occult.

UHR: You actually have a Master's in folklore studies, which is where you really began studying this stuff.

CRINKLE: That's right. When we talk about the occult, we're actually talking about a broad range of subjects—everything from alchemy to astrology and ESP. It might have to do with palmistry or tarot cards or Native American medicine cards. If you have an unorthodox view of religion, then some people are going to accuse you of being involved in the occult. It can mean different things to different people. For this reason, in some ways, the term "occult" has lost its meaning.

UHR: But if you had to generalize, providing a broad definition of it—what would you say?

CRINKLE: I'd say that those who adhere to occult practices— "occult," which means "knowledge or study of the hidden"—are interested in understanding their role in nature, finding out about their strengths and abilities, evaluating spirituality and the mysteries of faith in their lives. They are probably drawn more to the arts—literature and poetry and film—than they are to math or science. What they are definitely *not* interested in are activities like animal sacrifice, drinking blood, and killing babies. They leave that fun stuff to horror writers and filmmakers, who have a tendency to exaggerate for entertainment purposes.

UHR: But I've got a stack of news articles here that cover some pretty wild things, Barbara. Satanic ceremonies at daycare centers and pre-schools. Police finding pentagrams, animal bones, and makeshift altars in the forest. Song lyrics to call forth demons from hell. Even East Bay College was vandalized a few months ago with satanic messages and desecrated objects. If this is all just horseplay, why do kids get involved?

UHR: Well, there's always the possibility that it's *not* horseplay. I'm not saying that every instance of vandalism is harmless and should be ignored by the police. But kids are quite disaffected these days. They're angry, they feel displaced and unloved, and they're reacting to these feelings in ways that their parents don't understand. I think this disenfranchisement all began with two events—the Manson murders and the Vietnam War—both of which told the world that the age of innocence, what some people called the "utopian promise," was an outright lie. Your government will fly you thousands of miles away from home to fight an unjustifiable war and probably get you paralyzed or blown to pieces. Meanwhile, that good-looking protest singer who lives in the desert and promises to deliver "cosmic consciousness" to your soul—well, he's a megalomaniac cult leader who will trick you into stabbing innocent people to death in the middle of the night.

UHR: So the kids are pissed off—is that what you're saying?

CRINKLE: They're *very* pissed off, and they're using symbols—things like the pentagram and the upside-down cross—to convey their anger because they know that this kind of imagery is extremely provocative and will get a rise out of anyone who sees it. Now, in early history, the pentagram was a Christian symbol for the five wounds of Christ, the wounds he suffered during the crucifixion. It was a divine emblem—a symbol of faith. But then, in the 1860s, a French occult writer named Eliphas Levi presented the pentagram as a symbol of evil—of witches and warlocks and all the rest. As a result, the pentagram has come to represent everything from occult practices to ritual murder and black magic. It's just one of many symbols—like the swastika, for example—that has been misappropriated over time and used for forces of evil.

UHR: We have extreme reactions to these images and words because of their associations. When I see a pentagram, an inverted cross, even a goat's head, it's like my "Satan worshipper" antenna goes off. I think of *Rosemary's Baby*, the Manson family, and the Son of Sam. I think of Richard Ramirez, "the Night Stalker." All these terrible things. It's a natural reaction all of us have.

CRINKLE: Of course. But let's take that example you just gave about Charles Manson. As far as I know, he never said he was a Satanist. In fact, he told his followers he was Jesus Christ so he could manipulate them and gain their trust. What people like Manson do—and horror films are guilty of this as well, but to a much lesser degree—is they use the iconography of Satanism, witchcraft, black magic, whatever—to instill fear in others. Death metal bands do it too—in their lyrics and on their album sleeves. So when Manson ordered Patricia Krenwinkel to write "death to pigs" in blood at the LaBianca house, he was doing that because he knew it would freak people out—but not because he was a Satanist.

UHR: Barbara, I know this might be a sensitive subject, but you're no longer the editor of *Dark Roads* magazine.

CRINKLE: That's correct.

UHR: Now, the last issue that you worked on featured a story about a man, a young filmmaker named Billy Lee, who claimed he witnessed an event that could be considered a Black Mass. Does this type of thing even exist, or is it a just an old myth born out of horror movies, something that's not really real?

CRINKLE: During my graduate work, I read Aleister Crowley, Anton LaVey, even an interview with an Italian priest who claimed to have witnessed a Black Mass—and it strikes me as just a little too easy and predictable. I'm not saying that these people didn't involve themselves in strange activities, and that others could have been hurt in the process, but I don't think what they did or saw was a bonafide Satanic ceremony.

UHR: Were you involved in the writing of that story at all? Had you participated in the interview with the filmmaker?

CRINKLE: No. My book was about to be published around that time, so I didn't have much input on that issue as a whole. Harmony Allen, who's now the editor of *Dark Roads*, had basically taken over by that point.

UHR: I detect a bit of animosity in your voice.

CRINKLE: Quite the opposite; I have nothing but the utmost respect for Harmony. She's an outstanding writer, and she's entirely devoted to the pursuit of unique and interesting stories within the world of esoterica.

UHR: Okay. But can I ask you—what did you make of the story? Did it seem plausible to you?

CRINKLE: Well, I'm not one to discount another person's experience. But I couldn't help but feel that the young man's tale had more to do with the rivalries within their production team than it did with any genuine occult activity. I've seen *The Devil and My Daughter*, and I think it's fair to say that their personal conflicts affected the quality of the movie.

UHR: And, apparently, the police were unable to find a single trace of evidence to corroborate his story.

CRINKLE: I'm glad you brought that up, Roger. In a lot of stories like this one, there's the suggestion that people in positions of power—the police, or doctors or judges—are deeply embroiled in these satanic or occult groups. My views fall on the opposite side of that coin. I believe that the police work hard to protect us, to keep the big cities and the small towns like Monte Rio safe. They're out there solving crimes and arresting bad guys, not wearing masks and running around in the woods.

UHR: Monte Rio does have quite the reputation, though. There's supposedly a haunted hotel there, and a haunted bar and restaurant. In the farmhouse in Highland Dell Grove, people claim to have seen strange lights, and smell foul odors and even blood. Billy Lee, the filmmaker who told his story to *Dark Roads*, was quite descriptive of what he saw.

CRINKLE: I suppose that's my sticking point. He was *too* descriptive, almost to where it seemed like a set-up, like parody. The masks, the purple robes, the candles, the severed body parts—it was all caricature. I guess I'm just a skeptic at heart!

UHR: Lee claimed that the satanic ceremony was being recorded on videotape. If that tape was ever recovered, and if there was footage on it that supported his claims—in other words, if he had *proof*—would you believe his story then?

CRINKLE: Believe it or not, some of the world's most evil people have recorded their crimes in one way or another. Myra Hindley captured the moans of her child victims on audio tape. Charles Ng and Leonard Lake recorded their murders with a video camera. Jerry Brudos, "The Shoe Fetish Slayer," took photographs of his female victims before he killed them. Now, in the Monte Rio story, I think it's doubtful that any video footage is going to just appear out of the blue, but if it did—then my first thought would be that it was all a cruel hoax. Something the filmmakers did to promote their current film, or perhaps the sequel. Now, if the footage had any truth to it, especially if we're talking about illegal activity involving satanic crime, then the tape belongs in the hands of police. The public would never get the chance to see it—and that's probably a good thing.

UHR: In your book, you have a chapter devoted to demonic possession and its connection to mental illness. Can you talk about that for a moment?

CRINKLE: Well, as you know, demonic possession appears in the Bible, and many cultures all over the world have documented cases about it, with photographs, eyewitness accounts, interview transcripts, and audio recordings as evidence. But one of the difficulties with demonic possession is that there's no right way to define its stages or its symptoms. For this reason, demonic possession can easily be mistaken for the manifestation of certain mental illnesses, including schizophrenia and other dissociative disorders. Also, what some people believe to be possession could really be an externalization of the victim's fear—fear of rejection, fear of death, fear of losing someone they love, fear of parental neglect, whatever it might be. Even in *The Exorcist*, the most famous demonic-possession film of all time, there's the suggestion that these terrible things are happening to Regan MacNeil because she's a child of divorce and her father is a deadbeat dad.

UHR: I always thought, if demonic possession was real, then the demon would force its victim to do something really terrible. And I don't mean speak in Latin or use bad words, or even desecrate a church or kill an animal. I mean, something really, *really* terrible.

CRINKLE: I hate to break the news to you, Roger, but the evidence of demonic possession and of deliverance—the removal of the evil spirit from the body—is fairly generic. Physical contortions, strange facial distortions, fetid smells, cold spots—these are some of the demon's favorite tricks, according to those who believe in or claim to have witnessed such phenomena. In other words, nothing that you didn't see in *The Exorcist*, *Beyond the Door*, or even *The Evil Dead*.

UHR: Now that reminds me. What about demonic animals?

CRINKLE: How do you mean?

UHR: Well, there has been a slew of what they call "natural" horror movies hitting the big screens lately—including *The Swarm*, *Prophecy*, and a wild movie from down under called *Razorback*. There's also *Cujo* and *King Kong Lives*. Films where Mother Nature has lost her way, usually in the form of mutated animals and homicidal beasts. Is such a thing possible in real life?

CRINKLE: Well, certainly. Cujo had rabies, after all. And from what I remember, the mutant bear in *Prophecy* was the result of a poisonous contaminant in the town's paper mill.

UHR: Yes, but what about a demon inhabiting the body of an animal? Don't laugh—I've read that it's possible! Something big and ferocious, like a grizzly bear or a mountain lion, becomes possessed by an evil spirit and then goes out and wreaks havoc on the world. Or, perhaps, a possessed person sends his evil spirit out in the form of an animal.

CRINKLE: I don't believe there are official documented cases of such things, but the Bible tells stories of demons taking over the bodies of pigs, frogs, and dragons. In Christian demonology, demons in animal forms are considered lowly creatures, which is why we often associate them with mud and dirt and grime. But think about the intention of the demon—he wants to seduce and then destroy you. Now, if I were to hazard a guess, you're more likely to be seduced by a beautiful woman than you are by a frog or an angry pig, correct?

UHR: Well, maybe it's both. The beautiful woman seduces you before the wild animal inside her rips you apart.

CRINKLE: Which is a good segue into a much more important issue. Are we talking about demonic possession or genuine mental illness? Hollywood would have you believe that demonic possession is far more prevalent in society than mental illness, but that's just not the case.

UHR: Barbara, I have one more question before we hear a word from our sponsors here at KUSF. Earlier you mentioned *The Exorcist*. At the end of that movie, Father Karras begs the demon to leave Regan's body and enter his own. The demon agrees, which leads to the death of the priest when he commits suicide by hurling himself out the window. What do you think about something like that? About demonic transference?

CRINKLE: I've read that a demon can enter a person's body only if he or she invites it in, or if God allows the transference to happen— so, in that sense, *The Exorcist* was quite accurate. At the same time, folklore tells us that demons can enter the body through our mouths or even our sexual organs. And the Bible speaks of the transfer of spirits—both good and evil—occurring through physical contact or through spoken word. You might be surprised to learn that certain sound wave ranges can cause illness in humans, a reaction that could be misinterpreted as demonic possession by those with a devout belief in the supernatural.

UHR: Wow, good stuff. All right, coming up after the break, your calls and more with our special guest, the one and only Barbara Crinkle, author of *The Truth About Black Magic Cults and Secret Societies...*

My Name is Nancy by Charlene Worsley (written for her Playwriting 101B class, Spring, 1987):

My Name is Nancy: A One-Act Play

Characters:

Dr. Clifford

Nancy Monroe

Mathilde (voice)

Setting: *The spacious office of a psychiatrist. Neatly-furnished with crowded bookshelves, a desk, a leather couch, and two oversized armchairs.*

The walls are bare, cream-colored, unadorned except for a framed reproduction of Pablo Picasso's "Bull," *eleven lithographs that depict the bull in various artistic forms—from the realistic to the abstract.*

Several windows are set along on the back wall, through which we occasionally see a drizzle of rain.

Stage left is a door that leads to the waiting room.

As the play opens, a bearded psychiatrist, 45, sits rigidly at the desk, examining a curved animal horn with a magnifier. He is dressed impeccably: an expensive suit with a red pocketchief, a red silk tie, and polished designer wingtips.

His study is interrupted by the buzzing of the telephone intercom on his desk.

MATHILDE, *with German accent*: Dr. Clifford, your 4 o'clock is here.

CLIFFORD, *into intercom*: Ah, I lost track of the time. Thank you for the reminder, Mathilde.

MATHILDE: Should I send her in?

CLIFFORD, *into intercom*: Erm…no. I'll come to the door.

Clifford places the animal horn into the bottom desk drawer; he then withdraws a key from the inside pocket of his coat, locks the drawer, returns the key to his pocket, and approaches the door stage left.

He collects himself for a moment—then opens the door.

CLIFFORD, *into the doorway*: Miss Monroe? Please come in.

Clifford steps aside so that the patient can enter. Nancy Monroe, 25, steps into the office, clutching a large handbag to her chest. She is nervous, her eyes darting about furtively.

Nancy is dressed in austere fashion—almost puritanical. Long-sleeve black blouse, buttoned at the throat; a black skirt that cuts just below the knee; gray leggings and burgundy penny loafers add a spot of color.

CLIFFORD: You may sit in one of the armchairs, or rest on the couch. I promise they are both equally comfortable.

NANCY: Which do most of your new patients choose?

CLIFFORD: They tend to choose the armchair. They believe the couch is too informal for a first session.

Nancy hurries to the armchair and sits down, still clutching the bag to her chest. Clifford sits opposite her in the other armchair.

CLIFFORD: Did you want to give your handbag to Mathilde? We keep all valuables stored safely in a closet in the hall.

NANCY: I gave her my umbrella, but I prefer to keep my bag with me.

CLIFFORD: That's perfectly fine, perfectly fine. *An awkward silence between them.* Dr. Drummond faxed your patient file over to me this morning. Can I ask you—why did you feel the need to change doctors? You had been seeing him for quite some time.

NANCY: Dr. Drummond is a nice man, an excellent psychiatrist, and I had many breakthroughs with him.

CLIFFORD: He and I attended Duke together. He's a good man.

NANCY: I agree. But he actually recommended I speak with you. He said you have treated patients before with my...problem.

CLIFFORD: Well, I will do the best I can to help. How would you care to begin?

NANCY: My file—did you read it?

CLIFFORD: Yes, I did.

NANCY: Then would it be possible to skip the preliminaries? My age, where I was born, what my childhood was like—things like that?

CLIFFORD: It's somewhat unorthodox, but I am happy to talk about whatever is on your mind. If I have questions about your background, I can always ask.

NANCY: If we could just pick up where I left off with Dr. Drummond, that would work best for me.

CLIFFORD: Not a problem. Let me grab your file from my desk.

As Clifford stands and retrieves the file from his desk, Nancy notices the Picasso lithographs on the wall. She forces herself to look away, pressing the handbag against her chest like a shield.

CLIFFORD, *sitting down:* Here we are. I'll just use this to refresh my memory and take notes.

A palpable silence during which Nancy stares at the floor. Clifford flips through the file for a moment, then clears his throat politely.

CLIFFORD: There's nothing to be afraid of here, Miss Monroe.

NANCY: I'm not afraid, Dr. Clifford. But I feel that I should warn you.

CLIFFORD: Warn me?

NANCY: My story—it's very disturbing.

CLIFFORD, *as gently as he can*: I've read the file, Miss Monroe. And let me assure you that this is a safe place to discuss all sorts of issues, including those involving violence, familial abuse—

NANCY: He bathed me in blood.

CLIFFORD: Excuse me?

NANCY: A virgin's blood. So that I would stay young.

CLIFFORD: You're referring to your grandfather. *Glancing at the file*. Ellis Shephard?

NANCY: That's right. At the house in Belmont. They kept a tub in the basement.

CLIFFORD: Your grandfather's house, correct? Where you spent your summers?

NANCY: Yes.

CLIFFORD: How often did this take place?

NANCY: My grandparents held the party once a month.

CLIFFORD: What kind of party?

NANCY: A dinner party. My grandfather called it a gala. They would invite all of their rich friends over—the men in tailor-made suits, the women in evening gowns. My grandmother dressed me in a ballerina-style skirt and sequined blouse, and I would serve cocktails and hors d'oeuvres to all of the guests. *A painful pause as the memory unfolds*. Spanish ham with olives and oranges. That was everybody's favorite.

CLIFFORD: How old were you at the time?

NANCY: I was nine when I spent my first summer there. And I visited consistently, every summer, until I was thirteen.

CLIFFORD: You never told your parents you didn't like staying in Belmont?

NANCY, *with great contempt*: I was raised by my mother, though I say that very loosely. She was far more interested in how many men she could take to bed than she was about my well-being.

CLIFFORD: And your grandparents died the next winter.

NANCY, *nodding*: They committed suicide. Together. With pills.

Clifford digests this information, glancing down at the file. Outside, the rain falls harder a storm brewing.

CLIFFORD: These parties your grandparents would have—there was drinking, dancing, even gambling in one of the back rooms.

NANCY: Yes. I remember the gambling. Poker and blackjack. And the German records. Such haunting melodies—like mourning doves.

CLIFFORD, *clearing his throat*: What would happen after the drinks and hors d'oeuvres? What would you do during dinnertime?

NANCY: I was under strict orders to report to the upstairs bathroom while the adults had dinner downstairs. There was a…well, a cleaning ritual of sorts. My grandmother would prepare it for me earlier in the day. A bar of lavender castile soap, shampoo, and conditioner. There was baby oil and a bottle of talcum powder. All laid out for me on a vanity tray.

CLIFFORD: What were these orders exactly?

NANCY: To turn myself into a princess.

CLIFFORD: A princess?

NANCY: The older men—the ones who stayed at the house long after the other guests had left—they had certain expectations.

CLIFFORD *briefly scans the file. Then, gently:* Expectations? For the basement ritual?

NANCY: Yes. Grandpa Ellis wrote down the instructions for me. After my bath and powder, I was to dress in the black robe hanging on the rack. I was to meet my grandmother at the top of the basement stairs, where she would give me the drink.

CLIFFORD: The drink?

NANCY: She told me it was fruit punch. I believed her because it was red and tasted sweet. But my memory work with Dr. Drummond has helped me to understand so much more about my past. *Nancy shifts uncomfortably in her chair, but she lowers the handbag to the floor.* The punch was drugged with a sleeping agent, Dr. Clifford. But I was too young! *With rising anger.* I was too young to know any better!

CLIFFORD, *leaning forward, tenderly:* Miss Monroe, your anger is entirely justified. You were only a child.

NANCY: They were supposed to love me.

CLIFFORD: Yes, they were. But those who are supposed to love us often hurt us the worst. *He closes the file.* Would you like to tell me what happened in the basement?

NANCY: I only remember bits and pieces—but sometimes it's hard to tell what's real and what's not. That's why Dr. Drummond sent me to you. He thought you could help me unlock more of my memory.

CLIFFORD: Absolutely. There are a great number of exercises we can try that are designed to improve your recollection of the past. If you feel comfortable doing so, why don't you tell me the rest of what you remember, and then we can move forward from there?

NANCY: I can try.

CLIFFORD: Would you like some water, or a tissue?

NANCY: No, thank you, Dr. Clifford. I'm fine. *Takes a ragged breath before erupting again.* Oh, when it comes, it comes in waves!

CLIFFORD: I understand, Miss Monroe.

NANCY, *in a voice teetering on madness:* My grandmother, drunk on highballs by then, would guide me down the stairs by my shoulders. The basement door, at the bottom of the steps—well, to me it looked like the entrance to hell. Grandpa Ellis had used a stencil to paint an image onto it—the image of a hoofed creature sitting cross-legged on a bed of fire.

CLIFFORD: That sounds like a very frightening picture, especially for a young girl.

NANCY: I never found out who or what the creature was supposed to be, but it terrified me.

CLIFFORD: The door was closed? And your grandfather, and the rest of the men—they were on the other side, waiting for you?

NANCY: Yes. That was an important part of the ritual. My entrance. The presentation of my entrance.

CLIFFORD: Go on, Miss Monroe.

NANCY: Before she opened the door, my grandmother would always whisper in my ear, "Remember—your name is Sylvia."

CLIFFORD: Sylvia?

NANCY: Dr. Drummond helped me understand this. You see, the cult wanted to transform me into an entirely different person—with new personality traits and behaviors. This new personality—Grandpa Ellis named her "Sylvia"—would actually *enjoy* the basement ritual, for her only goal was to serve the needs of the cult.

CLIFFORD: Dr. Drummond told you this?

NANCY: Yes—working together, we came to an understanding of the group, and what my grandparents were doing to me.

CLIFFORD: *Opens the file and leafs through it.* What happened after your grandmother opened the basement door?

NANCY: The richest men from the party—and sometimes their wives, reeking of stale perfume, their faces painted in garish makeup—

148

would be leaning along the basement wall, smoking cigarettes and drinking from snifters.

CLIFFORD: Were they not wearing disguises?

NANCY: No. They were still wearing their clothes from the party.

CLIFFORD: So you would recognize them, if you saw them again?

NANCY, *shaking her head*: Their faces are washed-out to me. Blurry, and faded, like ghosts. Dr. Drummond and I tried everything—from primal therapy to hypnosis—to help me remember what they looked like, but nothing worked.

CLIFFORD: What did your grandparents do at this point?

NANCY: My grandmother took a highball and joined the others. They looked like skeletons, all lined up against the wall...like corpses inside a tomb. My grandfather stood in the center of the group, dressed in a black dressing gown. *With overwhelming fear.* There were flickering candles along the back ledge, and a video camera attached to a tripod to record the events of the evening. And there was... there was a table in the middle of the room—it looked like a gurney!

CLIFFORD: Like what you might see in a hospital?

NANCY: Yes! Exactly! And I can see objects on the gurney.

CLIFFORD: Objects?

NANCY: Yes. Medical objects. Medical instruments!

CLIFFORD: Describe them to me.

NANCY: I see a scalpel. And a speculum. And surgical pliers. *A final, soul-cleansing breath.* And Grandpa Ellis asks me to pick up one of them. My choice.

CLIFFORD, *with a tremor in his voice*: For what purpose?

NANCY: *Frustrated.* I don't know, Dr. Clifford! The last thing I recall is the sight of my robe on the basement floor. The rest is...just black.

CLIFFORD: Where was the bathtub?

NANCY: Bathtub?

CLIFFORD: Yes. At the start of our session today, you said that your grandparents kept a tub in the basement.

NANCY: *Confused.* I...did?

CLIFFORD: Yes. You told me your grandfather bathed you in blood. You said it was virgin blood. I'm assuming this took place in the tub in the basement.

NANCY: Bathed me in...virgin blood? I have no recollection of that at all.

A long, tense pause as Clifford rises from his chair and places the file on his desk. He returns to his seat, watching Nancy with an intensity that makes her shiver. He steeples his fingers before him, deep in thought. Silence except for the driving rain outside.

CLIFFORD: Allow me to speak frankly, Miss Monroe. Dr. Drummond referred me to you for a very specific reason.

NANCY: I know. He told me you have treated other patients who have also experienced this kind of abuse. He said that you helped them to remember!

CLIFFORD, *in a careful, methodical voice*: Yes, that's true. I did help them to remember. I helped them to remember that no such abuse ever took place.

NANCY: I don't understand.

CLIFFORD: Miss Monroe, I have read your file, and I have listened to your story today. I have heard similar stories—and some much worse. Stories of boys forced into cannibalism. Stories of girls kept locked in cages and having horns and tails surgically attached to their bodies. Stories involving incest, murder, and sexual torture.

NANCY: Why are you telling me this? I don't want to hear this!

CLIFFORD: Because I want to help you. Please don't misunderstand me—I am not denying that we live in a dangerous world, a world filled with terrible people who often do terrible things. But I have a distinct feeling that if we examined the details of your case further, we would find even more discrepancies than your confusion over the bathtub.

NANCY: But Dr. Drummond—he believed me!

CLIFFORD: Miss Monroe, I spoke with Dr. Drummond on the phone just this morning, and he will concur with everything I'm telling you now. You are suffering from what I call a "factitious disorder," and it has caused you to fabricate certain details of your story. I would like to teach you how to understand the underlying causes of this disorder and help you to restore your memory in a way that is true and honest.

NANCY, *with desperation*: But my grandparents committed suicide! They killed themselves because they could not live with the guilt of all the disgusting things they did to me—and who knows how many others!

CLIFFORD, *softly*: Your grandfather, Ellis Shephard, died of a heart attack in December of 1978. Your grandmother, Louise, passed away in her sleep a few months later.

NANCY: *Her paranoia has taken over.* You're one of them! You must be! With your secret files and your monstrous paintings on the wall! *With a trembling hand she points at the lithographs of the bull.* Right there! It's the same creature painted on the basement door!

CLIFFORD: Miss Monroe, please—

NANCY: *Standing, her face a mask of rage.* My name is Sylvia!

Clifford leaps up from his chair, startled. A burst of LIGHTNING flashes from behind the windows, followed by rolling THUNDER.

There is a face-off as Nancy stares Clifford down, breathing heavily. The episode passes as she regains her composure and picks up her handbag from the floor.

NANCY: I'll see myself out.

Clifford makes a perfunctory gesture to stop her, but Nancy turns on her heels and exits through the door stage left.

Alone now, Clifford lets out a huge breath, resting his hands against the armchair. Then, determinedly, he sits down at his desk, picks up the telephone, and dials a number. He waits, nervously tapping his foot.

CLIFFORD, *into receiver*: Drummond? Clifford. Uh-huh, she just left. *Pause.* I disagree—this was a foolhardy exercise from the very beginning. We should have never allowed her to get this close. *Pause.* You're wrong. She's not like the others. She's stronger—more resilient. *Pause.* No. Listen to me. Get your kit and meet me in the parking garage. I had Mathilde yank the ignition fuse, which will buy us some time. *Pause.* Good man. Oh, and Drummond? Make sure to bring your pliers. We shall put them to good use this time.

As Clifford hangs up the phone, a WOMAN'S SCREAM explodes from the waiting room.

Alarmed, the doctor reaches into his coat pocket for the desk key and uses it to open the bottom drawer. He removes a PISTOL and a box of AMMO.

As he attempts to load the gun, the stage lights FLASH and go out. Clifford cries out in fear. He drops the bullets and they rattle across the stage.

CLIFFORD: Dammit!

He gets on his knees, crawling on the floor, pawing for the bullets in the dark. And then: the SLOW CREAKING of the door from stage left.

CLIFFORD: Who's there? What do you want?

Silence—except for the rain and the thump of heavy footsteps.

CLIFFORD: I have a gun! I won't hesitate to use it!

NANCY: That kraut bitch still wears the same cheap perfume.

CLIFFORD, *with genuine terror*: Mathilde? What did you do to her?

NANCY: The Nazis used the guillotine—what they called the *fallbeil*—to decapitate resistance fighters who rebelled against them. Let's just say I have returned the favor with an instrument of my own.

CLIFFORD: Miss Monroe—*Nancy*—listen to me! You're under a great deal of psychological distress. I ask you—no, I *command* you—to stop what you're doing this instant!

A bolt of LIGHTNING strikes behind the windows, illuminating the stage in disorienting flashes.

We see Nancy, her black blouse torn open at the neck. She is holding a short-handled ax, slick with blood. Clifford is on all fours just a few feet away.

NANCY: It was only by chance that I found that pederast Drummond. I needed a shrink and his was the first ad I saw in the yellow pages. I followed him for weeks. To the farm in Calistoga, where he keeps his prized horses. To the orgy in Marin, where he screwed your wife. And to your lovely estate in San Francisco, where the two of you hold your depraved rituals. And by then I knew—the two of you were there. At the house in Belmont.

CLIFFORD: Miss Monroe, you're mistaken. We're doctors…not Satanists!

As lightning flashes across the stage again, Nancy grips the ax with two hands, slowing bringing it behind her body…

NANCY: The police are on their way to Drummond's farm right now, where they will find his specialty tools, his cattle prods and branding irons, his electric cages, his Polaroid collection—and who knows what other evidence. *Nancy's breathing grows more labored as her hands tighten around the ax.* My grandparents, the scum-sucking cowards that they were, took their own lives before I could exact my revenge. *Now, she raises the ax over her head.* You will not have that luxury, you evil bastard. You will pay for all the things you did to me.

She lunges for the doctor, screaming.

CLIFFORD, *bellowing*: Sylvia! Stop!

The words freeze Nancy in her tracks. The ax trembles in her hands above her head while thunder rumbles in the distance…

CLIFFORD: You are being very naughty! You are to stop this behavior immediately and obey every word I say! Do you understand me?

Clifford scrambles to his feet just as the stage goes black again. His voice passes through the dark in a soothing whisper.

CLIFFORD: Sylvia, my darling, you've been an excellent hostess this evening, but the adults are going to enjoy their supper now. It's time for you to go upstairs and have your bath.

A flash of lightning as Nancy lowers the ax to her side...

CLIFFORD: I left a surprise on your grooming tray, Sylvia. Something I picked up for you when I visited Frankfurt last month. *Pause.* It's a very expensive perfume. Wear it tonight, and you'll be the prettiest belle of the ball. *Pause.* The door is behind you, Sylvia. I'm asking you to leave—now.

As darkness falls onstage, Nancy doesn't move.

CLIFFORD: *Growing agitated.* Sylvia, perhaps you did you not hear me over the din of the party. The noise in here is quite loud. I will tell Mathilde to turn her phonograph down. *With a reconciliatory air.* I don't like German music either; it's too discordant for my tastes, the singing voice too guttural. But for now—I am ordering you to leave the room this instant and tend to your bath.

Silence. The entire universe seems balanced on the head of a pin.

CLIFFORD, *through gritted teeth*: This will be your last warning.

A tension that eventually shatters.

CLIFFORD, *with demoniacal rage*: Sylvia, this order comes from on high! Lucifer, the Great Dragon, compels you! You will have nothing tonight—no attention, no praise, no reward—unless you adhere to his every word! *With a final bellow.* Sylvia!

A tremendous burst of lightning that bathes the stage in white light.

NANCY, *with flat affect*: My name is Nancy.

Then, with a scream of her entire soul, Nancy charges Clifford and brings the ax down onto his skull as the stage goes to black.

The sound of rain, gentle at first, then increasing violently. The low-pitched rumbling of thunder in the distance.

THE CURTAIN FALLS.

"Savage Summer: The Possession of Charlene Worsley" by Harmony Allen (originally published in *Dark Roads*, November, 1987, p. 2-5):

In the months following a shocking murder spree at a nursing home in California, a young man has come forward with a frightening tale of psychological devastation and paranormal terror—a tale that provides chilling insight into the brutal and senseless tragedy that has ripped the city of Oakland to shreds. Even the most seasoned readers of *Dark Roads* should be forewarned: what you are about to discover in these pages is a terrifying story of demonic possession, cult ritual, and sexual depravity—and it is not for the faint of heart.

Todd Wheeler, a college student and the special-effects designer behind the controversial *The Devil and My Daughter*, claims that the satanic subject matter of the film has seeped into the real world—and the consequences could be deadly.

Todd explains that Charlene Worsley, the star of the film and the subject of grim speculation these past few months, moved in with him after the *The Devil and My Daughter* was completed. From that point on, Todd's apartment in Berkeley became the nesting ground for an onslaught of alarming paranormal events, unexplained phenomena, and perverse sexuality.

"I had a crush on Charlene while we were making *The Devil and My Daughter*, and I think she liked me too. Her mother had just moved into the nursing home, and they had already sold their house, so I asked Charlene if she wanted to stay at my place. It was a chance for her to get some rest, and a chance for us to start something special," says Todd. "Instead, I witnessed a sweet and talented girl become a monster before my very eyes."

A horror movie infused with demonic power. An apartment that reeked of excrement. A young and beautiful woman, a virgin, suddenly overcome with aberrant sexual urges and supernatural transmogrifications…

When Berkeley police officer Anthony Ellison was first called to Todd Wheeler's apartment, he thought he had become the victim of a practical joke; the rookie officer was accustomed to being the butt of more than a few pranks by his fellow boys in blue. Then, when Todd shared his theories about what was happening to Charlene, the officer thought the crazy story was part of a publicity stunt for one of Todd's film projects.

"I was prepared to arrest Todd for obstructing official business," Ellison says now. "But it didn't take long for me to start believing that at least some of what he was telling me was true."

Understandably, readers of *Dark Roads* will have doubts about the spectral terrors that Todd Wheeler believes served as some kind of "direct pipeline" to the murders in Oakland. But no one can deny that Charlene Worsley was tormented by hyper-realistic nightmares and violent afflictions that caused her to act out against Todd and herself. And despite the theological beliefs of anyone who reads this article, a connection must exist somewhere between the harrowing events that Todd describes and the brutal slaughter of four innocent people in the Bay Area.

Todd spent two days with *Dark Roads*, walking us through the apartment in Berkeley and detailing his nightmarish story. He makes clear that, despite his interest in horror FX, he was not quick to jump to a paranormal explanation for the forces that slowly took control of Charlene.

"*The Devil and My Daughter* was a stressful experience for everyone involved, especially Charlene," Todd says. "I thought she was just tired and needed some time to gather her thoughts and unwind.

"But then she stopped eating like a normal person. Her sleep became erratic, she was having nightmares, and we began getting into fights over petty things. Who left the dirty dishes in the sink, who didn't do the laundry—that kind of stuff. I thought she was just going through a phase and that she would snap out of it," Todd says.

But when the talented FX whiz tells more of his mortifying tale, it becomes apparent that something far more sinister was asserting its demonic influence in the apartment.

"Charlene and Debra Morrow, her best friend, had been making horror movies together for years," Todd says, listing a number of film projects, including the darkly comic *Monsters in Your Pants*, that the talented pair made just to spook their friends and have a good laugh.

"The movies were silly. They had generic storylines, poor production values, and cheap effects," Todd acknowledges. "But that all changed when Debra and Charlene made *Blood Songs*, their first attempt at a serious horror film."

Todd believes that something truly menacing rose from the celluloid of *Blood Songs*—something with the burning-coal eyes of a demon and the razor-sharp horns of a bull.

"Charlene wanted to be the greatest 'scream queen' who ever was," Todd explains, "but devoting her entire artistic life to horror was like putting a target on her back. The demonic just needed to find an entry point—a way to pierce the target and get inside."

Todd interrupts his dramatic tale to show *Dark Roads* around the apartment that he and Charlene shared until her murderous rampage in Oakland. The front room resembles a war-zone, with stains on the carpet, dirty clothes tossed in every corner, and busted cassette tapes piled high next to the TV. Wrinkled flypaper hangs from the open doorway to the kitchen, its orange strip of adhesive crowded with the shriveled corpses of flies and other insects.

Todd snatches up one of the cassette tapes and rattles it in his hand. "*This*," he announces, his voice cracking with anger. "This damn thing is what started it all!"

According to Todd, the cassette contains songs by Carnal Season, the hardcore metal band that wrote the soundtrack to *Blood Songs* and whose lyrics of rape, murder, and demonic possession have caused outrage in the conservative media.

"While rehearsing for *Blood Songs*, Charlene listened over and over to this tape until it seeped inside her head like poison," Todd says, clutching the cassette as if to hurl it across the room. "Many of the songs are about a demon named Moloch that cannibalized children, made his followers drink blood, and sought out virgin women to humiliate and destroy."

Todd takes *Dark Roads* into his bedroom, where he has amassed a large collection of books on witchcraft and paganism, along with a battered copy of the King James Bible and several prayer candles. He picks up a dusty, hard-backed volume and opens to a page marked with a red ribbon.

"Right here," he says, pointing to an illustration of a muscular, bull-like creature with sharpened horns, flaring nostrils, and a halo of fire around its gigantic head. "That's Moloch—that's the motherfucker that took control of Charlene."

Just as Christian music inspires listeners to deeds of charity and good will, Todd believes that songs about Satan and demonic entities can conjure unholy spirits and cause people to commit atrocious acts of violence.

"With their music, Carnal Season summoned Moloch into this world and it glommed onto Charlene like a second skin. By the time she began work on *The Devil and My Daughter*, the demon had burrowed into her soul and took over her mind and body," Todd says angrily. "During filming she was a nervous wreck. Always losing her temper, always cursing people out and yelling at them. Her voice became hoarse and rough, like the inside of her throat was lined with rocks— and her skin broke out in these big inflamed pimples. I thought she was just overworked, but it was something far worse than that. Carnal Season had planted the seed. The demon seed! Now Charlene was possessed!"

With desperation rising in his voice, Todd describes some of the terrifying events that took place once Charlene moved into the Berkeley apartment. He recalls one night when Charlene acted like she was being "throttled to death" by a supernatural power.

"I could see red claw marks and impressions around her neck, choking her," Todd claims. "Charlene would dig her nails into her throat, fighting for air, until the entity would finally let her breathe."

Todd says that he saw murky images inside the apartment, including a severed torso squirming with maggots; a human skull matted with honey-colored hair; and a dead woman with a bulbous animal horn plunged between her legs. In one of his more outrageous revelations, Todd describes a rotting female corpse that would appear by his bed at night, its blackened fingers tapping some ghoulish death march on the headboard. The sight of the apparition would send Charlene into terrifying convulsions, causing her to scratch at her skin and hurt herself.

"If I tried to take Charlene to the hospital, she would immediately calm down and start acting normal," Todd says. "She said the doctors would blame me for the injuries on her body, and that I'd probably go to jail."

As time wore on, Todd noticed a disturbing correlation between Charlene's visits to her mother in the nursing home and the severity of the demonic attacks. "Charlene would put herself together for her mom. She would do her hair nice and cover her acne with makeup," he recalls. "They would have a pleasant visit together, reading books and watching old movies with the other residents.

"It was like she had a split personality. Sometimes, she could act friendly and composed—just like you or me. She even participated in a magazine article to talk about her mother's health, and she came across as entirely normal," Todd says. "The writer of the article thought Charlene was so sweet—and she was! She was one of the nicest people I've ever known."

But when the young actress would return to the apartment after visits to the nursing home, the sexual deviant known as Moloch would unleash its perverted wrath. Todd recalls one awful night:

"After Charlene would visit her mother, she'd come home like this sexual dynamo. She'd be all over me—kissing me, biting my neck and ears, rubbing me through my clothes. I'm not going to lie—I liked it. It was exciting and fun. But one night Charlene came home late and I was asleep. Before I realized what was going on, she had pinned me to the bed—the demon had given her supernatural strength—and she began ripping off my clothes."

Todd takes a ragged breath. Tears pool in his eyes as he reveals the next startling detail. "I was a virgin too, and I didn't want our first time to be like this. But Charlene forced herself on me. I didn't want to do it, but my body betrayed me and she climbed on top. That was how we both lost our virginity, with me held down by this madwoman with bloodlust in her eyes."

Todd says that as the malevolent spirits continued to haunt the apartment—making strange noises, moving the furniture around, and clogging the toilet with a putrid brown sludge—his sexual activity with Charlene grew more unhinged and even dangerous.

"I'm not going to tell you all the things we did, and all the things Charlene tried to do to me—they're too embarrassing," Todd says, his face flushing. "But I was invisible to her. A tool for her to ride until she had her fill. She called me her human dildo. Her Sybian saddle. And her orgasms were these terrifying, snorting screams of pain and pleasure, where she would thrash and grind upon me like a crazed animal. Every night brought some new kind of horror, but I was in love with her by then and I didn't know what to do."

Charlene's behavior grew increasingly manic. She insisted that Todd make love to her at all hours of the day. She started cutting up her arms and stomach. She spoke constantly of lustful thoughts—and sometimes of murder. One day, just before Charlene was to go visit her mother at the nursing home, Todd sat her down on the couch. He told Charlene that she needed to move out.

"She didn't say anything. She just scratched at a cyst on her cheek and it popped open. When she saw the blood on her fingertips, it was like a wave breaking. She burst into tears and ran into the bedroom,"

Todd recalls. "Moments later, she came back out with a videotape and told me to put it into the VCR."

Todd assumed the tape contained one of Charlene's horror flicks—perhaps something she and Debra had made when they were kids. But when the first image appeared on the screen, he knew right away that what he was watching was all too real.

The tape showed a basement covered in dirt and grime. Candle flames danced inside animal skulls along the back ledge, and a hideous bull mask hung from a nail on the wall. The room was dark and empty, the corners cobwebbed and rippling with moving shadows.

"It looked like an underground film or a grainy home movie," Todd says. "I tried to get Charlene to stop the tape and talk to me, but she refused. She insisted that I watch it."

According to Todd, the tape showed a group of people walking into the basement from an upstairs area. They were all wearing masks and black hooded sweatshirts. A tall, lean figure joined them—clearly the leader, he was wearing a purple robe and carrying a metal censer.

"It was disturbing enough, just seeing them in that dark room, reciting their incantations or invocations or whatever you call them. The leader—he looked like a goddamn *skeleton*—wandered among the others, swinging his burner, letting the smoke waft around them. They were *inhaling* it, making these awful sniffing sounds. They were like drug addicts, getting high off the air," Todd says, deeply troubled by the memory.

But Todd claims the unthinkable was yet to come. Because then he saw something on the tape he would never forget. Something that made him fall to his knees. Something that made him lunge for the telephone and call the police.

"They brought a girl down from the stairs," he says, refusing to hold back his tears. "She was naked, bone-thin, a look of paralyzed fear on her face. It was Charlene. *My* Charlene. But on that night, she no longer belonged to me. She belonged to them—the men of the cabal, and the bull demon they worshiped."

According to Todd, the coven transformed Charlene into a human altar, decorating her spine with candles, eating communion wafers off her buttocks, and mocking her with vulgar insults.

Todd says that he stopped the tape when the man in the purple gown began to swat Charlene with a wooden paddle. "I couldn't watch any more. I looked at Charlene and asked her why she never went to the cops, but she was laughing! She was covering her mouth with her hand, dainty-like, trying to stop, but she couldn't. She couldn't control it. I can still hear that incessant cackling!"

Before he called the police, Todd demanded that Charlene tell him the entire story. In a croaking voice that belonged more to the demon than to herself, Charlene explained with disturbing glee how she became Satan's plaything for the night.

"During pre-production on *Devil*, Charlene became terribly jealous of Debra's relationship with our cameraman, this guy named Billy Lee," Todd recounts. "When Debra and Billy went location scouting one day, Charlene followed them. They had gone to a house in the woods somewhere, a place frequented by biker gangs and Satan worshipers. From a distance, Charlene spied on Billy and Debra. She saw them working together, laughing, having a good time. She couldn't take it. She got drunk and passed out in a field, and somehow ended up in the clutches of these evil men."

Adding to the stomach-churning horror, Todd believes that the entire string of events—the decision to follow Debra and Billy, the kidnapping, the ritual in the basement—was orchestrated by Moloch.

"Moloch controlled those men, those degenerates. He used their ritual to complete Charlene's transformation—her final pathway to full-blown possession," Todd says. "No one could help Charlene after that. Not the police. Not me or her mother. Moloch, the double-horned demon, the shame of Ammon, was in control now."

Charlene said that she believed the cult was going to kill her after the ritual was over. "But the men of the coven had either left the house, or had gone upstairs and passed out drunk," Todd says. "They left Charlene tied up on the basement floor, unconscious, covered in filth. But she woke up. She tore off her restraints with ease. And with Moloch as her perverted guide, she found the tape hidden in a box of old shoes and children's toys. She grabbed it. She grabbed her clothes. Then she ran as fast as she could, for two miles, back to her car. The fact that the men kept her alive just to abuse her again probably saved her life," Todd says.

Berkeley police officer Anthony Ellison, 27, listened earnestly as Todd outlined all the bizarre and violent incidents that had led him to call the police. Charlene had taken a sedative and was sleeping down the hall, giving Todd and the officer some quiet time to talk.

"One of the very first calls I went on was a murder-suicide, so I had already seen some pretty awful things out there. But I had never heard anything like Todd's story," Ellison says. The iron-jawed officer admits to being a skeptic when it comes to supernatural phenomena. "The evil that men do is enough for me without having to worry about demonic possession."

But when Todd insisted that Ellison watch the videotape from beginning to end, the officer began to question his own beliefs.

"This isn't the first time that a murderer or an abductor has left a tape behind of his crimes, but these men were the worst I have ever seen," Ellison declares. "They committed acts of extreme violence on an inebriated woman, but they were also clearly involved in aberrant occult activity. I saw a chalice that looked dripping with blood. I saw a figurine of the Virgin Mary with a plastic penis on it. I heard verbal abuse that bordered on sadism."

Despite the unfathomable horror and illegal activity that Ellison witnessed on the tape, he says he was not convinced that Charlene was the victim of the supernatural until he met her for the first time.

"The tape was just ending when Charlene appeared in the doorway to the room," Ellison recalls. "She was a terrifying sight, all pale skin and spider veins, with scrapes on her arms and legs. And her poor face...it looked *boneless*, like she was wearing a rubber Halloween mask. And it was weird because right when she came in, a swarm of cockroaches gathered in the window, batting their wings against the glass and tittering about. The room took on this awful stench that made us gag. I don't know how else to phrase this, but it smelled like a huge fart. Like somebody's guts rotting from the inside out."

But Ellison reports that the strange incidents did not stop there. As Charlene entered the room and sat down by Todd on the couch, the kitchen lights shorted out and the TV turned on to roaring static. Ellison says that the young woman then took his arm and spoke in a sinister voice.

"He flops into my bed at night. I can show you—I can show you the indentation of his rump! The mildewed puddle of his waste! Oh, we play games. We sing songs! And he tells me dirty secrets. Secrets about my friends—the talentless traitors! Secrets about my mother— the whoring libertine that cheated on my father!" Charlene hissed at the officer, her voice toneless and low, like the slithering of a snake. Then her voice turned shrill, her brown eyes welling with tears and self-hatred. "I've done so many bad things—the library and the parish! The police—they're watching me! I must avoid them! But it's not me they want! It's what's *inside* me!" she cried.

Ellison then watched in transfixed awe as Charlene's face took on the mottled features of a ferocious bull. Then the acne-riddled visage of a snarling teenage boy. Then Charlene made a grunting sound, farted, and promptly fell asleep, her limbs as limp as rubber bands.

"I'm a sensible man. I understand that your eyes can play tricks on you, and in law enforcement you have to be careful about that. But I know what I saw that day," Ellison says in a resolute voice.

"Once I determined Charlene was not currently a threat to herself, I left the apartment with the tape and gave it to our Indecent Assault and Battery Unit. I also brought Todd to the station so that he could provide a written statement of how he came into possession of the tape and everything he experienced in the apartment," Ellison says.

Reflecting on his alarming tale, Ellison admits, "It was a down-the-rabbit-hole kind of story, but I couldn't let the case go, no matter how hard I tried. These were good people, Charlene and Todd. I wanted to help them."

But after Todd left the police station, Ellison was overcome with a painful stomach virus that forced him to miss work for over a week. "Vomiting, diarrhea, abdominal pain, night sweats—I had it all. I had to sleep on the bathroom floor just to be next to the toilet," he says. To this day, Ellison is unsure if his illness was caused by a genuine bug or by his sudden involvement with the paranormal.

"Perhaps it was a warning of some kind, the demon ordering me to stay away," Ellison suggests. "But I refused to listen."

As soon as he recovered, Ellison returned to the apartment in Berkeley to check on Todd and Charlene. "Charlene wasn't there—she was visiting her mother at the nursing home," Ellison says. "But Todd told me things were better. Charlene had started seeing a psychiatrist who put her on medication. It was then that I started wonder if Charlene was suffering from a psychiatric illness. Todd told me that her parents had divorced, that her father had been a violent man—I started to question everything I had heard and seen."

Just three days after that fateful visit, Charlene Worsley entered the Mercy Care Medical Center in Oakland and embarked on a homicidal rampage that has left Todd Wheeler, Anthony Ellison, and the entire Bay Area community rattled to their core.

"The demon deceived me into believing Charlene was going to be all right," Todd Wheeler says today. "But the demon also tricked Charlene—tricked her into believing her mother was a horrible person who deserved to die."

At the end of his interview, Todd tells *Dark Roads* that he has plans to move out of the apartment and somehow return to his normal life. He says that he will never work on another horror film again. Meanwhile, Officer Ellison remains optimistic that he and his colleagues can bring some kind of closure to at least part of this shocking story.

"Charlene Worsley's assault case will stay open until we solve it. We are working closely with the Sonoma County Police Department and are determined to locate the offenders in that video and bring them to justice. Despite public opinion about Charlene now, that videotape is on the forefront of my mind," Ellison says.

"The nights when I'm not on patrol are the hardest," the officer concludes. "I find myself driving around the city, wondering if I could have stopped Charlene. Wondering why a young woman like her, with everything to live for, would suddenly fall apart and do what she did. That's when I wonder if demons really do exist. But I also think—if I had gotten to that apartment sooner, if I could have reached Charlene, then maybe I could have saved all those innocent lives."

From "August Blood: An Oral History of the Mercy Care Murders" by Noelle Ramsey (originally published in *Intrepid*, January, 1988, p. 13-25):

    In the summer of 1987, Charlene Worsley, a 19-year-old actress and college student, walked into the nursing home where her mother was a resident and embarked on one of the most horrific and seemingly arbitrary murder rampages in California history. The victims, mostly the elderly, were attacked so viciously that even a city accustomed to violence was stunned into disbelief by the killer's callous indifference toward human life. The location of the crime was equally disturbing, shattering the peaceful notion that there are still some places left in society that remain safe and pure, unblemished by the horrors of the outside world.

    The senselessness and cold savagery of the slayings have turned Oakland into an epicenter of mistrust and fear. The East Bay city has a long and storied history of crime connected to drug and gang activity, but the killings at the Mercy Care Medical Center were beyond the pale. Several eyewitnesses, like shell-shocked soldiers surviving the atrocities of war, have chosen not to speak—their experiences too traumatizing, the memory of that tragic afternoon branded like a hot-iron scar into their consciousness. Of those who have come forward, their voices speak not only to the magnitude of the crime, but to the legacy of the victims and the troubled city in which they lived and worked. Here is their story…

I. THE MURDERS

    HELEN CABLE, *former receptionist at the Mercy Care Medical Center. She is 29.* I was working at Mercy for about three years before it all happened. It was a nursing home in every sense of the word. We wanted our residents to lead meaningful lives, to feel comfortable—an extension of their family life back home. Staff was focused on working with doctors in the field of dementia research, and they were making great strides. That's what makes this so terrible—I can't imagine what our residents were thinking on that awful day.

    I saw Charlene when she walked in. She said hi to me. She smiled. But it was unsettling because her face had broken out in these big cysts on her cheeks and jawline. She was a pretty girl, you could tell she was an actress—but her makeup couldn't hide her acne. Her skin looked like it was infected.

I noticed she was carrying a duffel bag over her shoulder, which I figured was filled with books for her mom. They read together in the afternoons, mostly clasics like *Wuthering Heights* and *Jane Eyre*...

She walked down the hall to the right of my desk, toward the physical therapy office, and I remember thinking that was odd because her mother's room was in the opposite direction, on the second floor. But then I got a call and didn't think anything of it until I saw her again a few minutes later.

SAMANTHA BANKS, *sister of Joycelyn Banks. Samantha is 45 and teaches high school science.* Joy had been a physical therapist at Mercy for about ten years. She loved her job, loved teaching patients about exercise and nutrition—but most of all she loved helping the elderly feel strong and healthy and alive again. Her favorite sport was skiing, or anything outdoors. Every winter she would travel to Squaw Valley or Sugar Bowl to hit the slopes. She was a very active person...

Records show that Joy never treated Ruth Worsley, the mother. She never had any interactions with her, and she had never met Charlene as far as I know. One of the tabloids said that Joy was Charlene's "test run," which makes me sick to my stomach...

They said Joy was standing with her back to the door, facing the filing cabinet in the corner of her office. I don't think she heard a thing. My sister was a strong woman, very fit. She would have fought back. Frankly, she would have whipped that girl's ass, if she had been given the chance.

COLIN RICKS, *Oakland Police Department homicide detective, 47 years old.* I arrived at the nursing home after it was over—after the shooting and evacuation. I worked from bottom to top, starting with the bloody footprints in the west hallway and lobby—those belonged to Charlene—and the body in the office on the first floor. That was Joycelyn Banks. She was slumped in the corner of the office—sort of crumpled in the corner. There was cast-off blood spatter and arterial spray on the walls and floor, and a line of blood droplets on the filing cabinet and desk. Due to the positioning of her body and the angle of the entry wounds, it was clear the victim was attacked from behind with a sharp and powerful weapon. My guess was a hatchet or a butcher knife. Turned out to be an ax. Short-handled and single bit. A vicious weapon, and rare in homicides.

There were no defensive wounds on Mrs. Banks. This was a rage attack with multiple stab wounds occurring in rapid succession—an attack that demonstrated an incredible amount of strength from the perpetrator. At that time, I had worked homicide for over eight years and I'd never seen anything that bad. And it was only the beginning.

CABLE: I never went back to Mercy after that. I never picked up my last paycheck. No one mailed it to me either. I got very depressed after the murders, and when all those reports came out in the news, I practically went into hiding. I felt so stupid and ashamed.

People—not just the police, but strangers *on the street*—would come up to me and ask, "Didn't you see Charlene after she killed Joy? Didn't you see the ax? The bloody footprints? Why didn't you call the cops then?"

But that crazy bitch tricked me. She hid the ax in her duffel bag. And after she killed Joy, she put a coat on to hide all the blood. The police found bloody paper towels in the bathroom, which means she wiped down her face and hands.

She walked right past me to the opposite hall. I was probably on the phone or writing something in the appointment book. Joycelyn was already dead by then. And there I was, sitting on my ass. I'll never forgive myself for it…

JUD MONTOYA, *former security guard at the Mercy Care Medical Center and currently unemployed. He is 30.* I was on my break, in my car in the parking lot. I was eating my lunch. I didn't see the girl go in or even know that something was happening until the cop's cruiser rolled up. Even then, I just figured one of the residents had kicked the bucket.

MARTELLE BIERCE, *former nurse at the Mercy Care Medical Center and co-author of the non-fiction book,* "12 Minutes of Hell: The Mercy Care Murders." *She is 45.* I passed Charlene on the last set of stairs going up to the second floor. There are large casement windows in that stairwell and the light is really strong, and Charlene's face was lit up, white with the glare of the sun. She looked ghastly—raccoon eyes, her face covered in open cysts. I wrote about this in my book, and it was probably a trick of the light, but her acne seemed to *ripple* under the skin. I've been a nurse for 20 years, and I've seen my share of skin disorders, lesions and abscesses, things like that, but her skin looked *alive*. It really unnerved me and I asked her if she was okay.

We had just passed each other on the stairs, and she turned to look at me, just for a second—and I knew something wasn't right. She was carrying this big travel bag, and there were flecks of blood on her cheeks. The blood could have come from her cysts—I wasn't sure.

She didn't answer me and hurried up the steps onto the landing around the corner. Something was wrong—I knew it—so I went to the lobby and told Helen to call 911.

Right at that time, just as Helen was picking up the phone, I saw the bloody footprints in the hall, and I followed them to Joy's office.

CABLE: The 911 operator took *forever*, she was asking the same questions over and over—but part of that was our fault, because we didn't know exactly what the problem was. I told her there was blood in the hallway and a suspicious person in the building, because that's what Martelle was shouting at me to say.

BIERCE: I turned into the office and saw Joy. In all my years I will never forget it. Her neck was gaping open, and her body was chopped up and shoved into the corner.

JOHN TANNER, *brother of Mark Tanner, the Oakland Police Department patrol officer who was the first respondent on the scene. John owns a house-painting business. He is 43.* My brother got the call from dispatch at 2:33 pm on August 5th. He was driving alone in his patrol car, on Piedmont Street, about three minutes from the scene. But in the communication between the nursing home and 911, Mark was told that a *patient* had cut herself and was bleeding in the lobby. The "suspicious person" was the patient! That screwed-up call cost a lot of lives.

So Mark walked into the building without the full knowledge of what was going on inside.

CABLE: When the officer came into the lobby, I was back on the phone, telling a different 911 operator that Martelle had found Joy's body. Martelle was hysterical, screaming that there was a killer in the building and that we needed to get everyone out. It was a totally hectic scene, and the officer had to spend several minutes just trying to calm her down. He didn't actually see Joy's body until at least 2:45. By then, Charlene had already made her way upstairs.

EARLIE BREWER, *retired United States merchant marine and former resident of Mercy Care Medical Center. At 63, Earlie lost his larynx due to throat cancer and has a stoma in his throat. Now 73, he must cover the hole with his finger to speak.* I was sitting by the window near the stairs. I saw the girl come onto the floor. She put her bag down and took the ax out. Then she walked into the game room. Both Anita and Abby were in there, playing Scrabble.

SHARON GONZALEZ, *a graduate student in Political Science and daughter of Anita Gonzalez. Sharon is 38.* When people ask me how my mother died, I don't know what to say! She wasn't stabbed. You can't stab someone with an ax! So what am I supposed to say? I always say "she was attacked," but I'm only being polite. The truth is, she was hacked into like a slab of meat.

BREWER: The girl was screaming as she did it. I could hear her, with every swing of the ax, just this awful, piercing shriek.

CABLE: The staff on floor were bringing the residents down, the ones who could move faster, as many as they could at a time. We heard a scream, and the cop told me and Martelle to get out of the building—to get everyone out of the lobby and far down the street as possible. We just started running, but helping the residents along as we could. It was chaos.

RANDALL THOMAS FLEMING, *son of Abigail Fleming and a hotel concierge. He is 46.* My mother was hit in the head with the ax—that's what the autopsy report says killed her—but that wasn't enough for Charlene Worsley. She just kept on swinging and swinging until there was nothing of my mother left.

My mother was funny and kind. She was fiercely loyal to her family and friends. She was patient. She was loving. She was generous with her time, always giving to others and lending an ear. She loved the ocean. She was actually one of the first women in the world to ever take an underwater photograph…

I don't think about the past anymore. The happy times. The birthdays. The Christmases in San Francisco. Ever since the tabloids published pictures from the murder scene, my brain refuses to cooperate with my memories. Now all I think about is how terrified my mother must have been, how helpless she must have felt in those final seconds before her death.

BREWER: I'm in a wheelchair, so I couldn't take the stairs like a lot of the others. I made it to the elevator just as she was coming out of the game room. Sally (*Anderton, a nurse at the facility*) was with me, and maybe two or three other residents. I looked up, and the girl was down the hall. She had taken off her coat and was covered head to toe in blood, her eyes rolling wildly in their sockets. My stomach lurched like I was going to puke.

SALLY ANDERTON, *former nurse at the Mercy Care Medical Center. Now a physical education teacher, she is 42.* It was sickening. She was wearing a lemon yellow dress, a summer dress, so the blood stood out. It was clumped in her hair, all over her face and clothes.

BREWER: I was telling Sally and the others to just go, get down the stairs, but they stayed with me. We were waiting for the elevator to come up. The girl was standing there, about twenty yards away, her chest heaving up and down. Her hair all stringy and wet, clotted with blood... she looked like a goaded bull, just waiting to charge.

ANDERTON: I didn't recognize her at first because of all the blood—plus I was scared out of my mind. I couldn't think straight. But then it hit me like a flash—Ruth. She's coming for Ruth.

BREWER: I didn't find out until later it was Ruth's daughter. I had seen her before—I watched *Singin' in the Rain* with her one time—but you couldn't recognize her. She didn't look human...

Our eyes met—just for a second. And there was no fear in her eyes. No hesitation. No regret. She looked like she had been waiting for this moment her entire life.

ANDERTON: The elevator doors opened and we all got inside— it was me, Earlie, and two other residents. I was punching the button a million times, like you see in all those scary movies. But the door wouldn't close! I could hear Charlene coming toward us, the ax clunking and dragging along on the floor.

And then, just as the doors were closing, I saw Ruth leaning in the doorway to her room. I will never forget that picture for as long as I live. She was so frail by then, like a stick figure, standing there in her blue terrycloth robe and nightgown. Her hair in curlers. She looked so confused.

I was screaming at her, "Ruth, c'mon! Let's go, let's go!" But of course she didn't understand. She just stood there, and I didn't go get her, and we took the elevator down to the lobby.

TANNER: The tabloids said my brother was some sort of mad-dog cop on the loose, which was totally false. He followed protocol. He called for backup and went after the suspect. He did everything by the book.

RICKS: For such a chaotic scene, Officer Tanner did an expert job evacuating the lobby and getting people to safety. The decision to go to the second floor without any backup was his call. He evaluated the situation and the risks involved. His objective was to neutralize or eliminate the threat.

MONTOYA: I ran into the lobby and tried to figure out what the hell was going on. It was a mess. The cop told me to get out, so I did. I don't carry a gun. I don't even carry a friggin' baton.

JUDITH PRITCHARD, *retired bookkeeper and former resident of Mercy Care Medical Center. She is 77.* I was in my bed, across from Ruth's room. I have a leg ulcer and can't walk without help. If the girl had come for me, I would have had no way of defending myself.

TANNER: According to witnesses, Mark went up the stairs on the north side, next to the physical therapy office. So he and the girl were like magnets, drawn to each other from opposite sides. He didn't have the element of surprise. There was going to be a confrontation.

PRITCHARD: I saw Ruth leaning in her doorway, and people were screaming for her to get into the elevator. She just had a robe on, and her face was entirely blank. She had no idea what was going on.

RICKS: Charlene was wearing sandals, beach sandals with straps, and her bloody footprints were all over the crime scene. But up on the second floor, the way the footprints were spread out—she had started running. Running *hard*. Her mother didn't stand a chance.

PRITCHARD: The girl was an inferno. Volcanic rage. That's the only way I can describe it. She swung the ax like a logger ripping into an old tree, and Ruth went down flailing.

RICKS: Ruth Worsley's autopsy indicated two deep vertical wounds to the chest, and one massive blow to the head. The sheer force of the attack knocked her over her bed and onto the floor, against the far wall. Eyewitnesses told us that Ruth died while her daughter stood over her body, laughing.

BREWER: Ruth was a nice lady. Her room was filled with scrapbooks of photographs that chronicled her entire life. She was a photographer and an artist and she still knew all these old dances from when we were kids. The Bunny Hop and the Cha-Cha. The nurses would use the scrapbooks to help Ruth with her memory. But there was only one family photo that she kept near her bed—Ruth and her daughter, taken during one of those gondola boat rides on Lake Merritt—and you can't reconcile the love and sense of wonder you see in the picture with what her daughter did that day. It had to be an extreme form of mental illness. There's just no other answer.

II. THE SHOOTING

TANNER: It was the first time my brother ever fired his gun in the line of duty. It might have been the first time he ever had to draw his weapon—I'm not sure.

PRITCHARD: I saw the whole thing. The girl walked out of Ruth's room, blood coming off her in droplets. She was breathing hard, huffing the air, *snorting* it—and I swear there was steam coming out of her nostrils. Little puffs of steam. The cop had just come from the stairs. He had his gun out. He was shouting at the girl to drop the ax.

RICKS: The entire incident—from when Charlene walked into the facility to the time of the shooting—lasted approximately 12 minutes.

TANNER: Mark gave three verbal warnings—you can read this in the report, and there are eyewitness statements to back it up. Not everyone had been evacuated. Many of the residents were still in their rooms, hiding in bed, under the covers, or with the doors barricaded. They could hear everything.

PRITCHARD: The girl raised the ax with both hands. Over her shoulder, like she was going to chuck it at the officer's head. He was hollering, "Put it down! Put it down!" But she just started laughing— it was more of a cackle, really—there was no humor in it. It was just evil. And her eyes—they looked *rotted* black. She began tightening her grip on the ax—almost like she was winding up, the way a baseball player does before going up to bat. She was smiling then—a *hungry* smile—with globs of spit dribbling down her chin.

The officer gave her another chance. [He said,] "Put the weapon down or I will shoot," or something like that, but he was shouting it.

And the girl said something then. She spoke in this low croaking voice—very guttural and thick. At first I thought it was only gibberish, but now that I have had time to think about it—I think she said, "Kill me." I'm almost positive she said "Kill me."

RICKS: Officer Tanner discharged his weapon three times, with the third shot being fatal. That fatal round struck the assailant in the chest.

PRITCHARD: She fell down—sort of slipped in all the blood and hit the floor. There was a terrible gurgling sound as she died. She was suffocating in her own blood.

ETHEYLN REEVES, *homemaker and former resident of Mercy Care Medical Center. She is 78. Mrs. Reeves recorded her statements onto cassette tape for this article.* It all happened so fast—I didn't risk going back to my room or down the stairs. There's a sitting area on the second floor by the window, where we keep magazines and books. I was just sitting there with a *Bon Appétit* in my lap. She didn't look at me. She went straight to her mother. There was so much hatred and anger in her eyes—she didn't look like the Charlene I used to know.

After, she came out of Ruth's room. Her face was smeared with blood. Now, at the time, I didn't know the word for what I saw. I've since looked it up, and I've also spoken with my brother, who teaches a class called Catholic Social Thought at a private college. Charlene's face—it was no longer human. Her face had *transmutated*—that's the word I had to look up. When I told Richard, that's my brother, what she looked like—almost bovine, with flaring nostrils, lips stretched back from the gums—he said it was demonic. In Christian demonology, Richard said, the devil often appears as an animal with black fur—a goat or a large horse. Sometimes a bull. This change, this transmutation, only lasted a few seconds before the officer was there, his gun drawn. He was a tall man—powerfully built and broad across the shoulders. He gave Charlene explicit instructions to put the ax down or he would shoot. But she brought the ax back like she might throw it at him, so the officer fired—three or four shots, popping like firecrackers—and she went down onto the floor.

I'll tell you something else. There was a moment, after her face returned to normal, but before she was shot…she was Charlene again. A beautiful actress. A devoted daughter. She had such pretty eyes, almost a brown-gold color. And there was something in her face. Something sad. A sad recognition. Of what happened. Of what she had become. So when she raised her weapon, she knew what she was doing. Charlene wanted the officer to shoot. She wanted to die. It was the only way she could stop herself from hurting more people.

PRITCHARD: There was a crack when she fell. It was her skull hitting the tile. Her mouth was pulled open in this awful silent scream, and the ax slid across the floor. Then everything was still.

REEVES: I was in a state of shock and couldn't move. I couldn't talk. I kept trying to focus on the police officer, looking at him, telling myself it was over and he was going to make it better. But he wasn't moving either. He was just standing there, his lips fixed in this little pucker. The gun was frozen at his side, and his arm, his shooting arm, was trembling. I think he was in shock too.

PRITCHARD: Then something happened. The floor was quiet, like a cocoon. What's the word? Stasis—that's it! It was like a stasis. I could hear sounds, garbled voices, the police shouting from down below. But it was like I was cut off from everything. I tried to blink away what I was seeing and clear my head. I thought I had gone crazy. Even now, I wonder if the trauma of what happened was making me see things. But I have talked with Ethelyn [Reeves] and our stories match up. We saw the same thing.

REEVES: It was a single plume of smoke, gray in color. It curled up out of her chest from where she had been shot. Then the building took on this acrid smell. The smell of soot and fire. Burning. I thought it was smoke from the gunshot—like you see in old gangster movies. I had to cover my nose, the smell was so strong.

PRITCHARD: It didn't move like regular smoke. It didn't rise to the ceiling or fade into nothing. It moved…it *slithered*. It was floating, pulsing in the air toward the cop.

REEVES: The plume went right into the officer's mouth. He sort of sucked it down, like a little kid does with a strand of spaghetti. He swallowed, a big gulping noise, and then he holstered his gun. He was in a daze—just lost in space.

At that moment a bunch of other officers came running onto the floor. They made sure Charlene was dead. They asked us, "Are there any other suspects in the building?" As if we knew. They started sweeping through our rooms. One of them helped the officer who shot Charlene get down the stairs, while others began checking on the residents and getting them out. When one of the officers saw Ruth's body, he turned around and began dry-heaving in the corner.

REEVES: My brother told me that demons are powerless to do evil deeds if they don't have a body to inhabit—a human or an animal. I am 78 years old, and I have been alive a lot longer than most of the people who will be listening to this cassette and reading your article. I have seen some s*tuff* in my time. And I believe that what I witnessed that day was the work of the devil himself, or one of his demons—and once Charlene was killed, it wasted no time. It entered that officer's body like you would walk through a door—just effortless. And I worry for that officer. I worry what will become of him.

RICKS: I've heard these supernatural stories about the shooting and Officer Tanner. I see the tabloids at the check-out counter in the grocery store, all the headlines. "Hero Cop Confronts Demon Child."

"Rogue Cop Possessed by Satan." Now, as a detective, you have to be open-minded. You have to be aware of what's going on in your community. We've had a few cases in Oakland recently that would blow your mind—occult killings, grave-robbing, animal mutilations. A daycare center run by a pair of old degenerates. I'm not saying that weird shit doesn't happen. But these tabloid stories are disrespectful and ignorant. They're exploitative garbage. If anything, Officer Tanner should be applauded for his courage in the line of duty.

III. THE INVESTIGATION

RICKS: By the time I got to the scene, there was a perimeter set up around the building. This was to keep the media out, but also your average citizens. It seemed like the whole city had shown up. Workers from the parking garage, pedestrians, bicyclists, people from the bus stop. Hardworking, caring people—they wanted to know what the hell happened, but they also were trying to help. Reporters were blocking traffic, lining up their cameras on the street. There was a minor car accident at the corner because of all the confusion, which caused even more of a mess.

VIRGIL BONDS, *retired Oakland Police Department homicide detective. Currently writing a non-fiction book about the Mercy Care Murders, he is 60.* It goes without saying that it was the worst crime scene of my career. It was just so bizarre and gruesome, totally off the charts. The first killing—Joycelyn Banks—it was quick. A minute or two, tops. But why was she killed? Charlene knew where her mother's room was. She knew Ruth wouldn't be on that floor. It didn't make a lot of sense.

Upstairs was a nightmare. There were a total of four bodies, and the amount of blood was considerable. We didn't have the crime scene techs collect it all—just samples from each room. We bagged the ax, and the girl's coat, which was soaked with blood. We took photographs. One of the victims was wearing a necklace made out of seashells, and they were scattered and broken all over the floor, and I remember telling someone to pick up every piece—I was getting obsessive and angry about it. Later, I found Abigail Fleming's wedding ring crusted over with dried blood. It was just obscene.

It was hard to maintain decorum in the crime scene. I wanted to move the victims out of there, out of that hell. I couldn't wait for the coroner to show up and take them—not for me, but for them. This place was their home. They didn't deserve this.

RICKS: Aside from the bodies, the hardest part was all the little mementos scattered around. Reminders of life. Jewelry, cards, dried flowers, cat figurines—you name it, it was in there. In the game room, all the Scrabble pieces, each one covered with blood. We tagged, bagged, and numbered what we needed, but everything else had to be chucked.

By the time the coroner reached the last two bodies—that was Ruth and Charlene Worsley—he had run out of plastic bags. Before he left for the scene, no one told him that some of the victims had been dismembered. He didn't know there would be pieces of them.

So we had to wait for him to bring more bags. I asked Detective Bonds to go down to the first floor while I stayed on the second floor. I went in and checked on Ruth Worsley—it was so quiet now, it was like keeping a vigil. Like listening for ghosts. Her room was her private sanctuary—a handmade quilt, a water pitcher painted with flowers, a book about Bigfoot, a music box that played "Moon River." She was on her side on the floor, in the fetal position, behind the bed. Her chest had suffered the most trauma, but there was blood around her mouth and throat. The coroner told me she had drowned in her own blood.

Charlene was just outside that door, legs and arms splayed in an X position. I understand how the press thought she was a monster. She looked like something out of a horror movie, but you could see the pretty girl underneath all that gore. She looked...*soft*. Like the clouds had passed. I knew right then I wanted to talk to all of her friends. I wanted to learn why she did this horrible thing.

DEBRA MORROW, *film director, screenwriter and Charlene Worsley's best friend. She is 20.* When I first heard, I didn't believe it. I felt absolute shock and sick inside. We had just finished our first big movie (*The Devil and My Daughter*) a few months before and we were so proud. It was everything we had ever dreamed of since we were kids. And then this. It had to be the onset of schizophrenia—maybe inherited from her father? That was the only thing I could think of.

Then *Dark Roads* comes out with this article about Charlene and everything that happened at the farmhouse in Monte Rio. I thought it was bullshit at first, but Todd Wheeler is a decent guy. He really loved Charlene. He wouldn't just make stuff up.

TODD WHEELER, *special-effects artist and Charlene's boyfriend. They lived together briefly before the murders. He is 21.* When Charlene moved in with me, everything went to hell. She was exhausted from making the movie, and she stopped taking care of herself. She refused to eat and became moody and distant. Her sexual appetite bordered on psychopathic. And she became obsessed with blood. She would cut herself and smear the blood on the bathroom wall, drawing obscene pictures with it…

As time went on she transformed into a monster; she had either lost her mind, or it was something deeper than that. I came to believe an evil power had taken hold of her. I saw things in that apartment I never wanted to see—ghosts, furniture and objects moving by themselves, mountains of shit piling up in the toilet no matter how many times I flushed it away. It was terrifying. And then one afternoon, when I was finally ready to end our relationship, Charlene showed me the tape.

RICKS: During the investigation, we found out from Indecent Assault and Battery that another investigation was going on. There was a tape that showed Charlene Worsley being assaulted at a party—but it wasn't just a party. It was a ritual put on by some very sick people. My first thought was, "This is it. This is our smoking gun." We hoped the tape would lead us to why Charlene committed the murders.

So we brought all the kids from *The Devil and My Daughter* in for questioning. I was now convinced that this was some kind of cult murder, and that there was a group behind it like there was with the Manson killings. But the kids were terrified—it was obvious they had nothing to do with it. They didn't know about any cult. There was no ringleader among them. They were as stunned as we were.

BILLY LEE, *screenwriter and cinematographer. He worked closely with Charlene on two films, both of which contained themes of Satanism and demonic influence. He is 22.* I've been into the horror genre all my life, but what happened at Mercy Care was like a real-life slasher movie. I saw Charlene's picture on the news and thought, "This is not the girl I knew."

The ritual at the farmhouse—that's what did it. That's what set her off. They abused her. They made her wear a mask with the face of a bull. They turned her into an animal. Why didn't she go to the police with the tape right away? What possessed her to hold onto it for so long and not tell anyone?

MORROW: There was a scene in *The Devil and My Daughter* where Charlene was supposed to take her clothes off. But at the last minute, she refused to do it and Todd had to make these flesh-colored wraps to cover her up. And I realize now—it was because of that night. The attack. The beatings. Charlene didn't want us to see what those men had done to her body.

WHEELER: Most people associate the bull with power, fertility, and male sexual energy. But the bull has also been used in religious rituals for centuries, and in some mythologies is considered a pagan demon. That night, at the farmhouse, those Satanists weren't trying to murder my Charlene. They were trying to transform her into a bull! A therianthropic transformation!

MORROW: The media just ripped us apart. We expected it to a certain extent, but we didn't know how bad it was going to be. I was a raging bitch for making what the tabloids called "the only film in the history of cinema responsible for a mass murder." People left death threats on my answering machine. They harassed my father at his job. They blamed me for the attack on Charlene at the farmhouse. And even worse things got sent to me in the mail—chicken bones, pentagrams, squares of fabric or silk with actual blood on them. Of course, I turned everything over to the police.

BONDS: We looked into every angle we could to determine a motive. Even though we knew Charlene was our perp, our thought was, "What can we do to prevent this kind of tragedy from happening again?" We were also concerned that a copycat homicide might take place, so we were being as vigilant as possible.

My other thought was drugs—maybe cocaine or hallucinogens. I got a copy of *The Devil and My Daughter* and watched it. There was some unusual and psychedelic stuff in that movie. I started thinking it was all connected somehow—the movie, the murders, narcotics—but that theory went nowhere fast. There was no evidence that suggested Charlene took drugs. Not even pot.

The college kids who worked with Charlene gave us a few leads. Debra Morrow sent us a copy of a play that Charlene had written for one of her theater classes; it was about a woman getting revenge on these Satanists who had abused her. We tried to find if there was any truth to the story, but we came up empty-handed. In fact, if anything, the play revealed a certain amount of pre-meditation on Charlene's part.

Similarly, there was a heavy metal group, a group called Carnal Season, that wrote the songs for one of Debra and Charlene's movies. This is a really strange band—they are connected to the murder-suicide of two teen girls in San Francisco, and they write songs about death and killing. We thought it was worth checking out. Maybe Charlene got mixed up with them, or we could link them to the assault in Monte Rio. But we interviewed the members of the group and came up with nothing.

MORROW: I was in the supermarket the other day and saw one of the tabloids with Charlene and Officer Tanner on the cover. I surprised myself by buying it. I was having a little pity party, I guess. But the article got me thinking about the nature of evil, and if evil can be transferred between people—like how a wire conducts electricity. It was the same theme we explored in *The Devil and My Daughter*. That's when I first started believing that Charlene was possessed. I have even tried contacting the officer's family. I want to know if he's okay. I want to know if the evil has...*prospered*. I know it sounds crazy, but I need to know.

TANNER: Mark is currently on paid administrative leave while the shooting of Charlene Worsley is under investigation. As for his mental state...I can't really comment on that right now. He's been through an extremely traumatic experience.

IV. CHARLENE WORSLEY

RICKS: Debra provided us with copies of all the horror movies she made with Charlene when they were kids. One of them was called *Monsters in Your Pants*, which was about a young girl who had this disgusting worm creature living in her under-shorts.

In my opinion, that movie reflected Charlene's psychological state. She believed she had an actual monster living inside her. Before you laugh, you have to understand—Charlene was suffering from a severe psychosocial disorder caused by her father's violent behavior and her parents' divorce...these things created a psychotic condition within Charlene's mind.

But despite the problems with her mental health, Charlene had a strong moral code. She wasn't promiscuous, or dishonest, or cruel to others. Although her teachers were worried about her, she earned good grades in school and she didn't do drugs. She and Debra Morrow had a deeply personal friendship that stretched back for many years. They supported each other. Loved one another. My point is, we learned things about Charlene we didn't expect. I'm not defending her actions, but the girl was severely mentally ill. Isn't her illness worth at least some sympathy?

WHEELER: I've learned a lot since the murders happened, and here's what I've come up with. You can choose to believe me or not—I don't really give a damn. But if you trace the roots of Carnal Season, you'll find out about their guitar player, this scumbag named Judas Grimm. Only before he became Judas Grimm, he was just some pizza-faced kid named Alex who wrote a heavy metal song called "Rise, Demon, Rise." Now, some people think, "It's just a stupid song, it can't hurt you." But who says that song *lyrics* can't conjure up a demon? The Devil doesn't give a shit about the difference between fiction and truth! After all, he's the Father of Lies!

I've done my research. Alex's father, a drug dealer from Barstow, was killed in a car accident—only it wasn't an accident! It was a demonic attack! He was gored to death by the demon that Alex summoned in his song—the bull-creature known as Moloch!

Moloch possessed Alex. He made poor little Alex *do things*. Alex set fires. Alex stole. Alex bullied his classmates and stabbed one of them in the eye with a pencil. When he was 19, he committed his first murder—he dismembered a prostitute and dumped her body on the beach somewhere. Then he changed his name to Judas Grimm, and created Carnal Season. And the monster killed some more! Mostly prostitutes and runaways, the forgotten people. Check the Bay Area newspaper archives between '78 and '86 if you don't believe me. *American Investigation* even did a news segment on it. It's all there, if you know where to look!

But being forced to live his life as a cold-blooded killer tormented Alex. His friends and relatives said Alex was losing his mind. I know—I've interviewed them! They said Alex was suicidal. Moloch was pushing him over the edge. He wanted Alex to kill some more. He wanted his kills to be bigger, crazier—Holocaustian in scope. Alex couldn't take it.

So Alex wrote a song—a vile song called "Transfer of Spirits"—in hopes that the ritual within the lyrics would pass Moloch onto someone else. Onto some poor, unsuspecting person. Onto someone dealing with her own shit. Onto someone whose mother was dying. By the time Charlene was done with *Blood Songs*, the infestation period was over. Moloch began to oppress her soul, symbolized by that terrible night in Monte Rio. He tormented Charlene. He exposed all her weaknesses and fears, her abandonment issues, her grief over her mother's illness. He broke her down. Turned her into his little plaything. *The Devil and My Daughter* was the last step, the final stage—and just look at what Moloch made her do after that!

Everyone is asking, "Why did Charlene do this? How could she kill her own mother?" The Bible says that Satan is a roaming lion looking for someone to destroy. And this demon wanted to destroy Charlene by forcing her to kill the one thing she loved the most. And that's exactly what Charlene did.

BONDS: I don't have much to say about Mr. Wheeler's claims. We've interviewed him. We've checked out his story, despite how irresponsible some of it sounds. We know where Alexander Grimm lives. We know how to reach him if necessary. But those cases, the prostitute murders, have been cold for years. And they're handled by another police department. More to the point, the evidence doesn't show any connection to the Worsley case.

Charlene Worsley didn't go to Mercy Care because of an evil spirit or because she trafficked with demons. She went there because she was an emotionally disturbed person, and because her mother lived there. And she wanted to kill her mother—maybe because Charlene blamed her for the divorce. Maybe because her father abandoned their family. Maybe she stopped taking her meds. We don't have all the answers yet, but one thing is clear: Charlene didn't care who she took down with her.

MORROW: I admired Ruth because she made a living in the arts and raised a daughter by herself. She was a bit of a hippie when Charlene and I were kids; her parents threw a lot of parties with trippy music and poetry readings. It was always a fun, freewheeling time at their house. Ruth would tell Charlene, "If you want to understand what another person values, start by looking at what they have and what they do." This is the advice that encouraged me and Charlene to make movies. We valued the freedom of expression available to us through the medium of film.

But sometimes I think about what *Ruth* valued, especially as her dementia took hold and her life no longer made any sense. And it was Charlene—it was her relationship with her daughter. That was all Ruth had left. And there is no way that Charlene willingly destroyed what her mother valued. I refuse to believe she made that choice on her own.

I admit, Todd Wheeler has made some outrageous statements in the alternative press about Charlene and what he believes caused the killings in Oakland. But, in some ways, Todd's story adds up. In some ways, it's the only story that makes sense.

WHEELER: When I did the spread with *Dark Roads* magazine, people accused me of exploiting Charlene's story to make a quick buck. *Dark Roads* doesn't pay for interviews, and they were the only publication willing to print the story. Besides, even if you don't believe in all the paranormal stuff that happened in my apartment, even if you don't look into Judas Grimm the way I have, that videotape speaks for itself. Those bastards need to pay for what they did to Charlene.

RICKS: From what I know, the investigation into the assault on Charlene Worsley has switched hands numerous times. Because of where the crime took place, there are some complicated jurisdictional issues, and some problems with the amount of manpower the law agency has up there. But I have absolutely no doubt that the Sonoma County Police Department is working hard at identifying the individuals on the tape, and I hope the law will take its proper course.

GONZALEZ: Now there are articles out there making Charlene out to be the victim. "Oh, she was such a sweet and innocent girl, she was beaten by these maniacs," they say. They want me to forgive Charlene for what she did! To feel bad for her. Well, I will *never* forgive her. I don't care if your mother had some brain disease. I don't care if you got shoved around by some Satanic gang. If your father was a doper and a dog killer. I don't fucking care! You knew what you were doing, you bitch. You went to an Ace Hardware store and bought an ax! You're a *murderer*. No, I will never forgive you.

CABLE: The tabloids say that Charlene was possessed by the devil, only a person possessed by Satan could do such a terrible thing, and all that hocus-pocus crap. I believe in something much more simple. Charlene Worsley was a cold-hearted killer, and that's all there is to it.

FLEMING: After the murders, I stayed at my parents' house so that I could take care of my dad and help him plan the funeral for my mom. One night I awoke after having a nightmare, and I heard this awful sound coming from downstairs. It sounded like the wailing of a cat. I thought maybe a cat or some other animal had been hit by a car, and that it had crawled onto our front porch to die.

But when I walked into the foyer and turned on the light, I saw where the sound was coming from. It was my father. He was sitting on the floor by the front door, keening, holding his head in his hands and shaking all over. Here was an ex-marine, a grizzled hard-ass of a man, and he was making this high-pitched mourning wail. I will never forget that sound as long as I live.

A drunk driver doesn't set out to murder another man. A soldier doesn't intentionally shoot and kill his best friend during a confusing battle. But Charlene Worsley had a plan that she executed with brutal and disgusting calculation. And for that, I hope she rots in hell.

"Hero Police Officer Committed to Psychiatric Hospital" by Dave Hill (originally published in *Oakland Express*, February, 1988, p. 2):

OAKLAND - The Oakland police officer who was involved in the fatal shooting at a nursing home in August of last year was committed to a psychiatric hospital after cutting himself with a kitchen knife and smearing his blood on the walls of his apartment.

In the early hours of Tuesday morning, Mark Tanner's brother made a frantic phone call to Oakland police, urging them to hurry to the apartment in Emeryville where Officer Tanner lived. According to the incident report, officers arrived to find Tanner covered in blood in the bathtub and gripping a serrated knife in his hand.

After paramedics arrived and treated his injuries, Tanner made several incoherent statements to police, including that a demon had flown inside his throat.

At that point a decision was made to take the officer to a nearby psychiatric ward for evaluation. His brother accompanied the police to the facility and provided the necessary background information.

Officer Tanner made national headlines when he ended the massacre at the Mercy Care Medical Center in Oakland in 1987.

In one of the most brutal and senseless murder sprees the world has ever seen, 19-year-old college student Charlene Worsley murdered four people with an ax, including her own mother, inside the nursing home before Officer Tanner shot and killed her.

Tanner was recognized for his courage in the line of duty at the department's award ceremony in October of last year, and many Bay Area residents have referred to him as a hero.

The report noted that Tanner had been experiencing depression and alcohol dependency in the weeks leading up to the shooting. He had recently ended a rocky relationship with his long-time girlfriend, Ashley Matsumura, 33, who was disheartened to learn of the incident.

"Mark and I had just broken up, and he was drinking a lot and consumed with the troubles in our relationship before the shooting," Matsumura said.

"But he never drank on duty. It was a casual thing, something to do after a long shift, but it was starting to become a problem," she added. "He was in a vulnerable state at the time, which is actually a testament to how brave he was on that terrible day."

Before taking Tanner to the psychiatric hospital, officers found several unusual items in his pockets, including a St. Nicholas prayer card, a tin of pills, and a crumpled letter from Matsumura, according to the report.

"I had written Mark a love letter," Matsumura explained. "I thought there might be a chance we could get back together once he had taken some time off and gotten some help."

Tanner's apartment was in disarray, with dirty clothes and torn photos scattered on the floor. The bathroom toilet was clogged with waste, and dirty dishes were piled in the sink. Officers reported a foul odor emanating from the apartment and strange writing on Tanner's bedroom wall.

Tanner, 39, had been put on paid administrative leave after the shooting in Oakland. A veteran officer with 11 years of active duty, his record contains no history of violations or complaints.

"The Satanic Age Continues" by Harmony Allen and Sean Crestwood (originally published in *Dark Roads*, November, 1988, p. 2-4):

The St. Augustine's Behavioral Psychiatric Hospital in El Cerrito failed to properly monitor a visit between a patient and his girlfriend, which resulted in a homicide that hospital staff and police detectives are still struggling to understand. California State officials are describing the strangulation murder of a psychiatric technician as a "preventable tragedy that occurred due to personnel not following standard procedure."

The police investigation into the savage beating and murder of George Nicholson, 42, by psychiatric patient Mark Tanner, 39, has led many to question the ability of the state to treat mentally ill patients and prevent them from harming themselves or others.

Mark Tanner is the former Oakland police officer who brought an end to the 1987 murder spree at the Mercy Care Medical Center by shooting 19-year-old Charlene Worsley, the perpetrator of those crimes.

Weeks after the shooting, Tanner suffered a nervous breakdown and was committed to the psychiatric hospital in El Cerrito, a city in the San Francisco Bay Area. He has been a patient at the hospital for 13 months.

El Cerrito homicide detective Stephen Bernstein, one of the lead investigators of the Nicholson murder, is now in the challenging process of peeling back the many layers of the crime scene.

"Violent crime is on the rise in nearly all East Bay communities. When you add the ax murders last year in Oakland into the mix, you have people living in fear of their city and of each other," the detective said. "In the senseless killing of Mr. Nicholson, hospital staff failed to intervene. That's what crime does; it scares people, isolates them, and stops them from helping each other."

At the time of Nicholson's murder, five staff members were on duty on the floor where the crime occurred, but only one of them was a security officer.

"It was strange. Eyewitnesses, which in this case primarily means the patients, reported that no one, not even hospital security, attempted to stop the altercation. Patients said it seemed like the staff was in a trance," Detective Bernstein said to the press.

Nicholson, who had never met Tanner before, was walking past the visiting room and saw Tanner and his girlfriend, Ashley Matsumura, 33, getting into what appeared to be an argument.

A spokesperson for the hospital, Rhonda Braga, said in a press conference last month that hospital staff will cooperate with police to identify the tragic circumstances that led to Nicholson's death.

"Individually and collectively, the hospital staff at St. Augustine is deeply troubled by this incident and wants to ensure the safety and well-being of our patients," Braga stated at the conference. "Working with law enforcement and improving our training practices here at the hospital, we will make sure nothing like this ever happens again, and we offer our condolences to the Nicholson family."

According to the hospital's official report, Tanner and Matsumura were sitting opposite each other in the visiting room, engaged in a somber conversation. There was no one else in the room at the time.

"Because of the nature of Mark's condition, our visit was restricted to only 10 minutes, but I told him that I would wait for him to get better. I wanted to rebuild our relationship while he received treatment," Matsumura said. "We were having a quiet conversation. Mark told me about a book he was writing called *Demon by the Lake*— a memoir. Everything was going as well as could be expected."

But Matsumura said the discussion took a chilling detour when Tanner said he thought he smelled a foreign scent on his girlfriend.

"He believed it was another man's cologne—that I was cheating on him. He became livid, his face twisting into this hideous mask. He began jabbing me with his fingers, accusing me of having sex with strange men.

"I stood up to leave, and Mark grabbed my arm and spun me around. I cried out, and that was when Mr. Nicholson rushed into the room," Matsumura said.

Her voice cracking, Matsumura said that it was hard to describe exactly what happened next.

"Mark didn't flinch—he was still holding on to my arm—but Mr. Nicholson was hurled across the room. I saw it with my own two eyes. Something picked him up into the air and smashed him into the wall. His head busted open. He was mumbling, trying to talk. I think he was asking for help.

"Mark then let go of me. He whirled around to face Mr. Nicholson, who was crumpled up on the floor, so now Mark had his back to me.

I heard choking sounds, gurgling sounds, like someone was strangling Mr. Nicholson and killing him," Matsumura said.

"But Mark was standing several feet away from Mr. Nicholson. He wasn't touching him! But Mr. Nicholson stopped breathing, and when I tried to get to the door I saw these big purple marks on his throat. Like purple indentations. His tongue was hanging out of his mouth, and his eyes looked like they were filled with blood."

The terror only increased when Tanner shoved his girlfriend to the floor, preventing her from fleeing the visiting room.

"By this point I was shouting, crying for help, but no one came," Matsumura said. "I had the feeling of being totally alone, like the entire hospital was empty except for me and Mark. He was going to kill me and then walk out and go back to his room. That's how it felt."

According to Bernstein, Tanner was an exemplary police officer, but he had developed a "mean" streak after the shooting in Oakland.

"It's under investigation, we're talking to his brother and going back and looking at a few things, but the record shows that he became a different kind of man while on administrative leave—an angry, unhappy man," Bernstein said.

On the morning of the attack and murder, Tanner tried to make an immediate appointment with a hospital psychiatrist, explaining to the scheduling nurse that he was having "disorienting thoughts" and that he felt "an animal presence growing inside" him. The nurse made the appointment for three days later, encouraging Tanner to get some rest and take his medication in the meantime, according to the report.

The hospital's policy indicates that staff should intervene during physical altercations between patients. But Ashley Matsumura claims that no one came to her assistance during her fight with Tanner.

"I stood up to run, but he belted me across the face, and I went flying against the coffee machine. My head hit the edge, and I nearly blacked out," Matsumura recalled. "I could see out the glass doors in the visiting room. All of the nurses and patients were gathering against the glass. They were tapping on it with their fingernails and creating a rhythm—it sounded like the flapping of a million soft wings. I thought I was losing my mind."

But it was in the next instance that Matsumura felt like she had truly gone crazy.

"Mark came at me fast, his arms outstretched like he was going to choke me. There was such fury in his eyes. He was no longer himself.

My vision was blurry, I had twisted my ankle and couldn't get up. All I could do was beg Mark not to hurt me.

"But suddenly he stopped. Just dead in his tracks. And his face morphed from animalistic rage into something softer…*someone* softer. It was the face of the girl. The face of the girl Mark shot and killed. I was looking at Charlene Worsley."

Charlene Worsley was the college student who in 1987 stalked the Mercy Care nursing home like a "boogeyman" from a slasher film and murdered four people, including her own mother.

Matsumura said that she observed a "horrifying power struggle" in Tanner's facial features as his countenance appeared to fluctuate between that of himself, Worsley, and a bull-headed monstrosity with black nostrils and blazing red eyes.

While the beast huffed and bellowed, the shifting composites of Tanner and Worsley battled back and forth, screaming at one another with words that Matsumura said rattled for days inside her head.

TANNER: She is mine! Let me have her!

WORSLEY: No! She loves you! Stop!

TANNER: It is my time now. My reckoning! I am the god of human sacrifice! The tender of Ammon!

WORSLEY: Shut up! You've taken enough! You've taken the old, the helpless! I won't let you take any more!

"Charlene was the stronger personality. I saw her face. I heard her *voice*," Matsumura insisted. "She was my guardian angel. She stopped Mark from killing me. She drove his head into the wall, knocking him out cold. Now—how exactly did that happen? I certainly didn't do it!"

Matsumura said Tanner's injury seemed to catalyze the hospital staff into action. The security officer rushed into the room and helped Matsumura to safety, while a nurse dialed 911 and patients scurried to their rooms.

Tanner was treated for his injuries at the hospital before being taken into custody by Contra Costa County sheriff's deputies. He has been charged with second-degree murder and second-degree assault.

"St. Augustine houses all of their patients together, regardless of their illness or condition. But Tanner never should have been allowed to visit with Ashley, or even be around other patients," Bernstein said. "There needs to be an immediate change of protocol and far superior training of hospital employees, state-wide, or else these tragedies will continue to happen."

Ashley Matsumura suffered minor injuries from the attack, but has since recovered and moved out of the Bay Area.

"I need to start my life over, far away from the city I called home for so long," Matsumura said. "There are just too many associations with death here.

"Mark is not evil, but there's something inside him that is," Matsumura concluded. "And I need to get as far away from that as possible."

"USC Senior to Make Controversial Murder Documentary" by Niesha Walker (originally published in *Trojan Weekly*, March, 1991, p. 3-4):

In a move that has stunned her former professors and outraged a victim advocacy group, USC senior Debra Morrow plans to film a documentary to coincide with the third anniversary of the Mercy Care Murders and the death of the killer, Charlene Worsley.

We Were Children Once: The Possession of Charlene Worsley will be produced and directed by Morrow, with camera work by junior Jason Rosenthal and sound by senior Madison Dupree. The trio, all Film and Television Production majors at USC, is currently writing a narrative outline of the project and scheduling interviews to be included in the documentary.

Actress Charlene Worsley was the 19-year-old perpetrator of one of Northern California's most barbaric crimes, slaughtering four elderly people, including her invalid mother, with an ax in 1987. The murders happened inside the Mercy Care Medical Center in Oakland where Worsley's mother was being treated for dementia.

Investigators believe that Worsley would most likely have continued her rampage throughout the nursing home had she not been shot and killed by a responding police officer.

Morrow and Worsley had been best friends for most of their lives and had made several independent films together, including *The Devil and My Daughter*, an unsettling and gory tale of demonic-possession that some say psychologically damaged Worsley and inspired her to commit the slayings.

Though a made-for-TV movie detailing the ax murders and the lives of the victims premiered on CBS two years ago, Morrow intends to use footage in her documentary that most people have never seen, including snippets of the low-budget horror movies that she and Worsley made as they were growing up.

"I want to show another side to Charlene, the kind side, the talented and loving side. She wasn't a monster," Morrow insists. "The documentary will present convincing evidence that she was possessed by a demonic power that *forced* her to kill."

If Morrow's statements sound shocking, she adds that her claim of demonic possession as a defense for Worsley's actions is only a small sampling from a much bigger story.

"There's a murderer out there," she warns. "He's about 24 or 25 years of age. He might still live in California. He enjoys killing prostitutes. He may have stopped killing a few years ago, making his movements harder to trace.

"This man *summoned* a demon into existence. He attached it to my best friend through a satanic ritual. And that demon fed on Charlene, robbing her body of sustenance, bleeding her dry like a vampire and destroying her mind.

"I'm not denying that Charlene killed those poor people. She walked into the nursing home. She wielded the ax. But she wasn't in control of her actions," Morrow argues.

Though Morrow's theory sounds outrageous, she is not the only one who subscribes to it. With the input of a Berkeley police officer and a young man who lived with Worsley before the slayings, she plans to chronicle her friend's life, including Charlene Worsley's relationship with her mother, the challenges of her acting career, and the demonic force that allegedly consumed her and caused her to commit the murders in Oakland.

News of Morrow's plans for the documentary caught the attention of Crime Victims and Their Families (CVTF), an advocacy group based in Los Angeles. Cindy Bray, a spokesperson for the group, has expressed shock and anger over Morrow's claims and has pleaded with the young director to abort the project.

"Arguing that Charlene Worsley was possessed by the devil is a feeble and vulgar attempt to deny Worsley's personal responsibility in the killings," Bray says. "More to our point, it is a tremendous insult to the families of the victims, who have already suffered so much.

"Our agency has sent several letters to USC, hoping the school will encourage Ms. Morrow to reconsider her approach or to cancel the film altogether," Bray adds.

Though she has yet to respond to CVTF's concerns, Morrow remains open to presenting additional narrative angles in her documentary. "I hope to honor all of the victims in this case, but without sidestepping the supernatural causes that led to the murders," she says.

As Morrow's production team continues to shape the scope of the film, the 23-year-old director has started to raise money for distribution costs, including marketing and legal expenses. Once all the bills for the project have been paid, Morrow says, any remaining proceeds will be donated to funding research in the field of dementia.

Anthony Ellison, the Berkeley police officer who was the first to expose an assault case involving Charlene Worsley and several unidentified men, has stood by Morrow in her unusual pursuit.

"I met Charlene before the murders, and I saw things that I can't explain. At first I thought that she was suffering from post-traumatic stress because of her assault, and perhaps that theory still applies," Ellison admits. "But there is some truth to Debra's story. There's factual evidence, and yes, spectral evidence, to support it. As a police officer, I will deal with the facts. That's my job. I'll let Debra handle the paranormal."

Morrow has even gone as far as naming the demonic entity that she believes came to possess Worsley's soul.

"Its name is Moloch, and it has the hideous, slobbering face of a bull," she claims. "In *Paradise Lost*, Milton wrote that Moloch was a 'horrid king' covered in blood, a demon that delighted in suffering and human sacrifice. In his memoir *The Gathering Storm*, Winston Churchill used Moloch as a symbol for Adolf Hitler, suggesting that the Nazi leader was possessed by the beast.

"It might sound crazy, but demonic possession is actually one of the most accepted and universal religious beliefs in the entire world. Horror movies like *The Exorcist* and *The Devil and My Daughter* have sensationalized the topic and turned it into gruesome spectacle, but the truth remains: demons can possess our souls and *spread* their infection—and that's what the documentary intends to prove."

To underscore her argument, Morrow plans to interview people who are connected to Worsley—her friends in the acting world, the residents of Mercy Care who witnessed the murders, and several journalists and paranormal researchers who have written about the case.

"It is true that there may be a tenuous link between Charlene Worsley and a rash of ritualistic killings that took place in the San Francisco area in the late 70s, early 80s. That angle will continue to be investigated," Ellison states. "While I have come to believe that the supernatural exists, it's going to be difficult for Debra to prove that Charlene was possessed. The evidence is immaterial—almost ethereal. People accused of murder have tried this defense before in court, and they have routinely failed."

And it is this impossible question of proof that has some people criticizing Morrow for her new project, accusing her of exploiting the victims of the murders, paying gross tribute to a heartless killer, and outright lying about Charlene's "possession" in order to draw attention to her project.

"She did the same thing with *The Devil and My Daughter*," claims a film professor at East Bay Community College where Morrow and Worsley were once students. "She vandalized the film studio here, made it look like satanic mischief, and got everyone talking about her movie.

"Four innocent people died in Oakland. The brave police officer who shot Worsley had a mental collapse and wound up in a psychiatric ward, and then he killed a staff member there. These are the real tragedies of this case," says the professor, who asked not to be named for this article.

Mark Tanner is the former Oakland police officer who shot and killed Worsley during her rampage at the nursing home.

After suffering a psychiatric breakdown weeks later, Tanner was admitted to a mental hospital where he attacked his girlfriend, Ashley Matsumura, during a visit and strangled a staff member to death.

Tanner was taken into custody and charged with second-degree murder. He is currently awaiting trial in Contra Costa County.

Meanwhile, Cindy Bray and the rest of the CVTF group remain hopeful that Morrow and her production team will look for ways to tell the story of the Mercy Care Murders without exploiting the victims and turning this shocking true crime into another ham-fisted rip-off of *The Exorcist*.

"Out of respect for the dead, we hope that Ms. Morrow will work from a place of good will and truth, rather than of morbid curiosity and superstition," Bray says.

Despite her critics and the controversial material, Morrow has every intention of moving forward with *We Were Children Once*.

"I started my career with a documentary, so in a lot of ways this project makes sense," Morrow says. "I want this movie to help people and protect them. To make them aware of the evil that's out there in the world. To let them know it exists and that it can come for them at any time."

Afterword

Louis Ackerman, otherwise known as Abaddon and the former lead singer of the death metal group Carnal Season, moved to Los Angeles and continues to write music. He is currently the singer and guitarist for the band Satanic Scorn, and he wrote the soundtrack to Matthew Benowitz's horror film *Urchin* (1989). In the press, Ackerman refuses to discuss the Mercy Care Murders or his former bandmate Alexander "Judas" Grimm.

Ruth and Charlene Worsley were buried in plots next to one other in a cemetery in California. Despite attempts to keep the site of the graves private, Charlene's headstone was so routinely vandalized that cemetery officials removed both of the stones and replaced them with less conspicuous tin markers.

In a private arrangement between the Oakland Museum and the extended members of the Worsley family, Ruth's photographs and art prints were auctioned off, with all proceeds donated to MINDFUL, a charity devoted to financing research into the causes of dementia.

In 1988, a theater company in New York drew intense criticism when it attempted to acquire the rights to and perform Charlene Worsley's "satanic" horror play, *My Name is Nancy*. The company abandoned the project after public outcry and a lack of funding.

In addition to *The Mercy Care Murders*, the much-ballyhooed made-for-TV movie that premiered on CBS in 1988, two other media projects based on this story are currently in the works: *Mercy Care: A Survivor's Journey*, set to air on NBC in the spring of 1992, and *Rivers of Blood*, a feature film directed by Ginger Stevens and slated for a limited summer release next year.

Anthony Ellison, who tried to help Charlene Worsley shortly before the killings, is still a police officer for the Berkeley Police Department. He continues to investigate the violent assault on

Charlene at the Monte Rio farmhouse and remains determined to see justice served in that case.

Alexander Grimm, the guitarist formerly known as Judas Grimm, moved to Medford, Oregon after his departure from Carnal Season in 1986. In March of 1989, his mutilated body was found in the parking lot of the Gypsy Dancer, a bikini bar known for prostitution and drug activity. According to police reports, Grimm had been robbed of his wallet and jewelry before being stabbed and castrated. Though the grisly homicide remains unsolved, *The Medford Times* published an article later that year about a "rabid wolf pack" of vengeful prostitutes killing their abusive pimps and johns. "Tensions on the south side of the city are mounting," said a Medford homicide detective at the time of Grimm's murder. "After years of abuse, the girls are taking matters into their own hands—with knives, tire irons, and broken bottles. These ladies will take your money, and then they'll take your balls."

Patty Howard, who ran away from home in 1985, was found living in an El Cerrito flophouse just three days after the show about her disappearance and the prostitute killings aired on the KICU television program *American Investigation*. After returning home to Pacifica, Patty graduated from high school with top honors. In 1991, she received her Bachelor's Degree in Music Education from San Francisco State University. Now 24, Patty still sings in her church choir and maintains a close relationship with her father, Moses Howard.

In 1989, **Billy Lee** began raising money to turn his script, *Monte Rio Massacre*, into a feature-length film. The film was to tell the true story of the bizarre ceremony that Lee witnessed at the farmhouse in the Monte Rio woods. But in the winter of that year, Lee was driving alone on a country road at night, toward Sonoma County, when his car was hit by a vehicle coming in the opposite direction. According to the police accident report, the vehicle crossed the center divider and plowed into Lee's car, killing him. The driver of the oncoming vehicle, a 36-year-old warehouse worker named Gordon Claiborne, also died in the crash. Though the police ruled the collision an accident, Harmony Allen of *Dark Roads* magazine called the incident an "obvious murder and satanic contract suicide." Allen argued that Claiborne, aware that Lee would be traveling down that road at that time, intentionally caused the accident in an effort to kill the filmmaker. As a reward for his sacrifice, Claiborne believed he would be reincarnated as Satan's "first lieutenant." Allen described Claiborne, who had a prior arrest record for unlawful assembly and property destruction, as "tall and grotesquely thin." According to Allen, the police discovered a box of votive candles, several videotapes, and a purple gown inside Claiborne's vehicle. The videotapes were confiscated by police and their contents remain unknown.

Ashley Matsumura left California and currently lives in the Pacific Northwest, where she is continuing her career as a paralegal. Though she has been approached by numerous media outlets to recount her volatile relationship with Mark Tanner and the tragic incident at the psychiatric hospital in El Cerrito, Matsumura values her privacy and has declined all requests for interviews. "People are always asking me about Mark, if I truly believe he was possessed, and about the murder of Mr. Nicholson," Matsumura said in her only released statement. "My story has never changed. Not a single detail. And when Mark's trial finally begins, whenever it begins, I'll tell the jury the same damn thing."

Debra Morrow graduated from USC film school in the spring of 1991. She abandoned her documentary, *We Were Children Once: The Possession of Charlene Worsley*, that summer. After meeting with the families of the victims in the Mercy Care Murders, Morrow concluded that her intended film would serve only to inflict further anguish on the families and the city of Oakland. "As an artist, I'm still learning how to handle the moral dimensions of my work. The bottom line is that my personal beliefs about Charlene will never change the fact that these innocent people died. They don't deserve to have their memory exploited by me or anyone else," Morrow says.

"Maybe someday I'll look at that old footage of me and Charlene and edit it into something I can be proud of, but I doubt it. I've learned my lesson. I don't want to make movies anymore. I keep a few pictures of Charlene and Ruth. I still have one of Ruth's original prints and the letter she wrote to me after my mother died. I have some of Charlene's personal belongings. And then there's this book, which presents the truth of her story as I understand it. For now, that's enough for me."

Mark Tanner was charged with the second-degree assault of Ashley Matsumura and the second-degree murder of George Nicholson. While awaiting trial, he remains an inmate at the Contra Costa County jail in California.

While a patient at the psychiatric hospital in El Cerrito, Tanner wrote his memoir, *Demon by the Lake*, which details the murders at the Mercy Care Medical Center and Tanner's belief that he became possessed by the pagan demon Moloch after shooting Charlene Worsley. The memoir was originally due to be published by Kensington Books, which, at that time, was headed by editor and publisher Lloyd Carroll. Carroll had arranged that the memoir would be publicized via a two-hour television "special event" on *American Investigation*, with host Ronald Grantham interviewing Tanner at the hospital as the climax of the show. However, after Tanner's arrest for the murder of George Nicholson, the release of the memoir and the TV special were canceled.

Todd Wheeler returned to his hometown of Bodega Bay, California, where he now works as a stevedore for Sonoma County. Though Todd has no interest in returning to the entertainment industry, he writes for *Dark Roads* magazine and provided the foreword to Harmony Allen's book, *The Encyclopedia of Demons and Monsters* (1990). Wheeler has also been a featured guest on KUSF's Underground Horror Radio Program. "My first mistake was relying on Hollywood to educate me about the demonic," he says today. "I never took the subject seriously. And then the devil possessed someone I loved, and by then it was too late, and I lost her forever."

About The Author

Josh Hancock is a teacher and author. His first novel, *The Girls of October*, was inspired by his love of all things horror--especially John Carpenter's *Halloween*, Tobe Hooper's *The Texas Chain Saw Massacre*, and William Friedkin's *The Exorcist*. His second novel, *The Devil and My Daughter*, was equally inspired by horror films, including Amando de Ossorio's underground classic *Demon Witch Child*. For reviews, book trailers, and more, please visit www.foundfootagefiction.com.

Also by Josh Hancock:

OTHER GREAT TITLES FROM

Burning Bulb

PUBLISHING

WWW.BURNINGBULBPUBLISHING.COM

BELLY TIMBER

From the writers of Darkened Hills, Detour to Armageddon and Night of the Living Dead comes a novel unlike any other...

In the 1800's, ordinary people learned the secret of the Kala and undertook extraordinary measures to rid the earth of this evil. This is their story.

For John McCormick, life on the Indiana frontier held nothing but promise. His settlement along the White River would soon become the crossroads of America. Friends and family from back in Ohio and other points east were all making plans to see what all the fuss was about in the newly-formed city of Indianapolis. Yes, things were good. John had his general store and his friend George Pogue had his blacksmith business. Claims were being staked and relations with the native Indians were amicable. The town was growing and nothing could be better... or so he thought.

In Ohio, an evil was brewing. The Lecky Family, a group of ruthless Mongolian nomads, had made their way to America and were practicing their cannibalistic religion of Kala with reckless abandon. No one was safe, not even John McCormick's family.

Burning Bulb
PUBLISHING

GARY LEE VINCENT'S
DARKENED
THE WEST VIRGINIA VAMPIRE SERIES

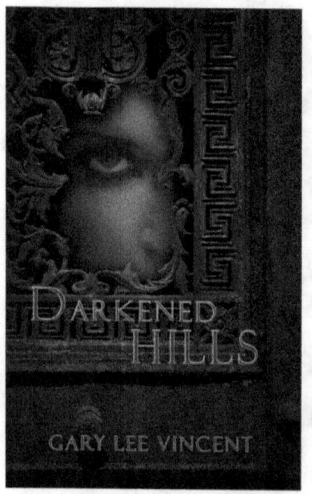

DARKENED HILLS

When evil descends on a small West Virginia town, who will survive?

Jonathan did not start out his life to become a rambler, it justworked out that way. William was a troubled youth with something to hide. Both were from Melas, a small town tucked away in the West Virginia hills... a town where disappearances are happening more and more frequently.

After the suicide of a wanted serial killer, the townsfolk thought the nightmare was over. But when a centuries-old vampire is discovered they find out the hard way it's just getting started. Dark secrets can only stay hidden for so long and when the devil comes to collect, there will be hell to pay. Can Jonathan and William find a way to stop the vampire before it's too late? Find out in *Darkened Hills!*

DARKENED HOLLOWS

In the heart-stopping sequel to the award-winning *Darkened Hills*, Jonathan and William must return to West Virginia to face possible criminal charges stemming from their last visit to the damned town of Melas, where both had narrowly escaped the clutches of a vampire seethe.

And as livestock start mysteriously getting murdered with all of their blood drained, worried farmers are searching for answers - leaving the local Sheriff and his deputy racing against time to learn the cause before a more violent crime is committed.

Burning Bulb
PUBLISHING

WWW.DARKENEDHILLS.COM

GARY LEE VINCENT'S
DARKENED
THE WEST VIRGINIA VAMPIRE SERIES

DARKENED WATERS

When the world goes to hell, the chosen must arise!

As Talman Cane orchestrates a flood of epic proportions in this third installment of the *Darkened* series the towns of Melas and Tarklin are caught completely off guard by the deluge. Hell-bent on finishing what they started, the evil brothers return to the lunatic asylum to take care of the witnesses and add to the ever-growing army of the undead.

Aided by Lucifer himself and the insane vampire demon Legion, the stage is set to channel all of the forces of hell to come forth. In an all-out race to survive, Jonathan, William, and Amanda soon discover they are up against impossible odds as Lucifer opens the Gateway to Hell, ushering in the zombie apocalypse and the End Times.

Find out who will survive this cosmic battle of the ages in *Darkened Waters!*

DARKENED SOULS

Melas and the Madison House are about to be rebuilt.
True evil is about to be reborne!

Young ex-priest and vampire-killer William is drawn back to the West Virginian town that almost killed him, where his vampire arch-enemy Victor Rothenstein still stalks the earth.

The town of Melas lies destroyed after the battle of the End of Days. But why is wealthy Jackie Nixon so eager to rebuild it using the bone dust of murdered souls?

Terrible evil has visited before, but the Gateway to Hell is about to be reopened in a horrific climax. And this time – it's personal.

WWW.DARKENEDHILLS.COM

Burning Bulb
PUBLISHING

BOB GRAY'S ATTACK OF THE MELONHEADS

"Melonheads is what I love. Give me a body count and gore, but don't forget the laughs. Anytime that I can be reminded of what makes Horror great it is a good thing. Melonheads does that and is something we should all support. Consider it highly recommended."
—*Screamsine.us*

Fifty years ago, a doctor sought to cure a terrible disease. Hidden from the world, Doctor Malcolm Crowe toiled in the dead of night while the world was sleeping, creating a new breed of mutant—all in the name of science.

Yes, he thought he could cure the sick children. But he was wrong.

Today, the results of his cruel and unconventional experiments have manifested into an evil never before seen.

Now, in Kirtland, Ohio, the town's unsuspecting residents are about to encounter the full onslaught of this unimaginable terror.

Can something be done before it's too late?

EVERYTHING HERE IS A NIGHTMARE
Collected Works Vol 1.

"Pyles makes it look easy. His characters come instantly alive with the cocksure verve and swagger of rock stars."
- Daniel Knauf, creator of HBO's "Carnivale,"
Executive Producer/Writer, ABC's "The Blacklist."

The critically acclaimed author of Demons, Dolls and Milkshakes returns with fifteen tales of horror and suspense with Everything Here is a Nightmare.

From zombies in the old west, to a young boy tempted by the Devil. From vampires with romantic longing, to an abandoned lighthouse haunted by vengeful spirits. From a serial killer getting unholy justice, to a haunted English race car, Nelson W Pyles invites you to explore a landscape of fear, suspense and horror.

Take his hand and hold on tight. Remember that whatever you find here, whatever you see, no matter what you might think it could be... know this: Everything Here is a Nightmare.

Burning Bulb
PUBLISHING

WOL-VRIEY
BIZARRO AND TRANSGRESSIVE FICTION

BOSTON POSH (BUD MALONE #1)

In 2028 AD, the USA is a nation ravaged by hungry dragons and dinosaurs. In Boston, Massachusetts, private eye Bud Malone is hired to rescue a kidnapped heiress. But nothing is as it seems.

Malone works to unravel a tangled web involving Boston Chinatown, a 200-year-old woman with a 9-year-old body, white robots, a human-liver-eating psychopath, a golem, a porcelain dragon, and a snake goddess with a crush on him. There's also a woman obsessed with chicken sex. Then Malone meets Posh Lane, a gorgeous call girl who's desperate to quit her pimp.

Romantic sparks ignite between Posh and Malone, but Posh's past suddenly catches up with her in a BIG way. To save Posh, Malone agrees to run a quest for Earth's new rulers, the Forks. But, Malone has no idea that agreeing to the Fork's odd request will send him on the weirdest trip he's ever been on in his life.

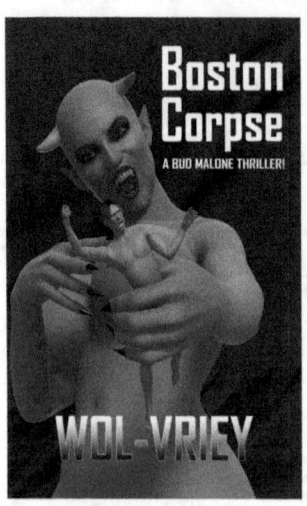

BOSTON CORPSE (BUD MALONE #2)

MAGIC CAN BE MURDER! - Drag queen Lucy Tang is back in Boston, and is hell-bent on settling her vindetta against casino owner Sookie Ling. And suddenly, Bud Malone, PI, has the case of his life to resolve.

When Boston's robot police force are baffled by a mind transfer case, they come to Malone for help. The one person who can likely help Malone out here is the witch Soledad Bathory. But Soledad seems to know a lot more than she's telling him. It's a case not made easier when Malone meets Soledad's beautiful cousin, Josephine 'Slave' Bailey. Slave has her own plans for Malone, most of which involve teaching him BDSM and making him her new Master.

Oh, and Rick Rogers owes Sookie Ling a whole lot of money, a gambling debt that's going to be literally Hell to pay!

BOSTON CORPSE - Not your average detective novel!

Burning Bulb
PUBLISHING

WOL-VRIEY
BIZARRO AND TRANSGRESSIVE FICTION

VEGAN ZOMBIE APOCALYPSE

In the post-apocalypse worlderness, zombies rule the earth. They're allergic to meat, and brains literally make them explode. Zombies now eat blood potatoes, parasitic tubers grown in the flesh of humancows corralled in maximum security farms. Two fugitives meet in the ancient ruins of Texas. The first is Soil 15-f, a womancow who's escaped her farm a week before she's due to be killed and her blood potato crop harvested. The second fugitive is Able Kane, former head necros food technician, now sentenced to death for heresy. But Soil is no ordinary humancow.

Unknown to herself, she's the vegan zombie agricultural revolution, and the zombies desperately want her back. And the necros equally desperately want Able Kane dead. He's fled with a forbidden discovery which will reshape the world for the worse if used. And Able is just hardheaded/misguided enough to use it.

MELANIE NEMESIS CATCHPOLE

In Springfield, Massachusetts, Melanie Catchpole is hired to fetch back a magic teddy bear worth millions of dollars from a warehouse across town. Problem is, the warehouse is down in Springfield's O-Zone-that totally weird sector of the city where Bizarro fell to Earth. The 'O' is a fairytale land, a place where dreams and nightmares literally live and breathe.

Worse still, the gingers—mutant cannibals—prowl the O. The gingers have already eaten everyone else Melanie's employers sent to get back the magic teddy bear.

Accompanied by the handsome but ruthless Doug Fisher (who she finds sexy but doesn't dare entrust her heart to), Melanie enters the O-Zone. Melanie and Doug are instantly caught up in an adventure they'd never have believed credible even if written as fiction . . . and Melanie's used to experiencing the very weird as the norm.

And now, additionally, there's a mystery to unravel: What does the dark, freezing-cold being called The Fixer want with Mary, the barkeep's daughter?

Burning Bulb
PUBLISHING

WOL-VRIEY

BIZARRO AND TRANSGRESSIVE FICTION

BIG TROUBLE IN LITTLE ASS

From Bizarro master storyteller Wol-vriey comes a truly we
western tale that will leave you awe-struck and on the edge
your seat...

In the town named Little Ass, tight-assed prostitute Rosa ov
hears a gunslinger's plans to assassinate rancher Edison Be
nett. Once the badass Bennett learns of the plot, he ensur
there'll be hell to pay for any attempt on his life!

Yes, it's going to take all of gunslinger Jude's shooting prowe
his eclectic collection of strange firearms, a trusty horse that
quires an owners' manual, and the help of the lovely and
vigorating Nell (who's EXTREMELY odd when the going g
weird), to survive the Bizarro hell that Edison Bennett unleas
es in order to hold onto the land that he'd stolen from Mada
Zizi.

BIZARRO 101 (A BASIC PRIMER)

Welcome to the strange place:

A collection of 37 flash fiction stories designed to introduce one t
the Bizarro/New Weird Genre.

Weird, dreamy, nightmarish, absurd, sad, surreal, humorous . . . t
collection of tales is all this and more.

***

*"This primer is the very essence of any and all styles and types of Biza
writing. Wol-vriey collects, distills, and bottles up these 37 tiny stories for y
sensory enjoyment. This is an absolute must-read for anyone new to the ge
because it demonstrates the scope of what Bizarro is, and what it can be."*
—Teresa Pollack, Bizarro commentator and blog

Burning Bulb
PUBLISHING

ANTHOLOGIES
BIZARRO AND TRANSGRESSIVE FICTION

THE BIG BOOK OF BIZARRO SPECIAL KINDLE EDITIONS

OTHER AWESOME COLLECTIONS

 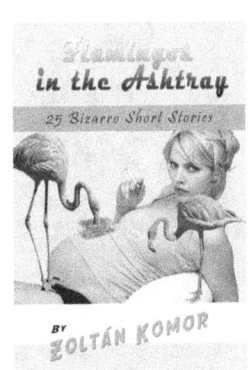 

ANTHOLOGIES
BIZARRO AND TRANSGRESSIVE FICTION

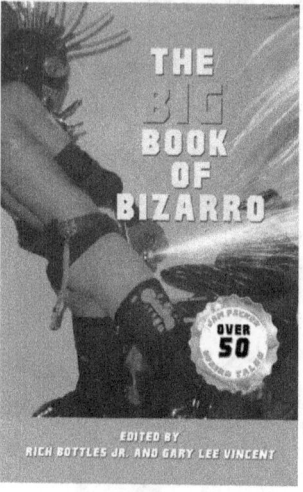

THE BIG BOOK OF BIZARRO

The Big Book of Bizarro brings together the peculiar prose of an international cast of the most grotesquely-gonzo, genre-grinding modern writers who ever put pen to paper (or mouse to pad), including:

NIGHT OF THE LIVING DEAD horror writers John Russo & George Kosana; HUSTLER MAGAZINE erotica contributors Eva Hore, Andrée Lachapelle, & J. Troy Seate and established Bizarro genre authors D. Harlan Wilson, William Pauley III, Wol-vriey, Laird Long, Richard Godwin and so many more!

From Alien abductions to Zombie sex, The Big Book of Bizarro contains OVER FIFTY STORIES of the most outrélandish transgressive fiction that you'll ever lay your capricious and curious hands upon!

WESTWARD HOES

Nine outlaw writers rode into town from obscurity to pen nine tantalizing tales of horror and fantasy, and leaving once they branded their own personal marks on the weird western genre and became living legends of the American Frontier experience.

Like drunken Indian scouts, the writers fervidly tracked down and captured the Western genre, tore off its fashionable veneer and ravished its exposed essence.

So belly up to the bar with your favorite soiled dove and enjoy perusing these thrilling tales of Old West debauchery, danger and desire; compiled by the publisher of The Big Book of Bizarro and featuring the bizarro novella *Big Trouble in Little Ass* by Wol-vriey.

Burning Bulb
PUBLISHING

DAVID J. FAIRHEAD

THE FALL

Hopelessness... How do you protect your loved ones when Hell itself opens its insidious mouth?

Horror... Nightmarish Creatures invade your world and there is nowhere to hide.

Blood... How long can you hold out before they come for you?

Pain... Where do you run to avoid being eaten alive by monsters with a voracious appetite for your flesh?

Screams... While you selfishly run for your own life.

Questions... Who is to blame? Where did they come from? How many people survived...and how does the human race find the means to fight back?

THE FALL OF TOMORROW is man's last tale of desperation told by those that are striving to salvage some hope against a ravenous bastion of evil beasts bent on ruling our world.

DWELLING IN THE DARK

From David J. Fairhead, author of the FALL OF TOMORROW, comes DWELLING IN THE DARK- A soulful anthology of creeping terror to keep you up in the small hours with horror set in the past, present and future. Overlapping bits of puzzle fitting each other, before and after The Fall of Tomorrow.

A place where three children facing a monstrous foe can only pray that their bloody summer would just come to an end. Go back to the 1960's- THE COMMUNE where overindulging hippies use a mage's diary to control the end of the world, only to see first-hand that their drug induced visions have horrific ramifications. Where a young boy's visit to a haunted house becomes a lesson in RESIDUAL morality. The story, DEEPER- plunges two brothers into a sinkhole only to find they were being hunted by an insidious creature from its depths. Visit the old west as hero Dekker Collins battles evil gunslingers in DEMONEYE.

And so much more...!

Burning Bulb
PUBLISHING

WWW.FAIRLYDARKPRODUCTIONS.COM

WEST VIRGINIA-THEMED HUMORROROTICA

BY RICH BOTTLES JR.

HELLHOLE WEST VIRGINIA

From the heights of Mothman's perch high atop the Silver Bridge in Point Pleasant to the depths of Hellhole Cavern in Pendleton County, evil lurks within the shadows as the sun sets upon the haunted hills and hollows of West Virginia.

Bizarro author Rich Bottles Jr. blows the coffin lid off horror genre clichés with this tour de force cast of Eco-friendly vampires, beach-yearning zombies and sex-starved she-devils.

LUMBERJACKED

If you are easily offended or do not possess a truly depraved sense of humor, this story may not be the light summer reading fare you desire. As for the four feisty female freshmen stranded on top of West Virginia's third highest mountain, they have no choice but to experience the sick, twisted debauchery and perverted mayhem described deep inside the tight unbroken bindings of this horrific missive.

Lumberjacked takes the reader to a nightmarish world where character development and aesthetic integrity are prematurely cut short by the swinging axes of maniacal lumberjacks, who are hell bent on death and destruction in the remote forests of Appalachia. And at the climax, when paranoia crosses over to the paranormal, Lumberjacked makes Deliverance look like a family raft trip down the Lower Gauley.

THE MANACLED

What happens when twin brothers lease out the former West Virginia State Penitentiary with the false purpose of filming a documentary on supernatural phenomena, but their true intention is to make a pornographic movie?

Chaos ensues as the disturbed spirits of murdered convicts, along with the reanimated dead from the neighboring Indian Burial Mound, take their vengeance on the unwary and undressed trespassers.

Zombies, ghosts, mobsters and porn collide in this bizarro tale from horror author Rich Bottles Jr.

Burning Bulb
PUBLISHING

ZAKARY MCGAHA
BIZARRO AND TRANSGRESSIVE FICTION

SEA OF MEDIUM-TO-HIGH PITCHED NOISES

The zombie apocalypse is changing; the world is coming to an odd demise; and a serial killer tries to change his ways and redeem himself before it all goes away. Now, Crabby has entered the world he left behind; the world of the undead. And things are changing. Everything will come to an end. In this new wave of the apocalypse, everything changes every five minutes. And death would be an absolute luxury. Psychological torment meets physical bloodletting in Sea of Medium-to-High Pitched Noises.

PARK MASTERS

Bad breakups, Bigfoot costumes, ghost bears, and more. Park Masters is a wacky, intelligent, quirky comedy about the power relationships have on people, good or bad. Also, it's just plain fun!

Burning Bulb
PUBLISHING

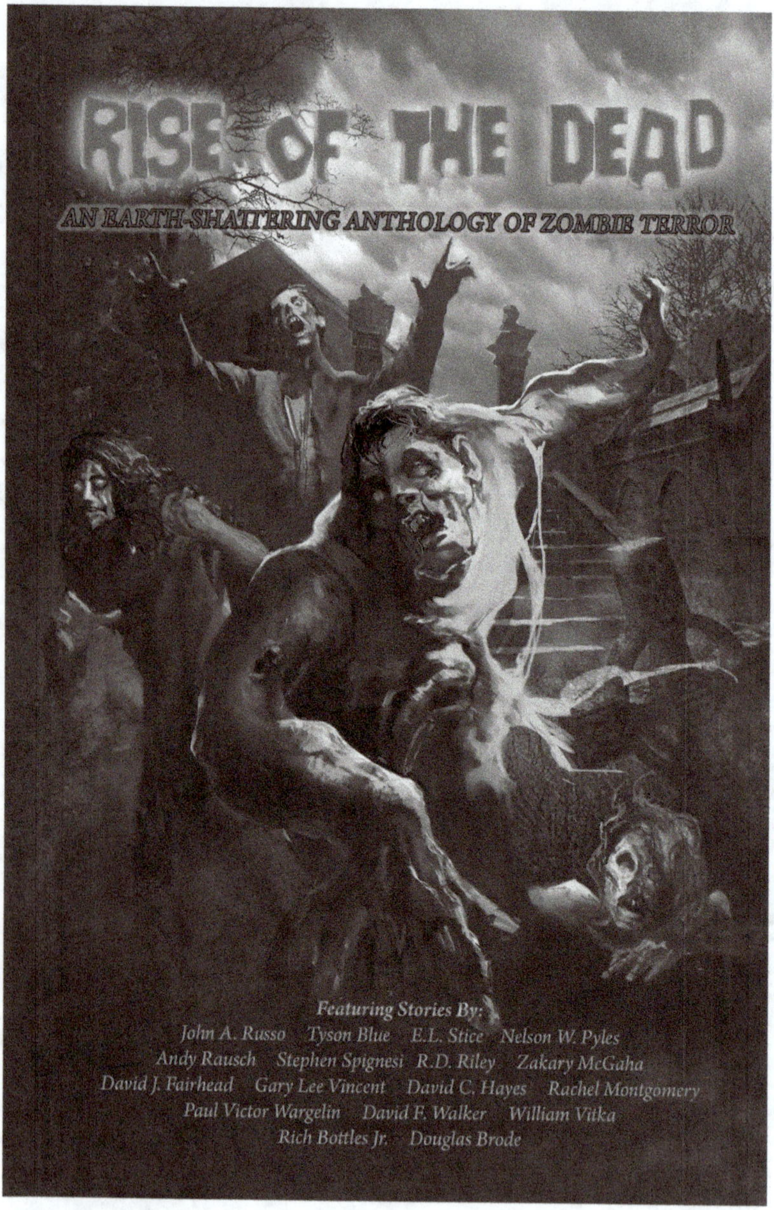
RISE OF THE DEAD
AN EARTH-SHATTERING ANTHOLOGY OF ZOMBIE TERROR
Featuring Stories By:
John A. Russo Tyson Blue E.L. Stice Nelson W. Pyles
Andy Rausch Stephen Spignesi R.D. Riley Zakary McGaha
David J. Fairhead Gary Lee Vincent David C. Hayes Rachel Montgomery
Paul Victor Wargelin David F. Walker William Vitka
Rich Bottles Jr. Douglas Brode

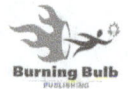

NIGHT OF THE LIVING DEAD

Why does Night of the Living Dead hit with such chilling impact?

Is it because everyday people in a commonplace house are suddenly the victims of a monstrous invasion? Or is it because the ghouls who surround the house with grasping claws were once ordinary people, too?

Decide for yourself as you read, and the horror grips you.

All the cannibalism, suspense and frenzy of the smash-hit move are here in the novel.

www.TheJohnRusso.com

Burning Bulb
PUBLISHING

THE BOOBY HATCH

With NIGHT OF THE LIVING DEAD, John Russo helped blaze a path in the horror genre that has never been equalled. In this hillarious erotic novel, he blazes a path through the wild, zany Sex Revolution of the 1970s.

Sweet, innocent Cherry Jankowski works for Joyful Novelties, where she tests sex toys ranging from the ridiculous to the sublime. But she can't find love or peace of mind and her efforts are hampered by a Peeping Tom, an exhibitionist, a cross-dressing boyfriend, a quack psychiatrist, and even her own product-testing partner, Marcello Fettucini, who can't get it up anymore and is scared of losing his job!

www.TheJohnRusso.com

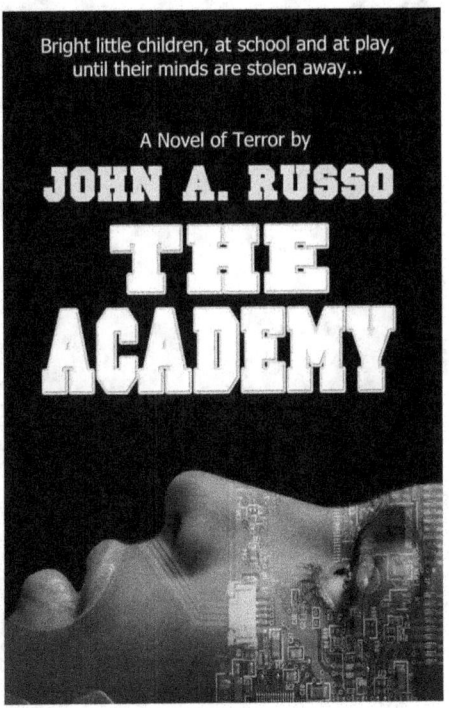

Bright little children, at school and at play, until their minds are stolen away...

A Novel of Terror by

JOHN A. RUSSO

THE ACADEMY

THE ACADEMY

The Academy. It's every parent's dream, turning their little darlings into geniuses, superachievers, perfect little children.

And if there's a problem, the Academy fixes that too. It's a simple operation. Just a little device. Then a teeny pink scar on a tender little skull . . .

One boy knows the secret. Now he wants his mind back. But it's much, much too late. Too late for anything but the ugly feelings. The bad feelings. The messy sexy feelings. The knife-cold hatred, the murderous rage, for total, screaming, blood-drenching revenge . . .

www.TheJohnRusso.com

Burning Bulb
PUBLISHING

"The most unique vampire story since 'SALEM'S LOT."
- George A. Romero

From Legendary Horror Writer
JOHN A. RUSSO

THE
AWAKENING

"A gripping plotline and good old-fashioned gothic horror."
- *Fangoria*

THE AWAKENING

For two hundred years, he has rested. Now he rises. Now he will be satisfied. Nothing can stop him. No one can resist him.

Benjamin Latham is young and handsome, his eighteenth-century mind wakened to a bizarre twentieth-century world. And there is the need deep within . . . an animal need, frightening, murderous, unholy . . . a vital need that must be fed.

And with his need comes a power over men and women to do his bidding, to quiet his dark craving . . .

Until the murders begin. And the inquiries. All suggesting the same hideous truth.

Now Benjamin must find a sanctuary: a lover, a partner, a friend. Someone who can share his darkness. Someone he can lead to . . . The Awakening.

www.TheJohnRusso.com

Burning Bulb
PUBLISHING

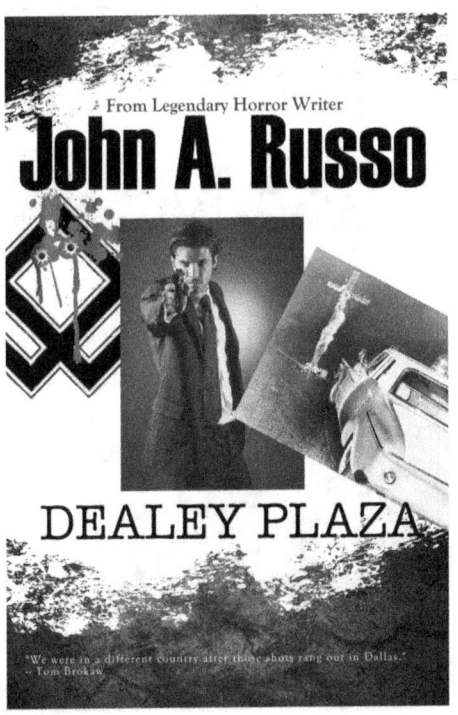

DEALEY PLAZA

From legendary horror and suspense writer JOHN RUSSO comes a harrowing tale where no one is safe!

Dealey Plaza is one of the most notorious places in America, and when youthful conspiracy buffs go there in 1964 to stage their own reenactment of the Kennedy Assassination, four of them are brutally murdered ~ the first victims of a hate-filled legacy that continues for four more decades.

The survivors of that long-ago Dallas trip, each of them now icons of the American way of life, are about to be honored ~ or killed.

Who will live and who will die? Will it be country-western star Lori McCoy? Her loving husband? Her scheming ex-husband? Or the case-hardened FBI agent and longtime friend who risks his life trying to protect them?

www.DealeyPlazaBook.com

Burning Bulb
PUBLISHING

LIMB TO LIMB

SUCH A PRETTY GIRL . . .
Tiffany Blake was a beautiful long-limbed dancer with a glorious future and the backing of a rich benefactor. Then a monstrous accident severed her leg at the hip.

SUCH A COLD, CRUEL KNIFE . . .
And now her fellow dancers are disappearing without a trace. One by one they fall victim to a dark and deadly pattern of evil – caught by the bloody, brutal logic that would have them pay with their lovely bodies for the cruel fate of another . . .victims of the sadistic madman whose flashing knife will make them writhe a gruesome new dance.

www.TheJohnRusso.com

LIVING THINGS

Beneath the shimmering Miami sun sprawls one of the Mafia's biggest empires, a glittering world of lavish beachfront mansions, neon-painted nightclubs, beautiful women, expensive cars—and absolute control over the state's billion-dollar drug trade. But, one by one, its ganglords and henchmen are falling prey to a new rival. His powers are fueled by monstrous ancient rituals; his hellish undead legions slaughter mobsters and innocent citizens alike, his unholy lust for power is virtually unstoppable.

Now a burned-out ex-detective and a brilliant anthropologist must enter a gruesome, nightmare world to fight this master of malevolence and illusion. Their time is short, their weapons few, and they face an ultimate, terrifying choice - annihilation or the loss of their souls to the eternal torment of those who never die. . .

www.TheJohnRusso.com

Burning Bulb
PUBLISHING

ELVIS PRESLEY, CIA ASSASSIN BY ANDY RAUSCH

"I can guarantee you. Read this book and you'll never look at Elvis the same way again!"
~ Douglas Brode, author of ELVIS CINEMA AND POPULAR CULTURE

SOON TO BE A MAJOR MOTION PICTURE

In 1970, singer Elvis Presley secretly met with President Richard Nixon. This new comedic novel imagines that Presley became a Central Intelligence Agency operative, eventually moving up through the ranks to become a skilled assassin.

Presented in an oral history fashion, the book tells us about Presley's secret transformation by the people who knew him best.

Did he fake his death in 1977? Was Presley involved with the Watergate scandal? The Iran hostage crisis? Communicating with aliens?

Read this book to find out the answers to these and many more questions.

Burning Bulb
PUBLISHING

MAD WORLD BY ANDY RAUSCH

"*Mad World* is dark, twisted, no-holds-barred fun."
—Jason Starr, author of *Bust*, *Slide*, and *The Max*

EVERYONE'S PLAYING AN ANGLE IN THE CITY OF ANGELS

Mad World tells the stories of a black hitman who doubles as a university professor, a Catholic priest who longs to be a gangster, a would-be author from Kansas, a gay phone sex operator who claims he's straight, a group of rich twentysomethings playing a deadly game of life and death, a vicious Mafia boss, and a sleazy Hollywood movie director. As each of their stories intersect, the body count piles up and the action comes nonstop in this tense, white-knuckle thriller by first-time author Andy Rausch.

"A wild ride. If you like it gangster, *Mad World* delivers."
—Daniel Birch, author of *Get Some*

Burning Bulb
PUBLISHING

BLOODLETTING: A TALE OF REVENGE BY ANDY RAUSCH

"Relentless… Addictive… The kind of nightmare you don't want
to wake up from."
—Heywood Gould, screenwriter of *Rolling Thunder*

He was just an average Joe. But when he finds his family held at
gunpoint by merciless thugs, he's told he must murder a Mafia
chieftain if he ever wishes to see his loved ones again.

Against all odds, Joe keeps his end of the bargain, but the criminals
don't. Now at his wits end, Joe is pushed beyond his breaking point
and forced to exact bloody revenge against those who've done him
and his family wrong in this powerful and violent novella by author
Andy Rausch (*Mad World*).

"Andy Rausch has a tight noir style that combines gritty, realistic drama
with a cinematic flair that makes for a powerful, compelling (somewhat
Stephen Kingesque), authentically visual reading experience."
—Stephen Spignesi, author of *Dialogues*

Burning Bulb
PUBLISHING

THE TAILSMAN

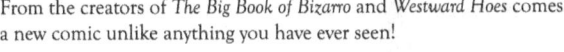

BURNING BULB

COMICS

From the creators of *The Big Book of Bizarro* and *Westward Hoes* comes a new comic unlike anything you have ever seen!

He's hot on the trail, looking for some *tail...*

Sly Franko was a man of the West, a forger of the wild frontier. Like the Country Western song that would be written years after he died, the words, "Faster horses, younger women, and more money," seemed to be the anthem of this horn dog cowboy.

Franko would ride into town on a blazing saddle, find the closest saloon to wet the whistle, belly up to a good card game, and find him a hot-loving hussy to get his cowpoke on with.

However, Sly might have met his match when a visit to bathroom leads to terror and death. Can Sly and his poker buddies solve the mystery before more of the townsfolk are murdered? Find out in this exciting premier issue of *The Tailsman!*

WWW.BURNINGBULBCOMICS.COM

THE HAGS OF BLACK COUNTY

by Michelle Bowser

Ruled by a committee of Hags, and fueled by toothless rivalries, Black County lurks just far enough out of the way to be completely unnoticed by the rest of civilization. Its inhabitants have been mentally warped for generations and the land itself seems to have the power to drive anyone unlucky enough to visit into ridiculous hillbilly madness. When a construction Company needs to bury a pipeline through its ludicrous hills and valleys, a twisted charm goes to work and every aspect of already bizarre Black County life takes a gory turn for the hysterical. Take a preposterous trip along with its citizens, both native and new, through escapades such as the Hag parade, the grand opening of Madame Skunk's House of Ill Repute, the demolition derby riot and the rabid, zombie clown apocalypse.

THE ABANDONED SOUL

by Daniel Sellers

After spending most of his 20s in a drug and alcohol fueled daze, a young man finally hits rock bottom. Having used up his friends and their good graces, he ends up squatting in an abandoned house. Forcibly sobering he begins to realize that he is not alone in this abandoned house. Left with one last friend and a mountain of regrets, he must decide if this presence is a guilty conscience, or a malicious hunter.

WE WISH YOU A HAPPY KILLDAY

by Jason Heroux

"We Wish You a Happy Killday" is the story of an international b eloved holiday called "Killday" where one day a year everyone over the age of fifteen is permitted to register for a license allowing them to kill one other person. But this year Chad Ovenstock doesn't feel like killing anyone. His friends and family urge him to participate in the festivities, but he can't seem to get into the holiday spirit. On the day before Killday Chad comes in contact with Ambrose, an old friend who suffered a nervous breakdown and is now part of The One Ant Army, a mysterious cult dedicated to making the future disappear. When the holiday finally arrives Chad refuses to participate and tries to survive on his own, surrounded by constant gunfire, countless corpses, and the nagging suspicion that Ambrose may have secretly brainwashed him into becoming a member of The One Ant Army cult.

Burning Bulb
PUBLISHING

www.ingramcontent.com/pod-product-compliance
Lightning Source LLC
Chambersburg PA
CBHW060917250626
47159CB00008B/3049